Elizabeth Wilson is Professo...
mental and Social Studies a...
London. She has long been inv...
ment, the lesbian and gay m...
She is author of a number o...
Dreams (Virago 1985), and *The Sphinx in the City* (Virago 1991),
and contributes to the *Guardian* and *New Statesman and Society*.
Virago also publish *The Lost Time Café* (1993), the first Justine
Hillyard mystery.

Elizabeth Wilson lives in London with her partner and
daughter.

Poisoned Hearts

Elizabeth Wilson

Published by VIRAGO PRESS Limited July 1995
20 Vauxhall Bridge Road, London SW1V 2SA

*A CIP catalogue record for this title is
available from the British Library*

Typeset by Keystroke, Jacaranda Lodge, Wolverhampton

Printed in Great Britain by Cox & Wyman Ltd, Reading, Berkshire

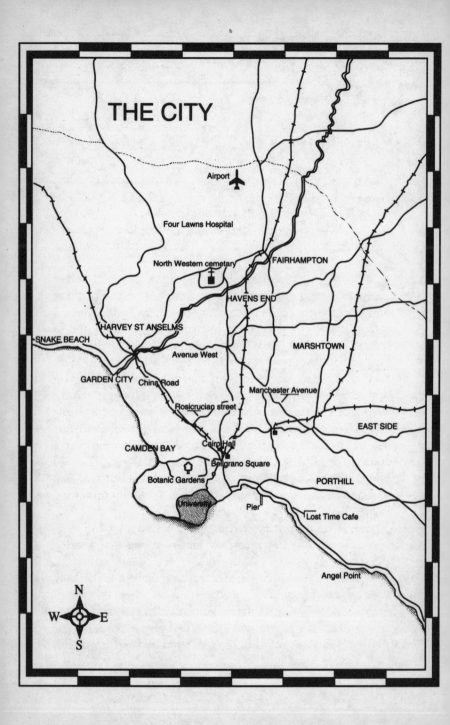

One

Well you know what happens in the dark,
When rattlesnakes lose their skin and their hearts –
The Velvet Underground

The journey back from the prison, I ended up in first class. I'd reserved an ordinary seat, but these four neanderthal types were sitting there, and when I showed them my ticket they just sniggered and refused to budge. I called the guard. He could see I was in the right, but he wouldn't stand up to them, not for a moment. Well, they could have knocked him down by just blowing on him, a wispy, grey little man due for retirement. Anyway, even if one of them had moved, I'd have had to sit with the other three making remarks or trying to get off with me. We all knew that. So the guard hustled me along to first. I couldn't think why I hadn't opted for that anyway. I could afford it. I sank back in the fat, moss green velvet seat, but it didn't make me feel any better. I was still protesting loudly.

'You're on a short fuse, aren't you?' he said.

Yes. It was the last straw, the end of a bad day. I hated the prison. It was the vilest place on earth.

When I stalked back past palaeolithic man to get a drink they sniggered again.

'Why don't you join the human race?' I quipped, but it wasn't exactly brilliant, and they didn't give a fuck.

I was still tense and full of aggression as I sat down with

my double vodka and tried to read my book. I didn't want to think about the day, the nagging worry, the low-level depression, but the novel depressed me too, I'd read it before, *The Wings of the Dove* by Henry James: a young, beautiful heiress dying of a mysterious, perhaps imaginary illness in deathly, wintry Venice. It was enough to give you hypochondria. I opened my newspaper instead.

In the depths of the city, someone was killing old men. The police were linking four murders now. All the men had been gay; and they'd been sexually assaulted. The detective in charge of the case had issued a statement: Evil, perversion, the usual clichés. Somehow he'd managed to imply that these crimes were more unnatural than the murder of young women – as if girls made appropriate victims, while grandfathers did not. This was real perversion, while women were the unfortunate victims of excessive but essentially normal enthusiasm on the part of their attackers.

Actually, anything could happen down in the dosshouses, the dead-end estates, the abandoned railways, those outlying parts of the city where no one went except the destitute. One old man had been killed in the vast North Western cemetery. A second had been bludgeoned to death in his bed in a squat, a third in his own flat. Now the killer had struck among the gravestones again – the cemetery was a notorious cruising ground.

I'd been there once myself – with a lover, as it happened. We hadn't *done* anything. Fucking among the brambles on a Victorian tomb . . .

Its gates were locked, but we'd climbed in at the back where the wall had crumbled and the wire replacing it sagged to the ground. The cypress-bordered avenue opened an imposing vista through the centre of the necropolis, but brambles and ivy had choked the narrow paths between the graves, and the grass grew waist high. The mossy tombs rose from this sea of strangely fecund greenery like the remains of a submerged civilisation, watched over by stone angels with folded wings and downcast eyes.

When we walked up the avenue it had been silent, too silent. They lay low in the daylight, Lennox had told me, the addicts on the east side, the gay men at the south end, where laurel and ilex trees surrounded secluded mausoleums, the sick and homeless to the north; but at night the place came alive. No silence then, he'd said, but the eerie laughter and shouting of restless outcasts from hospitals and asylums, the explosive coughing of the sick, the singing of the drunks. I'd wondered how he knew – lain low there himself for a while, I supposed.

I sighed, and went on reading. Myra's broadcast had also hit the front page. Myra Zone, my friend, transexual fortune-teller, formerly living on the margins in a garden city slum, now transformed into a media star through her gift for the Tarot, had dared to use her fortune-telling programme ('family entertainment') to discuss the killings. Yes, no doubt the serial killer was mad, she'd said, yet his crimes could not be divorced from the culture in which they occurred, could not be dismissed as some random attack by the Thing from Another World. The entertainment industry with its passion for serial killers and gruesome crimes and its lingering, ingrained homophobia surely bore some responsibility, while poverty and destitution made potential victims more vulnerable.

Telephone calls, faxes and letters had rained down on Channel Nine, objecting to this mild infusion of thought into a prime-time programme. Now the channel was threatening to terminate Myra.

My reading was interrupted by the woman across the gangway. She had a mobile telephone. I couldn't believe my bad luck. You'd expect them on a weekday, when all the businessmen have those naff conversations with their opposite numbers or mistresses – although for that matter these days you can't get on a bus, not that I often do, without finding someone curled up with their instrument and sharing their intimate lives with an unwilling audience – but on a Sunday you hoped for peace and quiet. I thought of pointing

3

out to her that those phones give you brain cancer, but then I decided not to. Serve her right.

However much she was annoying me, it was too big an effort to change seats yet again. I glared, but then as I really looked at her for the first time, my anger melted away.

It was the colouring that did it. It's a cliché, but her skin really was opalescent, it had an extraordinary radiance. Her hair, an angelic golden halo, made her look like a saint in an early Italian painting, her eyes were two shards of intense blue as she returned my stare. Her nose was slightly hooked, her lips too narrow for her large white teeth, her eyes deep set and small, but I couldn't take my eyes off her.

She wore a tight little purple suit; it looked very expensive, and her smooth legs were curled up sideways on the seat. The hand not holding the phone to her ear was playing with a bit of paper on the table in front of her. It was a pinkish, lightly freckled hand, with short almond nails.

Somehow you at once imagined that hand stroking a man's balls, guiding a prick, massaging, pleasuring, efficient as a nurse, impersonal as a prostitute – but she looked too rich to be a nurse.

Her voice had a hard little edge to it. 'It's Miranda . . . is that Tracey? . . . yes, well I'm in the train. Is everything OK? . . . Umm . . . and what about the French order? Did it . . . you did? Super.'

She listened for a while – something more intimate maybe, for she said, 'Mmm, it's very difficult . . . you have to make a decision some time though . . . mmm . . . you can't let him – ' After a while she started to frown and shift about in her seat. Bored now by the confidences, she said brusquely: 'Is Dean there? . . . What? Oh I haven't *seen* him, we've both been doing so many things – '

I lost interest and looked out of the window, my thoughts drawn back to the prison. My clothes reeked of the cigarette smoke they'd soaked up in the visitors' waiting room. And how I hated the way you were dragooned by overweight, pudding-faced men with their bunches of keys, keys they didn't even use because everything was electronic. That was why I never travelled first class when I went there. You had to get into role, and then – well, it was all part of the penance, part of the mess of unresolved feeling.

The woman in purple caught my attention again. Now she was talking to – her husband, was it? 'Yes . . . if you like. The French order – no . . . Are you in for dinner? . . . Then I'll see you this evening, darling.' She sounded indifferent about that.

She punched the numbers again, a little hurried now, and played with the bit of paper, frowning. She waited. No one answered. She gave up finally, pushed the phone down into a large leather bag and flipped open her copy of *Vogue*. Then, instead of reading it, she looked back at me and smiled across the gangway.

'I hope I wasn't disturbing you. They're a menace, aren't they? Just another of our little toys.'

'That's OK.' I no longer felt annoyed. She uncurled herself, eased herself out of her seat and came to sit across from me.

'The thing is – it's so useful for my business. But I suppose it's like everything, faxes, video transmissions, internet, you can't imagine how you lived without them.'

I was about to ask what she did, but she handed me her card. Printed in plain black lettering: MIRANDA MARS – MM DESIGNS. An address in smaller print ran along the bottom.

It took me a few seconds to gather my wits. Then I said: 'Oh! I just love your stuff. That wonderful boutique – it's my favourite shop.'

She looked pleased. Her eyelashes were long and darkened, and I inhaled her scent, Chloé, sweet and heavy. She still looked hard at me, a blind, blue stare. I smiled back, but her gaze puzzled me: how to interpret its strange insistence.

'I was sure I'd seen you somewhere – perhaps there. Not

that I go to the shop that often.' She went on staring at me. 'I know. There was an article about you in a magazine. You run that café, don't you? What did they call it? The capital of the new Bohemia.'

As she said it I somehow had a feeling she'd known all along. I felt embarrassed. I hate talking about myself, my work. Don't know why – it makes me feel self-conscious, pretentious somehow. 'The Lost Time Café, it's just a place where people hang out,' I muttered, and switched the conversation back to her. She was more than happy to talk about the rag trade, one of those women with a passion for her work, a passion for clothes. Clothes being a passion of mine as well, we got on like a house on fire.

The train rushed towards Kakania. The city I'd lived in forever: shit city – one of the biggest cities in the world, the great capital city, rotting, fermenting and slipping slowly into the sea; a city that, like all great cities, raised decay to the status of an art form. Now we were streaking through the outlying hills, gilded by the diagonals of the autumn afternoon sun, now we thrummed and galloped across the Harvey St Anselm bridge. Then the train plunged through the cuttings between high walls crowned with white stucco terraces and cliff-like black brick housing, burrowing through mile after mile of the stony landscape until the tracks opened out on to a view of the Cairo Hall, the new concert hall – a fanciful neo-Assyrian building covered with turquoise and terracotta tiles – before the train entered another tunnel and creaked and screeched to a halt alongside the platform under the echoing glass roof of the terminal.

When Miranda Mars stood up she was shorter than I'd expected. She held out the plump, pink hand. It was slightly moist to the touch and squeezed mine firmly.

'I have a card too,' I said, and took one out for her. 'You must come to the Café some time.'

'Oh I've been dying to . . . only there's never any time. But now I've met you I will. Really.'

I was taking time folding the messed up sheets of my newspaper. 'Don't wait for me,' I said, and she didn't, but when I got on to the platform I could still see her ahead. She looked square and chunky from the back, and walked in a sturdy, determined way, the way toddlers trot along. For a while I kept her in sight, but my pace was lethargic and other passengers soon separated us. I glimpsed the halo of hair again at the barrier, and the last I saw of her she was marching towards the taxi rank.

I'd probably have forgotten all about her, only three weeks later, by one of those odd coincidences, our paths crossed again.

Two

It was at the Cairo Hall inaugural concert. Myra and I arrived early. We wanted to see the celebrities – and be seen ourselves. I wasn't famous like Myra, of course, but *Fascination* had run an article: QUEEN OF BOHEMIA – JUSTINE HILLYARD'S LOST TIME CAFÉ TAKES THE CAKE, there'd been a late-night TV arts feature item, 'Millennial Boho', and a fashionable ceramics artist had created a series called 'Cakes' for me – a pottery chocolate gâteau, a plate of coconut fancies, a china doily, all of which were now hanging on the Café walls.

We walked up the steps and into the hotly lit foyer. Already there was a crowd. Men and women milled about on the marble pavement like extras on the set of *Intolerance*. Some stood by the bar in twos and threes; in the centre of the hall, loners, waiting for their friends, drifted up and down; poseurs leant against mosaic columns; important-looking elderly couples stalked across; a burst of laughter came from a group of glamorous youth near the entrance. Many slid sideways glances at us – well, mostly at Myra – as we strolled towards the bar. In her purple robe she certainly stood out.

The vast atrium made a suitable stage for her. It was primitive, it glittered. There were staircases like waterfalls and columns like the Acropolis. The floor was white marble. From the far-off ceiling candelabra plunged crystal rapiers down towards us. On the rear wall a gold mosaic mural dimly gleamed.

'There was a lot of fuss about the design,' I said.

'I'm not *surprised*. And all for the greater glory of Cairo Enterprises Inc.'

Some time in the nineteenth century a refugee shopkeeper from Poland had started to make pickles, and now Cairo was a household name all over the world, a food empire that funded supermarkets, paper making, spilled over into health charities and drugs, and, most recently, had propelled Lord Cairo into high political office. The Cairo Hall was more than just another building, it was a monument to the Cairo name, fixed it in lights for ever.

'Oh look – there's Francis.' And Myra strode towards him, her brocade dress dragging along the floor with a rasping sound.

Francis stood near the bar, elegant in a dinner jacket, aloof as a stork, with his long, thin legs and bony face. When he saw us he waved his hand in a languid yet hurried way, a sketchy little gesture, but as he came forward to meet us, his shoulders stooped, his head bowed, his movements were tentative and apologetic. The stork did not spread his splendid wings. It was as if they'd been clipped.

I kissed his dry cheek. Like many thin, tall men he had kept an air of distinction and usually still seemed youthful, but this evening in the dazzle of our surroundings he not only looked his age – fifty five – but even rather ill, pale and papery. Myra with her flowing white locks and massive physique eclipsed him.

'Let's have a drink,' he said. While we waited at the bar he looked around. 'So here we are at Aaron's . . . well, what is it – a wake, a memorial? Actually, it's not about Aaron at all. Have you seen the programme? Not a word about him, nothing but the bloody family, their services to private medicine, to architecture, to the environment. So far as Aaron's concerned, it's a conspiracy of silence. Christ.'

'Let me see.' I held out my hand for his copy.

'They'd hardly want to remind us he committed suicide,' said Myra. 'But why a memorial concert at all, then, and after all this time? How long *is* it?'

'Six – seven years. No, nearly eight. God – I can't believe it.' And Francis smiled grimly, knocked back his gin and signalled the barman. 'Doesn't seem that long.'

I leafed through the programme. We were to hear a famous conductor, the new resident orchestra, and, best of all, Delphine Jordan, hailed as the most exciting soprano since Sutherland; a tactful choice for the new venue, but Francis was right, nothing to do with Aaron Cairo. There were the usual paragraphs about the musicians and advertisements for luxury foods and choice restaurants (including the Lost Time Café, I'm afraid, and the MM Designs boutique), but the main idea, as Francis had said, seemed to be to sanctify the Cairo family, and it was Lord Cairo, not his dead brother, who smiled out complacently from the frontispiece. Only one inconspicuous sentence at the bottom of the list of works to be played informed us that the hall was dedicated to the memory of Dr Aaron Cairo.

Francis lit a cigarette. A woman at the next table ostentatiously fanned the smoke away, but Francis didn't notice, the last of the hard-core smokers. A no smoking zone was merely a challenge to him, he was militant about it, strange in someone who in some ways was so sensitive. I could see he was miserable this evening, so I didn't like to remind him, but just squeezed his arm instead.

'I suppose they thought they had to do something,' said Francis. He paused, pulled on his cigarette. 'Nigel Cairo was junior health minister at the time. When Aaron shot himself it made an embarrassing story – the two brothers at loggerheads, Aaron fighting the reforms his brother was pushing through. Cairo did get quite a lot of stick over it. I mean in the media.'

A waiter asked him to extinguish his cigarette.

'Oh – yes – I'm so sorry, of course – ' but he took a final drag and made a big performance of grinding it into the marble floor, to the disgust of our neighbour.

'And now they've built this casino. Place reminds me of Las Vegas. So inappropriate. Quite difficult to have hit on anything he would have liked less. But they can have it both ways, can't they. More publicity, and they can pretend it's in Aaron's honour.' He smoothed back his flat, silky hair and looked around desperately, staring out at the gathering crowd as if into a great empty space.

Myra observed him, but said nothing. I was puzzled. He and I were old friends, but this mood of distress came as a shock. I couldn't remember him ever even mentioning Aaron Cairo before.

When I say old friends – I'd known him since for ever, known him since he'd been one of my father's science students at the university. He and my parents were involved in serious left-wing politics then. I was just a kid. I mean, really a kid. He was seventeen years older than me, but as the years went by the difference in age mattered less. Before I'd gone to live in California our friendship had been intermittent, but since my return, three years ago now, we'd become quite close. I was fond of him, although I sometimes felt that there was a null, dead space at the centre of the relationship, where sexual attraction could never be. Or perhaps that was just some deep reserve in each of us, a mutual reticence that paradoxically bound us together.

From time to time he'd turn up at the Café with some young man plucked from an unpromising life among the workless, and steer him through the throng with almost paternal pride. Often the young men rebelled against all the mothering, the advice about late nights and over-indulgence, the attempts to interest them in worthwhile careers, sometimes they became clinging vines he was too kind to shake off. It didn't help that he was a psychiatrist – he got caught up in endless intense analyses of their personalities. He was a sucker for pathos, too. What was endearing about him was that unlike most people, whose skins thicken as the years go by, he seemed to grow more vulnerable, as if life was scraping away his defences against pain and suffering.

'I don't know much about Aaron Cairo,' I said. 'I was in California so long.'

'You knew we worked together.'

'No, I don't think I even knew that.'

'Aaron was a wonderful person. He was dynamic, creative – and he fought for his ideas when the going got tough. Lived for his work – a bit too much, I suppose. Lacked a sense of proportion in a way. His opponents called him fanatical. Some of the staff at the hospital said he drove them too hard. But it was himself he drove, really. Of course, his wife's illness didn't help. But I'd never have said he was clinically depressed. Not even a depressive personality, well, maybe, just slightly, but then that doesn't necessarily lead to depressive illness, any more than a schizoid personality leads to schizophrenia.

'When I heard – I was in Boston at the time, on a sabbatical – I didn't believe it at first: that he'd committed suicide . . . I never thought he was depressed. I'd left about a month earlier, he wasn't depressed then. And I know about depression. I know the really determined suicides are the ones no one suspects for a moment. Then they kill themselves and it comes as a terrible shock to their friends and relations. Well,' and he smiled grimly, 'in his case me. But – he really wasn't. Anxious, preoccupied, there was a lot going on at the hospital – but suicide! Even now it seems extraordinary. I'd never have thought he'd lose his nerve like that. Really haunts me, you know.'

'No, I didn't know,' I murmured, dismayed. Other people's pain must never be allowed to creep too close: death, disappointment, failure, the corrosive desperation of lives that touched one's own without contaminating it, that burnt great holes in life's fabric, gaps that could never be repaired. I skirted round it so carefully, that abyss, those black holes of screaming despair, I was so careful to keep it at arm's length.

I scanned the crowd, in search of a different topic of conversation. 'Oh look – there's the unfrocked bishop. What on earth's he doing here?'

'Barnaby Tenison-Joliet's the best self-publicist since Andy Warhol,' said Myra.

'He'd hardly care for the comparison.'

'He's not unfrocked,' Francis corrected me pedantically. 'He left because of the women. He said they should be burned at the stake. Only he didn't go over to Rome like the rest of them, went the other way. Now he's a holy roller in the very worst part of town.'

By this time the foyer was jammed. A television crew was assembling itself. We were surrounded, smothered by lavish gowns, confident voices, made-up faces, port-wine complexions. A woman with red hair and an emerald green dress which plunged both fore and aft was tracked by the cameras. I hoped *my* dinner jacket, worn with nothing underneath, and with high heels and a diamond-studded dog collar, looked a tiny bit camp, but Myra said rudely:

'You look like you've escaped from that Japanese all-women drag troupe.'

Oh dear – kitsch, not camp. Well, it couldn't be helped now, and actually I felt quite good, although no one tried to photograph *me*.

Myra said, 'Who are all these people?'

'*Tout le monde*, darling.' There were celebrities from the arts and the music world, well known television faces, Francis pointed out some psychoanalysts, occasionally a politician sidled through with that expression they wear on such occasions of self-importance mingled with shiftiness. The usual charity-show crowd made up the numbers, but – most important of all – John Carson was expected: the media magnate.

A bell rang. The audience drifted towards their seats, settled down, seething and murmuring like a beehive, a murmur that rose by half an octave when the Duke and Duchess appeared in their box, followed by Carson. Then the lights dimmed. The voices sank.

The master of ceremonies was a TV psychiatrist – an odd, covert reference to Aaron Cairo, perhaps. This guy interviewed the famous, was famous himself for making them cry in front of the cameras. But there were no confessions today.

13

He spoke briefly, praising the Cairo family, and in particular their generosity in replacing the old concert hall, bombed by terrorists six years ago, as he reminded us. Only just before he introduced the conductor and the orchestra did he remind us in whose memory the hall was built.

The music cocooned us, and in the semi-darkness I watched the amethysts on Myra's heavy fingers gleaming dimly. She and Francis seemed absorbed in the music, but I found it hard to concentrate. There was a piece by Vaughan Williams, a Mozart symphony. I wondered if it was a selection of the dead psychiatrist's favourite music, but if it was, no one said so.

Francis had been invited to drinks behind the scenes in the interval, and took us along as well. 'Frankly, I was amazed,' he muttered, 'but I suppose they had to pay some sort of lip service to . . .'

We never heard what it was the Cairo family had to pay lip service to, for at that moment a woman turned towards him with an eager yet painful smile.

'Ruth!' he said, and introduced her as Aaron Cairo's sister, Lady Gardiner. She looked like the photograph of Lord Cairo in the programme, had the same heavy black hair, the same powerful, masculine face, with moist eyes like prunes and a large, crooked mouth, in her case darkened with maroon lipstick. It was all wrong with her skinny body and her ultra-feminine silk dress, a mass of yellow accordion pleats with a huge, picture collar. She looked mid-forties, but could well have been older. Her movements were quick, as if she was trying to be youthful, but the effect was rather one of enormous tension.

A waiter stood beside us with canapés on a silver salver; another held out a tray of flute glasses filled with champagne. Ruth Gardiner gestured us to some chairs. She seemed mesmerised by Myra. Her skirt fanned out as she leant towards her, and her triple rope of pearls dangled forward. 'I've always longed to have my fortune told.' She smiled guiltily. 'But my husband doesn't approve of anything like that.'

'If you ever wanted to talk to me.' Myra handed her her card.

'Oh – oh I don't know . . .' She flushed, and laughed, but she snatched the card almost with desperation. Her bony hands were hung with rings, two set with large diamonds, the third a chunk of topaz. She turned to Francis.

'How do you like the concert? Aaron would have loved it, wouldn't he?' She was staring almost pleadingly at us. 'I'm so glad it's finally happened. I felt it was so important to do *something*,' she said in a low voice. 'My brother, my *other* brother – ' she looked round as she spoke – 'was always against the idea. He didn't want all the old stuff about Aaron raked up in the press. But I absolutely insisted. Though for all the good it's done . . . Nigel absolutely put his foot down about a speech, a formal tribute, anything like that. Still, Aaron's name is up there, in the foyer. Did you see?'

Francis shook his head.

'The mural at the back. You must have a look.'

'Don't worry – people will remember Aaron,' Francis said, 'his work was so important. And – well I'm sure you know this – there's a revival of interest in it now, in his approach, his writings. I'm helping organise a conference.'

She looked uneasy. 'Nigel isn't too happy about that either.'

Francis looked quite angry: 'But what right has he to object? It's none of his business.'

'I know, but . . .' She shrugged hopelessly, twisted her pearls, bit her lip.

Francis placed a hand lightly on her arm. 'Don't let it upset you. Just remember – Aaron was a wonderful man. That's what matters.'

Ruth's face reflected every nuance of her changing emotions, and now a vivid smile replaced the grimace of a moment ago. 'Oh he was! Wonderful. Dedicated – and he had. I don't know what to call it – presence, didn't he? A radiance, almost. He'd come into the room and it was – as if a light had been turned on. And he was so good to Monica.

It's a horrible illness, you know. But he never – I mean he did everything he could. Absolutely everything. That's why, after she died . . . I suppose it was just too much for him.'

She looked away, and I saw that now she really was close to tears.

'This evening was bound to bring it all back,' said Francis, 'I feel the same myself. These last few weeks, I've thought more about it than I had for – I don't know how long.'

Ruth Gardiner nodded and pressed her lips together. 'It's brought back all the anger. I mean, the way the police – they were so insensitive, all those insinuations, the questions, the suspicion – of course, you were away at the time. But it was all so strange . . . they even suggested . . .' Her voice trailed off. Then she said: 'Why couldn't it have been an accident? Don't you think it could have been?' She looked almost pleadingly at him. 'And then there was the money.'

'Ruth – I think Gilda wants to talk to you.' It was Lord Cairo himself, tall and beefy. He towered over us. His sister sprang guiltily to her feet.

'Oh – where is she? Oh – over there, of course – just excuse me – '

Since Lord Cairo made no move to sit down, we all three somehow found that we had stood up. Lord Cairo had merely nodded coolly at Myra and me, not bothering to hide his distaste at this unwelcome proximity to such a subversive couple, and at once went on the offensive to Francis.

'Frankly,' he said, 'I could never understand why Aaron became a psychiatrist. Important work of course, most important, but isn't it a bit morbid? Minister of the Interior was telling me the other day – now you're taking on some of the more dangerous offenders – pretty tough assignment – shouldn't fancy it myself.' He stood there, smiling insolently at Francis, daring him to argue, almost picking a fight. 'And now, all this new interest in Aaron's work. Plans for a conference, some papers to be published, I understand. Is that wise? Some of Aaron's ideas were rather controversial, weren't they? I understand you're keen on the idea, but

– well, maybe we should have a chat about it some time. Ring my office, why don't you.'

He moved off. Francis looked rather white, and muttered: 'Was that some kind of covert threat? Foul man. Ploughing back his millions into the bloody Far Right. Even though he's in the government.'

'Really?' Myra looked startled, and so was I. 'That's sailing close to the wind, isn't it?'

'Can't stand them,' said Francis. 'Let's get out of here. Oh God, there's Derek.' Another tall, florid man had materialised by the drinks table. A flop of brassy hair fell over his face. He took a glass of wine from the table, looked round, saw Francis and moved towards us. Seen close to, he looked older, despite the sumptuous hair. His skin was scaly, lined in grooves and folds like that of a tortoise.

'How's things? Enjoying the concert?' he boomed with professional geniality, but his eyes, like chips off an iceberg, glanced everywhere but at us.

'Derek Leadbetter,' said Francis stonily.

'Did you know Dr Cairo?' I enquired.

Leadbetter laughed. When he laughed his shoulders shook up and down. I couldn't see what was so funny. 'I'm the medical director of Four Lawns Hospital,' he told us.

'Sorry, I didn't explain, he's my boss.' Francis was looking around, as if for an escape route.

'I knew Aaron pretty well – tragic, really.'

The four of us stood there in awkward silence. Then Leadbetter showed signs of animation. 'There's Nigel,' he cried. 'Excuse me.' And he eased his way through the guests in the direction of Lord Cairo.

We returned to our seats for the second half of the concert. Now it was the soprano's turn. She was wonderful. She wore a clinging mermaid dress of shimmering eau de nil, and sang a couple of Verdi arias, then Berlioz's *Nuits d'été*, followed by Richard Strauss's *Four Last Songs*.

For the first time the place came alive. There were cheers, wave after wave of applause. They wouldn't let her go. When she returned to the platform for the fourth time she waited for silence. Then she spoke.

'You all know – ' and her voice came clear to the expectant crowd, 'that this evening is in memory of Aaron Cairo. I want to share with you my own memory of a man without whose help I would not have been here tonight. Dr Cairo believed in free health care for all, and especially for the mentally ill, always a neglected group. For that reason he saw very few private patients, but when I was still in my teens I had a nervous breakdown and, exceptionally, he agreed to treat me privately. I was very ill, and had it not been for him I doubt if I could have continued to train as a singer. The song I am going to sing now is dedicated to him.'

A murmur ran through the audience, then quietened again, as she clasped her hands and prepared to sing. She was going to sing unaccompanied.

And she sang: not an aria, but the song – originally I think from some long forgotten revolutionary war – which the terrorists' supporters had sung during a big trial, the previous year.

When she finished, the silence was extraordinary. Then, as she walked slowly off the stage, a section of the audience began to clap. So did we – and gradually the applause swelled, but in our part of the stalls most of them stood rigid, silent, furious.

Afterwards, in the foyer, the audience milled around, trying to recover. Yet after all, it was only a song. It doesn't take much to upset the shits. I tried to get over to speak to Delphine Jordan, but she was being mobbed by the press. Francis went to the gents and Myra and I strolled to the back of the hall to take a closer look at the mosaic.

Huge, it depicted scenes from the life of Aesculapius, the Greek god of healing. Aesculapius stood in the centre with a serpent twined round his stave. A scene to the left showed Apollo, his father, a halo of golden hair standing out about his head. Presumably the subject matter was intended as some sort of homage to Aaron Cairo; and, as Ruth Gardiner had told us, there was an inscription to him above the mosaic.

We stepped back to get a better look, and at that moment I saw her: Miranda Mars.

It was she, quite definitely. She was coming down the stairs. In her radiance she stood out, although she was dressed in black; indeed, the black only enhanced her luminosity. As I watched her, she turned and saw me across the glittering hall. She stared, at me and at Myra. I nudged Myra.

'There's that woman I met on the train, Miranda Mars, remember I told you? Look – up there.'

'The dress designer?' Myra looked up.

Miranda Mars waved, smiled, and started towards us, but as she did so a tall blond man came up behind her, on her left, she turned away abruptly, and moving across to the further side of the wide stairs, was lost to view.

'Sorry I was so long – fearful queue. It's too small in there. Badly designed.' Francis was beside us again.

Myra mopped her brow and fanned herself with her programme. 'Can we get something to drink? Half-past nine,' she complained, 'the middle of the evening, what a terrible time for it to end.'

Francis cast a haunted look around the crowd. 'Can't stand it here. Let's get out.'

'Yes,' I agreed. 'Come back to the Café, it's terrible here.'

As we were jostled through the crowd, I looked round for the woman from the train, Miranda Mars, but she had disappeared.

Three

As we came through the door of the Lost Time Café, the roar of talk and laughter hit us head on. I felt better at once. This was home.

At a glance I took in the familiar scene. The big front room, somewhere between a junk shop and a private house, was crammed with tables and chairs of every description, with bookshelves, pictures, ornaments and cushions haphazardly placed. Nothing matched. A blue glass vase of red gladioli stood on the piano. Curving down the length of the room on the right-hand side was the long, old-fashioned mahogany bar, with its brass rail, retained from the days when the place was a dockside pub. Through a wide, columned archway and up a step was the secretive, exclusive back room with its sofas and banquettes and little alcoves.

The big round table still stood midway between the piano and the bar. Even after all this time I half expected to see the familiar faces from the old days – Wilma, Jade, Lennox – but they were long gone, and the women's writers' group had colonised the centre table. Dressed in red, blue, purple, white, they were flung back and forth in their chairs as they argued, with hands shaping thoughts, and bursts of raucous laughter. A huddle of *Daily Post* journalists in the smoking section seemed to be hatching some plot, perhaps against their new editor, Urban Foster. In the back room I glimpsed Verity Planchette, the poetess, and her circle of adoring admirers.

Only a deeply lonely person could do what I did for a living, especially as I didn't even need to make a living. I had more than enough money already (inherited wealth, I'm afraid) so I must be doing it for psychological reasons. My customers were my friends, and they came to see me. They came to see me without my having to ask, and that's brilliant for someone shy. I never had to take a risk, I never had to make the effort. All I had to do was wear my out-rageous clothes, clothes that hid me perfectly, so that I looked out from behind them as if from behind a mask or a screen, invulnerable, unscathed, and surveyed the perfection I'd created. I simply had to wait, and that's what I did. I sat at my table in a recess at the back, with a cup of coffee or a margarita. My friends came to me, they called me darling and kissed me, and there was gossip, there were shrieks of laughter and arguments and sometimes maudlin tears.

The Café was the velvet underground of our bleak times. We were the Romans in Britain when the Roman Empire was crumbling away. Somewhere along the coast the barbarians marauded, but they hadn't reached us – not yet. We were aristocrats in Renaissance Italy, holed up to escape the plague in a country palazzo and passing the time by telling porno stories. Yes – when I read in the newspapers of bubonic plague spreading from Zaire all over Africa and threatening Europe, when I read about civil war spreading from the East, I thought how like the Romans in Britain we were.

We were like skaters too, gliding and spinning to the music, unaware that the ice was melting. The water was over our skates, it was over our ankles, we were sinking fast, it would soon be up to our necks and we'd be swimming for dear life. Not yet, though. Not quite yet.

We'd gone into internal exile, and the Café was where the exiles and the double agents (which was all of us) met. No – I was kidding myself, we were merely the spectators, spectators with a ringside seat.

We were the dissidents, the *out*, the official dissidents at least, and everyone was paranoid. Gennady and I used to look around and wonder which of the regulars was the man from the Ministry of Fear, who was the informer mingling with the *bohème dorée*.

The other – the real – dissidents were underground, in prison, met secretly in houses, in the abandoned underground system . . . who knew where.

Gennady was my manager. Now he nodded, to show he'd seen me. He was my right-hand man, in fact he did the work, freeing me to play hostess to my favourites. Like most of the Russians, he'd come over during the civil war, originally to help the Socialist Opposition back home. But the longer he'd stayed and the more hopeless his mission, the more he'd got locked into life at the glittering end of shit city.

I went over for a quick word, then took a couple of bottles of champagne up to the balcony, which bulged out over the front room at the top of a curving stairway. Up there, the decoration had a whiff of 1930s Hollywood boudoir, with drooping silk gauze flowers, gilt furniture and cheap pastel colours. Myra loved it. That's where she told fortunes, saw her clients. She didn't believe in making appointments. Everyone knew that on Tuesdays and Fridays you could just turn up and see her. Usually there was a queue, but if, exceptionally, no one came, she read her books up there. She knew about Jung and Zen, Sufi and the Qabalah, all that stuff, but her real interest was some sort of psychological alternative to Freud.

She was seated at her table now. I poured the champagne. Francis lay on a sofa, his long legs crossed elegantly at the ankle.

We mulled over the Delphine Jordan gesture. Extraordinary! We couldn't stop talking about it. It had cheered Francis up no end, as you can imagine: a cool, stylish slap in the face for Lord Cairo.

Eventually we calmed down. Francis grew broody again.

'You know his death's a mystery.'

'What?' Myra looked at him. 'Oh – Aaron Cairo.'

'Suicide . . .' mused Francis, 'but why on earth would he kill himself? It never made sense. And everyone knows it.'

Myra said: 'Did you think that at the time? Or is it only now? Sometimes things change in retrospect, don't they? I mean, it's eight years ago, isn't that what you said – eight years – and you haven't been thinking about it all that time.'

'No. You're right. I'm being absurd.'

'I didn't say that,' said Myra. 'What I'm asking is why it's started to bug you now.'

Francis emptied his glass, refilled it and drank again. 'Don't know.' He stared at his feet. 'Why are people interested in him again? Why have I started working on the papers he left behind? I've had them all this time. When I got back from the States, the stuff was all there, lying around at work – the research he'd been doing. Been meaning to do something with it ever since. But I never have, until now.'

'Perhaps you couldn't cope with it then,' I said.

'I wish I had, I wish I'd looked into it right away, instead of letting it hang around, everyone trying to shove it under the carpet. His death I mean, not the research.'

'How did people do that?' asked Myra.

Francis shifted about on the sofa. 'Well – the line the family took was he was depressed because his wife had died. She'd had multiple sclerosis for years. He'd have liked children, a big family, he was kind of quite traditionally Jewish in that way, but because of Monica's illness they decided against. But I was around at the time she died, and I don't think it made him suicidal. I really don't. But I suppose the Cairos preferred that explanation to the idea that his death had to do with the row over the hospital and the health reforms. That was very embarrassing for them, for Lord Cairo at least.'

'Yes, of course,' said Myra.

'Derek didn't like that explanation either – the doctor we met this evening. He never liked Aaron, loathed his guts in fact. Basically it was the old struggle: drugs versus psychotherapy. Do you treat mental problems as though they're physical, or do you try to talk to patients about them? Many of us do both, but there is still a level of polarisation. Also, Aaron should have got the medical directorship. But no, Derek was the drugs boy. Pump everyone full of tranqs, and it'll all be OK. Psychotherapy takes too long. Everyone prefers the quick fix these days, especially the government. Rewards and punishments. Take your pills for ten days on the trot and you'll be let out of the ward for half an hour. Lay off raping women and you might get a job sweeping the floor of a Cairo supermarket. And of course it's worked. Huge success. Money's poured in from the drugs companies. We're the richest hospital in the country, even without the special patients.' He laughed bitterly. 'Though the new wing essentially *is* a prison of course – a prison for all the people they'd rather have hanged. Really crazy but harmless patients who can't look after themselves are just kicked out, and we're left with the ones who come through the courts. Sometimes they're not mad at all.' He stared gloomily into his champagne. 'Well – I'm exaggerating. But d'you know what I think – ' and he sounded a bit drunk now – 'I think Aaron got in Derek's way. Derek could have driven him to it, he knows how to put the knife in. Or he could even have – '

'Hi sweethearts!' It was Myra's new girlfriend, Marky, a tough little bruiser with spiky black hair.

She and I flirted. I didn't mean it, that went without saying. I wouldn't have dared to try anything on with Myra's squeeze. It was just a safe little game, and if I played it a bit too hard this evening, really camping it up, that was because my glimpse of the woman from the train, dressed all in black with her halo of pale gold curls, had been so tantalising. I'd been so sure she'd say hello again, but suddenly she'd turned away.

Myra said: 'Francis, why don't I throw a spread?'

He looked at her. There was a little tingle of aggro in the air. Their relationship was always slightly barbed. They argued endlessly about therapy and superstition. In one mood Francis would say: we're in the same business really, don't you think? I'm just as much a witch doctor as you are at the end of the day. In another mood he'd be the white-coated scientist and accuse Myra of pandering to people's basest instincts and playing on their credulity. It was always the same argument: whether psychoanalysis was a perverted kind of fortune-telling, or fortune-telling a cheap imitation of therapy.

Now Francis said, rather piously: 'Aaron didn't believe in that sort of thing. Used to say there's no rational basis to it all.'

'Oh, the Tarot is quite rational in its own terms. Quite as rational as Freud.' Myra smiled sweetly. 'Anyway, you don't have to believe. It's just a method. Which of course is exactly what the psychoanalysts say about psychoanalysis, isn't it?'

I knew why Francis had such mixed feelings; it was a very sore point indeed, and as I'd feared, he couldn't keep away from it now.

'I wouldn't know, I'm not an analyst,' he said huffily, as if it were our fault. 'As you well know, they wouldn't have me on account of I'm gay.'

Marky was appalled. 'You're saying you can't be a psycho-thingummy because you're queer? Are you really saying that? Shit. And you carry on working with the shits?'

Marky was a twenty-three-year-old radical dyke, and had only a hazy idea of what the world outside queer culture was like. Compromise to her was tantamount to selling your mother. I was just as shocked as her, though, when Francis said cravenly:

'Well . . . maybe we do have more psychological problems. Aaron thought so.'

'Jesus! What are you – some kind of masochist or some-thing?' cried Marky. 'Not that there's anything wrong with masochism,' she added hastily.

'Well, you know, being attracted to your own sex, it is a kind of narcissism,' said Francis.

'What about children?' I said. 'You know, people adore

their own children, they see themselves in their children. Is that just being in love with yourself as well?'

I thought I'd got him in a corner there, but he only smiled: 'I'm afraid so, yes. Freud said precisely that.'

'But that's OK, right? So this stuff, loving yourself, narcissism, it's good when it's with children but wrong for gays. What's the difference, then? Is it the sex? It's OK so long as there's no sex? Or what?'

Marky could contain herself no longer. 'I call that self-oppression,' she said passionately. 'That's all part of it, making queers feel bad about themselves. In my job, I have to read the local papers, monitor them for gay issues. And you know there are so many of us out there being persecuted because of stupid ideas like that. Queer bashing, murder, the bottom line is all about homophobia and what you're saying is just dressing it up in an intellectual way.'

'Perhaps you're right.' Francis looked uneasy. He disliked gay activism, it made him uncomfortable to translate his private life into a public issue.

'Who is this Aaron anyway?'

'Aaron Cairo,' I explained. 'We went to his memorial concert this evening. Psychiatrist. Francis worked with him – he committed suicide. One of the grocery Cairos.'

'Well, there you are, he topped himself – shows he wasn't so clued up after all.'

Francis winced. I said quickly: 'Marky works for the *Gay Herald*,' – as if that helped. Although the two of them had met several times at the Café, it now dawned on me now they'd never actually talked to each other before.

'Oh really?'

'Anyway, all that Freud stuff is mumbo-jumbo, isn't it?' said Marky.

'You have to admit that psychoanalysis is less irrational than the Tarot,' said Francis.

'*I* don't admit that at all,' said Myra. 'It's your definition of the rational that is so constricting.'

I was afraid they were going to have a real quarrel. 'Why

don't you throw a spread, Myra?' I said quickly. 'Ask the cards why Aaron Cairo committed suicide.'

'Oh, the cards don't tell you things like that. That's not a very appropriate way to approach divination.'

Marky said disloyally, '*You* look at the cards to tell you things.'

'Go on, do it.' I was getting into the idea; it was just spooky enough to give me a frisson.

Of course it was all superstition, but I always fell for it. Everyone did. That's why Channel Nine hadn't pulled her programme in the end. The ratings were huge. The fans who watched her every week and read her syndicated columns had flooded Nine's offices with protests, more than outweighing the original protests about her 'political' remarks.

The Tarot Zone had started as a breakfast item, predictions for the day, quite routine, but had developed into a cross between a game show and one of those 'real life crime' programmes such as were popular a few years ago. The difference was that members of the public came on the programme to discuss unsolved crimes of which they, or one of their 'loved ones', had been victim. Myra made inspired suggestions and astute predictions. People said it was almost uncanny. In several cases the police had been forced to re-open or step up their enquiries. That didn't endear her to the authorities either.

'Go on,' said Marky, 'you gave them a lead on that murder the other day. And the FBI use psychics in difficult cases,' she added inconsequentially.

'It's just the Tiresias effect, my dear. I expect they'd have reached the same conclusion themselves. They just believe it more coming from me.'

'What's the Tiresias effect?'

Marky's ignorance of classical culture clearly shocked Francis: 'Tiresias was the soothsayer of the ancient world.'

'Tiresias was changed from a man into a woman,' Myra said. 'He was walking in the woods and came upon two huge entwined snakes. When he struck them with his stick he became a woman. Some years later, he saw the snakes a second time, struck them again, and changed back into a man.'

'What's that supposed to mean?'

Myra smiled. I couldn't help feeling she rather patronised Marky sometimes. 'It is rather a strange legend. Zeus gave Tiresias the stick or wand with which he struck the snakes. Later, Hera, Zeus's wife, queen of the gods, became angry with Tiresias, and made him blind, and it was then that Zeus granted Tiresias power to foretell the future. Either then or later, his gift of second sight was associated with his magic status as a man-woman.'

'I can understand the part about the change of sex,' I said, 'and the blindness . . . sort of . . . but what do the snakes mean? I know, don't say it, phallic symbol. Sex. But that's so obvious.'

'Because a symbol seems obvious doesn't mean it isn't valuable or truthful,' Myra said. She took her pack from her bag, unwrapped it from the indigo silk scarf in which she kept it, and placed the cards on the table.

'What actually *happened* to this guy; your friend?' said Marky.

Francis frowned. He spoke reluctantly, as if it was painful to go over it all again. 'Aaron was shot. He was found in his Audi. It was parked at the edge of the Botanical Gardens. His wife had just died, couple of months earlier. The gun was there. There was a powder burn. The angle of the shot was consistent with suicide. Fingerprints on the gun. The only thing the police thought a bit odd was the way he'd fallen. He was all crumpled up against the steering wheel, and the gun was still in his hand. The police said they'd have expected the impact of the shot to hurl him backwards against the seat and the gun might have got flung away too, even hit the windscreen or the side window or something. The inquest was adjourned initially. The police weren't sure what to think.'

Marky was staring at him, her brown eyes big and round. 'So what was the alternative? You mean, like – *murder*?'

'Yes. Actually I do believe he was murdered.'

'*What*?' I jumped, and Myra looked up sharply.

'They seemed to have this idea to begin with it might have been a hold-up gone wrong. But no money was taken. And the car was just parked, it didn't seem to have been forced off the road or anything. So if it wasn't suicide it'd have had to be someone who knew him, they must have been *in* the car. Well – they could have held him up before he set off, I suppose, got in, made him drive them to the gardens. Or hid in the car. He lived miles away, in another part of town. But small-time guys don't hold up cars like that. And professionals would have worked it all out, they'd have known he had nothing worth taking.'

'What are you saying, Francis?' I couldn't believe he'd sprung this on us. This was a crazy idea – although he was wrong about hold-ups. A few months ago a woman's car had been hijacked. Two boys rammed her. They were drugged up. She'd been murdered. But things hadn't been quite that bad in 1990 . . . had they?

'I tell you what it was – gangster scenario,' said Marky cheerfully: 'they could have been kidnapping him for a ransom. The Cairos are loaded, aren't they?'

I wished she'd shut up. I wanted to think.

'They wouldn't have killed him then, would they?' said Francis. 'Not at once.'

'Maybe one of the family bumped him off, then.'

Myra made a warning face at her girlfriend. 'Francis,' she said, 'are you serious? After eight years you have suddenly decided Aaron Cairo was murdered?'

'I know it sounds bizarre. It's because I've been going through his papers. There are all sorts of notes – most of them are quite scrappy, but – nothing he was writing then shows any signs of depression at all. You get this feeling of enthusiasm; he really felt he was getting somewhere.'

'Well – let's throw a spread.'

Myra laid out the Celtic Cross. Two cards at the centre were placed one across the other. Myra turned them over.

'The six of Swords . . .' A cloaked, hunched figure, man or woman, was being ferried across a river. Six long swords were stuck round the edge of the barge, so the passenger appeared to be seated in a cage. 'Some people say that this is like the River Styx,' said Myra. 'A journey – '

'Death,' murmured Marky.

'No – although it signifies a break, an ending – his wife's death, maybe.' She paused, then pointed to the card that covered it: 'Against it we have the five of Pentacles.'

Two beggars staggered through the snow past a brightly lit church window. 'This is a card about not having money. We'll come back to that.' She turned over more cards. 'Look at the card to the right – the nine of Swords: grief, agony. And then below you have the three of Swords, reversed. All this is very consistent with the death of his wife. Mmm . . . reversed, the three of Swords may mean grief mitigated, so perhaps her death *was* a relief, like you said –

'But then to the left and above we have the Queen of Cups and the four of Cups.'

The Queen of Cups was seated on a throne at the edge of the sea, and stared glumly at the goblet she held out in front of her. Myra liked her: 'The Queen may represent a person, in which case it's normally someone . . . well, what can I say, it's so obvious – someone with everything: life, vitality, creativity. Someone solid, attached to life. That could represent her – his wife – as well. What might have been . . .

'The four of Cups, on the other hand, that's not so rooted in reality, it's more of a fantasy – a fantasy of children, perhaps? The children he couldn't have? Or . . . it's as if he couldn't appreciate what was there, what was real, and wanted something . . .' She looked questioningly at Francis, who shrugged and shook his head.

'Now this five of Pentacles: there *isn't* money in all this. That card's about the absence of money – although again, it's also about not being able to get . . . sustenance, support when the person could get it if they knew where to look, or if they could look . . .'

'Oh, but he was rich,' said Francis. 'You know, the Cairos – they're billionaires. They all have some of it, Ruth. Aaron, all of them.'

Myra looked sharply at him and then back at the cards, but she didn't say anything. At the side of the cross itself she had laid out a line of four cards. Starting from the bottom, she turned them over one at a time. 'The Knight of Wands,' she said, 'suggests – again – new energy, something hopeful, although it might be rather undirected. In the next two cards, too, there's a sense of hope. The High Priestess is a card of the unconscious, of spirituality. So you have his life bounded by these two aspects of female strength, the Queen of Cups and the High Priestess. Then, above the Priestess you have the Hanged Man, that's a symbol of transformation, not of death.'

It was true that the Hanged Man, a youth dressed in red tights and a blue tunic, looked serene rather than tortured, although suspended upside down by one leg from a crossbar formed of a living tree. His other leg was crossed horizontally behind the first, and his arms were folded behind him too. His golden hair hung downwards in a halo, like Miranda Mars's hair, or Apollo on the concert hall mural.

'The last card is bad.'

A yellow dawn was breaking. In the foreground a knave stole away from some war tents carrying five huge swords, leaving two more stuck in the ground. 'That's a card of treachery, trickery,' said Myra, 'and it's the card that comes at the end. As if that was what it all led to. Something really nasty. I don't know . . . a betrayal, a raid, an ambush, the one that got away.'

'His death,' I said, stating the obvious.

No one else said anything. Francis stared at the cards in silence. We all just sat there. I looked at Myra. After a while she said: 'There's nothing about suicide here . . . something very wrong, though, but I'm not sure what. The four of Cups must be important. And the Knight. Some scheme – some wild scheme, maybe?'

I drove Francis home. He lived up on the cliff, the university quarter. As we looped round the big square on the way up, he said: 'I'm having so much trouble with this paper I'm trying to write about Aaron's work.'

'It's really got to you, hasn't it.'

'Talking about it helps. It's been on my mind for days. I'm more and more certain. Only – I don't know what to do.'

We reached his flat. His hand was on the car door handle. He looked at me: 'You think I'm crazy, don't you?'

'Of course not.' Not true. I tried to ease round to face him, but the steering wheel got in the way. 'Bit of a bolt from the blue, this murder theory. I mean, why *now* after all this time?'

'I told you. Going through his papers . . . Look, why don't you come up to the hospital. You've never been, have you? It'll give you a better idea of what I'm talking about.'

I didn't see how. I looked at Francis, his drawn face, the cigarette stubs in the car ashtray. The thought of madness made me nervous.

'We can have a longer talk,' he said.

'Of course I'll come,' I said.

Myra and Marky had been discussing Francis. I lay down on the sofa on which he'd earlier reclined.

'So what's your verdict?'

'Edgy, wasn't he?' Myra fanned out her pack, picked out a single card at random, and turned it face up: 'Ten of Swords. That's bad.'

'Let's talk about something else,' said Marky. 'This shrink stuff makes me depressed.'

'I'm worried about him,' I said.

'He must have had these suspicions for years,' said Myra, 'just buried them. And now they've resurfaced.'

'Murder – that's heavy,' said Marky.

'D'you think he felt guilty?' I asked. 'He wasn't here when Cairo died – feels he could have prevented it . . . something like that?'

'That's probably it,' said Myra, and put her cards away.

Four

The following Tuesday, women's night at the Café, I was drinking at my table on the parterre with my ex-husband Occam, and wondering how soon I could get rid of him.

He'd only recently returned from California, having spent years in LA. I'd originally married him so I could go and live out there too – and had done for a while. We were divorced now, of course, but he was still a friend. He was currently earning a precarious living as a kind of freelance academic.

Tonight he was upset. His boyfriend had ditched him and he was trying to ward off his despair in the glowing, manic space of the Café. His brown eyes, his sensual lips, the way he laughed recklessly as he talked, were all part of his manner of naked self-exposure. His emotions seemed so near the surface, compared with those of other men I knew; Lennox, for example, or Francis. I'd been worrying about Francis ever since the concert.

Myra joined us, and at that moment Occam spilt a bottle of wine, sending it spinning with a fine gesture, a sweep of his arm which was meant to express his despair, but which got out of hand. Red wine went everywhere. Luckily I was wearing purple trousers, but Occam's white cords were ruined, and wine dripped on to Myra's shoe. She stepped backwards. 'For Christ's sake be careful!'

Occam only laughed. He put his hand in the pool of wine that wobbled across our table, and licked his palm.

'Henry bloody left me.'

Myra, who could always be trusted to be worldly-wise after the event, and sometimes during and before as well, said: 'Henry's unstable. He has no ambitions, he just nances round getting off with men.'

'Oh shut the fuck up, Myra. You know nothing about him, *nothing*, nothing at all, nothing – ' And Occam stood up, swaying and staggering.

'I'll call a cab. It's time you went home, sweetie.' I escorted him to the door and made sure he'd left before I returned to my table in the back room.

'About Francis,' I said.

Myra was about to speak, but something caught her eye. I looked up too and saw Miranda Mars. Still dressed in black, she moved inexorably towards me. Her movements were so definite, almost brutal.

'Hallo!' She held out the small, plump hand for me to shake. 'You see, I'm here.' Then, turning to Myra: 'I love your programme,' she said.

Soon we were drinking champagne; at least I was. Miranda Mars was eating an apple flan topped with cream.

'You'll think I'm pathetic, I've wanted to come here for ages, but I've always been too nervous. I don't like going places on my own and my husband hates this sort of scene. Then I heard about the women's night. What a wonderful place! You must tell me all about it. How did it start?' What gave you the idea?'

She asked question after question: wanted to know what it was like to run, whether it took up all my time, whether I had children, how long I'd done it, how much money it made.

To be that shamelessly nosy was somehow endearing. Her questions were so direct, bang, bang, on the line, no beating about the bush. She sucked you in completely, zoomed in on you with all the finesse of a tank, acting out of instinct, not reserved and cerebral like me, but downright, seeing life in black and white, no half-tones. We took off on a rollercoaster ride of mutual admiration. I hardly noticed when Myra stole away upstairs. It was good for me, I was enjoying myself. Lately, I'd lacked admirers. As we talked, I watched her jagged profile, which was in a different mode from the rest of her body, as if belonging to another, thinner person. I watched her plump, pink freckled hands as they made those confident, caressing gestures, and once again I was somehow led to imagine how they might caress a man. She had an air of being in charge . . . but, yes, that was it – clinical, efficient, not really sensual. I wondered if she ever made love with women. Her manner to me was rather flirtatious, and yet . . . somehow I didn't think so.

'Dean and I – that's my husband – we don't go out, don't enjoy ourselves enough.'

I'd noticed the sapphire eternity ring on her finger, but even a ring like that is less conclusive than an ordinary wedding ring. Yet I didn't exactly fancy her, it was just that I couldn't stop looking at her, and I disliked the owner-ship implied by that word: husband, it has such exclusive implications, even today.

I watched her obsessively. The greed with which she demolished the apple tart was so childlike, as was the way she looked around with open fascination, commenting on a famous actress at a far table, and some weird cult film women nearby.

'I love your suit,' I said. It was so simple, a tight little jacket, buttoned lopsidedly with buttons made from bits of driftwood, a flowing skirt with an uneven unhemmed edge, and a *faux* petticoat of coarse net hanging visibly beneath.

'My own design.' She slipped off the jacket (lined with silk hessian) and showed me the label: MM DESIGNS.

'We've built the business up together, Dean and I. It's a real bumpy ride, the rag trade, but we've done OK so far. You'll have to come out to the factory one day. I could design some things for you.'

MM Designs was very new: a hot fashion ticket since her wedding dress for Saffron Queen, the porn star. That had been a sleazy concoction of leather, see-through plastic and satin, but most of her designs were a bit less crude, a bit more avant-garde than that; the media labelled them 'witty', and their hallmark was a mixing of unrelated or contrasting bits and pieces into a coherent design.

'It's so exciting,' she said, 'but it could all change overnight again.' There's going to be a downturn soon, I can feel it. And then you know, it's difficult, trends are so hard to predict now, it's very media led – '

Later she started to talk about what, I guessed, was the real reason for her visit. 'I'm thinking of a Bohemian collection. I'd like to talk to you about it, I'm sure you'd have lots of ideas. I should just sit here, I'd get so much inspiration. We could even use the Café to hold the show – ' she looked sideways at me – 'if you thought it was a good idea, that is.'

'Brilliant.' I was pleased – but disappointed as well. Business propositions came so much easier to me than amorous ones. Lucky with money, unlucky in love, they say. I'd have preferred her to have been smitten with *moi*. But: 'Be a huge success,' I enthused. 'Such good publicity for both of us. We could be photographed together – you know . . . the Café Queen, wearing something made by Miranda Mars.'

'Oh, no one wants a photograph of me. Just you – here. With the models.'

It was a seductive idea, but I wasn't absolutely convinced. The Café didn't need publicity, it had plenty of that already. A fashion show would be a lot of work, most likely more trouble than it was worth. Just for the sake of a few glossy photos in the colour mags. There was also the problem of selling the idea to Gennady. Gennady's whole aim – mine too – was to make the guests feel at home. It was their home from home, and model girls and catwalks and noisy music felt a bit too commercial.

'I'll have to talk to my manager.'

She'd finished her cake and now her hand delved into a bowl of Japanese snacks. 'It wasn't just for that I came, like I said, I've wanted to see it for ages. The Café's famous after all.'

It was 1 a.m. when she stood up to leave.

'It's not frightening here, is it?' I said. 'You'll come back soon, I hope.'

'Of course,' she said, and treated me once more to the intense blue smile. Then she said: 'I wish you – both of you, of course – I mean your friend, the fortune teller – would come round one evening, have dinner with us. I'd love it if you would. I can see you have to be here a lot – but you must have evenings off, you can surely get away sometimes.'

This was rushing things. A cold wind of aloofness and suspicion made me think that perhaps I didn't like her so much after all. Maybe she was just a little celebrity hunter, and all this nothing more than an elaborate sales pitch, just to have the famous Myra Zone round to dinner, to show off to her rag-trade friends.

'Well . . .' I said, cautiously.

She pinned me down at once. 'What about Saturday week?'

Well, what could I say? It might be amusing. I watched her stalk away between the tables, like a cat that had got the cream.

Five

Four Lawns Hospital was right at the edge of the city. On my day off, Monday, when the Café was closed, I drove up China Road, took the expressway through Harvey St Anselm's and out to the north-west suburbs where the golf-courses met the hills. Francis had – typically – given me minutely detailed directions, and I was looking out for the tall stone pepperpot gateposts well in advance. The gates were open, as he'd said they would be, and the road wound upwards through a coppice. At the top of the rise it opened out suddenly into a park with a lake to the left, and when I drove round the curve I faced a Victorian palace in imitation Renaissance style, with square turrets, rounded windows, and patterned brick. The sunlight fell flatly over the silent edifice.

The hall, pompously panelled in dark wood, was just as empty. I looked round.

'Can I help you?'

The voice came from nowhere. Then I realised that a uniformed woman, almost completely concealed by a large tub of plastic ornamental ivy, was seated behind the wooden counter at the back. A notice on the wall behind her stated: ALL PASSES MUST BE SHOWN.

I explained why I was there.

'Yes, Dr Vaughan is expecting you. Through the swing doors, right to the end of the corridor and up the stairs. Here's your pass.'

It seemed rather casual to send me trekking off into the

hinterland of this asylum armed only with a plastic pass, and I wasn't at all optimistic about finding the way. Beyond the swing doors there was no carved wood, no baronial grandeur, but unplastered walls of green-painted brick, and a sour-sweet smell – top notes of pine disinfectant strong enough to rip the lining of your nose away, undertow of stale piss. There was also more silence: a flat, abnormal silence, not the active, busy quietness of an ordinary hospital.

A stony corridor stretched in front of me towards infinity. Outside, the October sunshine shone brightly, but the walls of this mausoleum sweated cold. I felt chilled to the bone. The corridor was empty, but as I walked down it I sensed the spoilt lives murmuring just out of sight and earshot, as if the silence walled up some seething rage.

Every ten yards or so a passage led off to left or right. Down one such passage I glimpsed a shambling figure in shrunken clothes shuffling slowly towards another dead end. Far away a door slammed. Once I heard howls, quickly cut off. Along another side passage came the clash of plates and trolleys. I walked on and on, and still I met no one.

The passage ended in a door. I opened it. The passage continued, but curved slightly now, and when I rounded the bend, I came to a fork. I stopped, having no idea which direction to take. I hesitated, then set off to the left, but after a few yards the corridor abruptly widened into an ante-chamber with glass doors opening on to a great room. A hunched figure was lurching towards me. Her face had caved in, she munched on toothless gums, wore what looked like a nightgown and socks wrinkled round her ankles.

'Lilian! Lilian!' came a voice, 'come back.' I heard foot-steps. I should have stayed and asked for help, but I turned and ran: this creature, reduced from human to animal, frightened me. I reached the place where the passages diverged, and this time I went to the right. This was a second endless vista, infinite regress, one corridor leading to another corridor, leading to a dead end.

I passed through three doors before I came at last to the

stone stairs. I hurried up them as if pursued. Then suddenly, on the first floor, I was in a different world. Here it was like a country house. White-painted, pannelled doors opened off a landing. I heard a printer clacking from beyond an open door, but when I looked in the room was empty and the machine was eerily spewing out paper all on its own.

Then I heard Francis speaking in an adjoining room. I looked round the door. He was on the telephone. This inner room was obviously his office. He waved, signalled for me to wait.

'Sorry,' he said when he came into the outer office, 'secretary's at lunch. Oh listen – before I forget . . . my spare set of house keys,' and he rifled through a desk drawer, muttering about burglaries on the Cliff, and the need to change the locks. When he'd found them, he said: 'OK, let's go.'

I followed him down the stairs. At the bottom, instead of turning back into the endless corridor, Francis opened a door which led into the garden. A gravel path skirted the vista of lawns and shrubberies and led towards what had once been another wing of the hospital, but was now a ruin.

'It's almost the last of the big Victorian asylums – a few others, up North, that's all. Once I'd have laughed if you'd told me I'd ever be sorry to see them go. We all wanted them razed to the ground, sooner we got rid of them the better, thought we'd replace them with modern community hostels. Never guessed that when they were finally knocked down everything would be so different – patients sleeping on the street, down the old Underground tunnels, in the North-Western cemetery. It makes me so angry. My whole life's work, bleeding into the sand. Christ! Why doesn't someone do something? What's happened to us all, for God's sake? We can't say boo to a goose.'

'Your hospital's been saved, though.'

'But what for! I'd rather it'd been turned into a theme park. There were plans to do that, you know – turn it into a theme park. A *madness* theme park. A museum of madness. Imagine – tableaux, famous inmates, actors hired to play patients and nurses. You'd watch people screaming in strait-jackets, or having the water cure. The ruin was going to be a creepy vampire haunt or something – wasn't there a lunatic asylum in *Dracula*? Only then they discovered they still needed somewhere for the really dangerous ones.'

I thought of those invisible lost souls whispering and shrieking in some limbo beyond the corridor along which I'd walked, and the ancient relic with whom I'd come face to face. Actually, I thought, the hospital *had* survived as a kind of ruin haunted by its own inmates.

'Now what have we got – a ward full of Alzheimers, and the psychopaths the privatised prisons can't handle; plus a few really dangerous patients who fortuitously haven't killed anyone. Meanwhile the perfectly harmless addicts and schizes we used to treat were shovelled out of here and end up in prison. Look over there. That's what it's really been saved for – the special wing.' He gestured towards a new block, a raw, square redbrick building behind a high wire fence, which rose beyond the ruin. 'The gay serial killer will be banged up in there some day – if they ever catch him.'

Special: what a word – meaning, in this case, not child-hood treats or dearest friends, but human monsters it was safe to hate.

'All thanks to dear Derek,' he said. The skin on his face stretched more tautly. You could almost see the skullbones at his temples.

I wondered why Francis had stuck it out so long – but I knew why, really: he hadn't been accepted as a psycho-analyst, there were few hospitals to work in, and even fewer posts for psychiatrists in the so-called community. As he himself had said on more than one occasion, a nurse with a bottle of pills and a hypodermic would do just as well at a third of the price. The profession he'd trained for had been transformed, and had pushed him to its margins, when it was too late for him to change.

We walked across the lawn and he led me through the

gap where a wall had once been: 'This place was built on the radial system,' he said. 'Jeremy Bentham's Panopticon – spokes going out from a central point from which everyone could be seen. Perfect surveillance. It was never finished, though. They only completed two of the spokes.' I followed him through the ruins. We passed another shrubbery, came up behind it against which the massive new block had been built, doubled back, and re-entered the main building by a different door.

Now we were walking along another corridor, or perhaps it was the same corridor, the one I'd walked down before. Wherever you went, it seemed like you were in the same place, going round in circles. Like the circles of hell, I decided, or the Minotaur's labyrinth. The difference was, the monsters here were safely locked away. Unlike the monster outside in the great city, the serial killer, who was waiting for his next victim. I wondered if we'd ever know his name.

Francis opened a door and we were in a large, high-ceilinged ward. Red flowered curtains, and cushions on the rows of easy chairs could not disguise its grimness. We were back in the nineteenth century. The inmates sat and stared into space.

'Over there,' he said in an undertone, 'the Pike twins. They were two of the patients Aaron was researching.'

I looked across the room at the two young men playing a game of draughts. They were the youngest people there, about thirty at most. We went over and stood beside them. They both looked up.

'Hi, Dr Vaughan – see, I'm winning.'

His voice was flat and stilted, his smile bland. His brother didn't smile. They were identical. It was quite uncanny to see the two pure oval faces, smooth, coffee skin, with light, limpid eyes as they stared glassily up at us.

'Well done, Michael.' Francis's tone sounded almost equally forced to me.

As we walked back to the door, I muttered: 'You mean they've been here *eight years?*'

'Oh – much longer than that. They used not to speak. Michael does now, he talks for both of them. But only in a passing the time of day kind of way. Can't imagine how Aaron could have treated them – unless he tried to decode their private language.' We were back in the endless corridor. 'Aaron's treatment of the twins was especially controversial,' Francis explained, 'it was so obviously a case for drugs, they both seemed to be so deluded. If anyone lived in a world of their own, it was them. They went through a very bad period, quite violent. I hadn't realised until I read Aaron's notes. But Aaron insisted they weren't locked up, no drugs . . . of course after he died, that all changed. It was drugs with a vengeance then. Their relationship is so strange, love-hate, Melvin's very dependent on his brother, Michael resents it at times, but he's slightly more tuned to the outside world, so inevitably . . .' Francis shrugged. 'There's enormous hostile dependency deep down, I suppose.'

'What was his research all about?'

'I'll tell you at lunch – we are having lunch, aren't we?'

'Of course.'

He shepherded me down another short side passage. 'We won't actually go in – '

Uneasily I looked through the glazed door. In another huge, high room the patients walked up and down. One woman with stringy grey hair circled a table in the centre. Round and round she walked with grim determination.

'These are some of the dangerous patients who aren't in the special wing. We can't even help them much with drugs.'

It was just a room with people in it – an ordinary room, as ordinary as those photographs of the electric chair. I wondered what it felt like to have only one life, and spend it in that room.

'Let's go,' I said, 'I don't like it.'

He led me back to the main entrance hall, and out into the sunny autumn day. I unlocked the Lagonda. Francis did not drive, and I'm sure he regretted it every time I gave him a lift. He'd never come to terms with my style. I drive in dark glasses, whatever the weather or the time of day, and I have to have opera playing loudly on the stereo. So behind the wheel I am more or less blind and deaf, which protects me from the unpleasant and often provocative behaviour of other drivers. I simply do not notice if they use obscene gestures, cut me up, force me into drag racing, or alternatively off the road, or go berserk if I happen just to nudge their sacred heap.

'My treat today,' I said. 'I'm taking you to an Italian restaurant.'

La Donna è Mòbile catered for a wealthy clientele in the high suburbia to the north-west of the city, halfway between Four Lawns and the centre. It was expensive and very straight, but at least it wasn't difficult to park, and Francis had wanted somewhere we could talk and no one would know us.

I made for the patio, but Francis frowned. 'I want some really secluded corner.'

'But it's almost empty.'

'It's too cold out here.'

I looked at his white face. 'Cold? It must be twenty-four degrees.'

'There's a nippy little wind.'

I didn't argue. We made for a gloomy corner of the pseudo-Mediterranean interior, and sat face to face, each barricaded behind a giant menu.

The waiter hovered. The food was déjà vu, full of clichés like black linguine and tiramisu. 'I'll have a spinach salad,' I said.

'Not very Italian,' said Francis. I'd like – let's see. I think I want . . . *scaloppine marsala*,' he said with an exaggeratedly perfect Italian accent, 'with broccoli, garlic bread, *acqua minerale* – no, wait, perhaps . . . yes, make it *fegato Veneziano*. And not broccoli. Fried potatoes and, er, *insalata mista*.'

'And I'll have a margarita,' I said.

The waiter brought the drinks. The margarita had been frothed up and poured into a bulbous goblet, all wrong, it quite spoilt my enjoyment.

'You drink too much, Justine.'

I ignored this, but watched him as he looked all around conspiratorially. He was smoking – of course – and the hand that held the cigarette was trembling slightly. I wished he wasn't so upset, it was upsetting me. I so much wanted things to be all right for him – and clearly they weren't. He'd often talked of his frustrations at work, but this mood of bitter desperation, and the obsession with Aaron Cairo were new, and filled me with formless anxiety.

'Justine – what I'm going to tell you is absolutely confidential. You mustn't tell anyone, not *anyone*, you understand. Except Myra, of course.' He stared at me. I waited for him to say more, but he didn't.

'Well – go on.'

'You really won't talk about this?'

'Of course not. What is it?'

'I wasn't joking the other evening. I do really think Aaron was murdered.'

'I wasn't sure how seriously – '

'Shut up,' he muttered as the waiter placed garlic bread and ordinary bread and olives between us. He left, and Francis muttered: 'Sorry – maybe I'm being a bit paranoid.'

'You certainly are. Why all this secrecy all of a sudden? You were talking quite openly the other evening.'

'I believe Aaron stumbled on something. The more I go through the work he was doing the fishier it gets ... I've thought about it so much more, even since last week, you see.'

The main course arrived. The waiter tried to rape my salad with his twelve-inch pepper grinder. I ordered a second margarita.

The spinach was delicious, laced with garlic croutons, smoky bacon, olives, mushrooms and avocado, and the dressing was aromatic with a whiff of sage. Francis was cutting up his liver into tiny pieces and he pushed the fried potatoes to the side of his place. I leant across and forked some up.

'I'd better explain from the beginning,' he said. 'To begin with, you see, I was so hung up on *why* he committed suicide that I couldn't get past that at all. But once it dawned on me that maybe he didn't, the whole thing opened up. There was never any reason for him to kill himself, but there was a lot going on at the hospital then. I knew something was wrong, the minute I got back from Boston, but I never did anything about it.' He fiddled with a piece of bread, rolling crumbs into little grey pills. 'The way I look at it, there are two possibilities. In the first place: Derek.'

'Derek?'

'You know, the medical director. Leadbetter. We met him at the concert.'

'Oh Francis, surely you're not suggesting he had anything to do with it?' He was really worrying me now.

'They were rivals. weren't they? And the thing is, Derek *hated* Aaron. I've always been convinced that in order to get the directorship – ' He stopped, and looked at me very hard. 'You musn't tell *anyone*,' he repeated.

'Of course not.'

'Really not. Seriously. This isn't gossip for your Café friends.'

'OK, OK. I won't tell a soul. My lips are sealed.'

'Derek was absolutely set on getting that job. He'd been at it for months. Cosied up to the governors. Look, he even managed to get Lord Cairo on his side – supported him up to the hilt over all the reforms. Kowtowed about the special wing. It was revolting. But he took a lot of the staff with him. Put the fear of God into them about job losses if they didn't go along with the new ideas. Said there'd be prison officers in there instead of medical personnel. Gradually the hospital divided into camps: for and against. Then vague rumours about Aaron began to circulate – just little, tiny things. Of course, you couldn't pin it on Derek, he was much too clever for that, but they must have come from him, must have.' He poked at his food.

'What sort of rumours?'

'Oh ... the most ridiculous little things ... charges of favouritism ... all sorts of spiteful rubbish. But it didn't work. Not really. So then perhaps Derek got a bit desperate and – well, draw your own conclusions.'

'But Francis – ' This was crazy. I felt sad, depressed and anxious as I gazed at his tense, drawn face. Why did it matter so much to him? Why was murder preferable to suicide? But I knew the answer. Suicide always seems like a failure of nerve, a denial of all that person stood for – especially if you admired them. Worse still, it's the ultimate reproach to the living, to those who are left behind, an endless punishment of guilt.

'You mustn't feel guilty about Aaron,' I said.

The gaunt smile stretched his face. 'Oh, but I do, I do.'

A trio of smooth-suited businessmen entered the restaurant and Francis lowered his voice. It had already been an undertone. Now he was whispering, which was a mistake, because it drew attention to the fact that he felt he had something to hide.

'But there's a second set of possibilities.' He signalled the waiter. 'Coffee? Pudding?'

I sipped an espresso and watched him eat a fat slice of chocolate gâteau.

'I don't think I've told you about his research?'

I shook my head.

'He trained as a psychoanalyst, but the irony was he didn't believe in private practice. However, as you know, psychoanalysis is an incredibly expensive form of treatment and it's hardly ever available for free. You heard what Delphine Jordan said the other evening; he treated her as an exception – he loved music and she was so talented – but in general he was committed to treating patients in the public domain, and so he evolved a controversial method with groups in the hospital, patients and their families. But in order to develop his theories, and also his techniques, he still needed to see some patients individually and in depth. So he devised his special research programme. At the time he died he had just six patients. Two of them were the twins, whom you met, and there were also four women. One of them died, the other three have left the hospital. He was doing some very confrontational stuff with them. It's just possible one of them could have blown a fuse.'

'What? Got out of the hospital and shot him?'

'I know it sounds impossible. I admit that.'

'If you're going to start suspecting patients, anyone from the hospital could have killed him, surely.'

'But only *his* patients would have a motive. You see, Aaron was interested in relationships between siblings of the same sex, that was the link between the six patients. That's why he picked them – because of their relationships with a brother or sister. And they all had a history of violence. The twins murdered their mother. One of the women, Valerie Walsh had killed her stepfather, who'd abused her for years. There was another woman with religious delusions, she'd tried to kill her sister. Another, Françoise Lange, she was only in her teens, she'd suffocated her newborn baby sister. The sixth patient died. Obviously the twins' relationship was extremely unusual. And Valerie Walsh had a very close bond with *her* sister – murdered the stepfather when he made a pass at the younger girl. Well – Aaron took them all off their medication and plunged them into this very tough therapy.'

He paused while he beckoned the waiter to bring more coffee. 'But you're right, it's difficult to see just how it could have happened. But it wasn't suicide. Of that I'm convinced.'

'After all this time, though, what can you do? How could you ever prove anything?'

'I realise I'd have to have some proof. I'm not stupid. But the police did entertain the idea of murder, after all. Don't you remember, I told you the other evening.'

'But that was to do with a hold-up or something.'

'That's what they said. But maybe the family brought pressure to bear. That wouldn't have been difficult. It was the Cairos who went on and on about how depressed he'd been. Monica and all that. You see, if Derek and Lord Cairo were up to something together . . .'

I could not believe he was saying this: 'Francis, you're not suggesting your boss and a government minister *murdered* him? That's absolutely ridiculous.'

'Not really.' He looked mulish. I watched him. I knew that once he'd got a bee in his bonnet he was the most obstinate person in the world.

'What are you going to do, then?'

He didn't answer, just looked across the room and squinted over his cigarette smoke. We'd have been better out in the open air, it wouldn't have got in my eyes then.

'I don't know . . . yet.'

'Don't let it become an obsession.'

He laughed. 'It already has.' After a while he said: 'Actually, I thought you might help me. Why don't you have a look through his notes – then still see if you think I'm crazy?'

'Oh Francis, don't ask me.' I moved back in my chair, as if to escape his insistence. It was such a typical Francis lost cause. I didn't want to get drawn in – but I would be, I knew: an unsolved mystery, of course it fascinated me.

Six

That first dinner party at Miranda's – I shan't forget it. The address had surprised us. They lived in Marshtown, in the north-east inland part of the city. It was an area with a grim reputation: you didn't go there unless you absolutely had to.

We slipped down from the expressway into a cramped, decrepit, nineteenth-century village, where abandoned gardens had grown into forests of thistles penned in with corrugated iron, and whole families sheltered in what had once been allotment huts – every façade from which the bricks had begun to tumble sheltered anything from two to eight squatters. Yet the little crooked streets that turned off from the main road were empty and abandoned, as if no one dared venture on to them. The road snaked round a pond and then we were back in a twentieth century of the shoddiest kind: cheap hamburger joints and kebab huts, used car dealers, their rusty forecourts encircled with coloured pennants, a bingo hall that had once been a cinema. The only building with any sign of life was Tenison-Joliet's shack, also built from corrugated iron. A neon cross pulsed above it, some children were sitting on the steps and a disciple, who stood out in his scarlet T-shirt, was talking to them, perhaps teaching them. On the side of the shack someone had painted a gigantic figure of the risen Christ, his hand raised, two fingers stiff in blessing. He wore blue and red robes, bore a striking resemblance to Tenison-Joliet himself, and his whole body was surrounded by a red and yellow halo, which looked more like the flames of hell than the light of resurrection it was no doubt intended to represent. Still further on we passed a wasteland of ruined buildings, once a public library and swimming complex.

'It *can't* be out here,' I said.

'You've missed the turning – there's a roundabout, go on till you get to that and then turn back and it's on the right. About five turnings along.'

When I finally found the side road, we entered an even earlier time. The Lagonda whispered past cramped old terraces and came to a dead end behind a graveyard shaded with rusting chestnut trees.

'I think it's the other side of this. We can walk through.'

'Is it safe to leave the car here?' I already knew the answer – it never was, but there was no alternative.

The neoclassical church cast a massive darkness over the graveyard. Its columns, two storeys tall, supported a heavy triangular pediment of unadorned grey stone. The doors, large enough for a cathedral, were chained together.

We strolled past the tombstones, arm in arm. The sallow evening sun emerged between two clouds and striped the graves with lurid bands of light. The chestnut trees leant forward towards one another, a little jostled by the wind, which worried at their ragged leaves, tearing the first few away to rustle along the ground like scraps of brown paper.

By the time we reached Miranda's street the golden bar of light had gone from the sky. It would soon be quite dark.

'Look! How weird – out here in this wasteland.'

We stood at the end of a row of magnificent Georgian houses. Somehow this lost corner of the city had escaped the destruction of centuries, had survived the Victorian railways, the 1920s factories and the postwar council estates. Fanlights, ironwork railings, balconies and columned porches, were all intact.

The house belonging to Miranda Mars stood apart from the others. It was detached and double fronted, almost a mansion; a garden surrounded it, and a smartly trimmed high box hedge shielded it from the road. It might once have been the vicarage, I thought.

All at once I felt excited, energised, curious. 'Wonder what it'll be like inside.'

A Filipino maid opened the door, and Miranda trotted towards us with arms outstretched. Her dress, made of some soft, almost transparent material, shot blue and green, floated round her. As she embraced me her scent was heady and sweet. Then as she drew back she noticed my outfit and gave a little shriek.

'Oh! Your trousers! Oh my God!' she said.

'Don't you like them?'

'I – I don't know.' She laughed. She seemed slightly hysterical, but pulled herself together. 'Come and meet the others.' Beyond her I saw three or four guests standing with drinks in their hands, but the room was what caught my attention. The whole ground floor had been gutted to create a stark, vast open-plan room, decorated in the bomb-damage style so fashionable two or three years ago. In places the brickwork was jaggedly exposed, as though the plaster had fallen off the walls, and what plaster remained had been treated to look stained and blotchy. Everything had a half-finished, half-abandoned look, the furniture was lop-sided and strange 'found objects' had been attached to the walls – a stuffed stag's head, a very kitsch landscape, a peeling poster, a piece of driftwood.

The maid held out a tray with champagne cocktails and Manhattans. Miranda introduced us to the other guests: a big-business lawyer and his wife, two gay men in the dress trade, a lanky fashion journalist called Rusty. I assumed this was a nickname on account of her hennaed hair.

I wondered what impression we made, Myra and I. Myra wore a midnight blue trouser suit. Her white hair pulled back into a plait like an eighteenth-century wig made her face look even more Hanoverian than usual. She towered above me. I felt tiny in my leather waistcoat and skintight snakeskin jeans.

I lifted my champagne glass to my lips. Miranda was smiling at me. Then her expression changed as she looked beyond my shoulder. I turned. A tall, stooping man in a black suit stood at the foot of the spiral staircase. He held a little girl by the hand. The pair made an eccentric contrast. The child was about three years old. Light brown ringlets fell round her face. She was the daintiest creature, as solemn as her mother was sparkling, and gazed at us with round black eyes. But he – there was something almost Frankenstein about him, an unfrocked priest, Oscar Wilde after *Reading Gaol*. A lock of straight, greasy black hair hung over his face, which was doughily misshapen, as if his slack mouth and simian jaw had got pushed sideways, his nose pushed back into his face. His skin was rough and blotchy too.

'Dean – my husband.'

Dean smiled and said the right things, but all his attention was focused on the child. 'And this is Isobel,' he said. 'Say night night, darling.'

'Don't want to.' The child stared at us, bleakly unforgiving. 'Want to stay downstairs. Stay downstairs with you, Daddy.' And she put her little arms up to be held. He picked her up, and she kissed him fiercely. There was something touching about the child's love for this repellent man.

'No darling, Daddy will put you to bed now.'

She shook her head with tragic intensity. 'No, no, no, no. I want to stay with all these people.'

'Take her up, Dean – '

Myra was staring thoughtfully at the man who, unbelievably, was Miranda's husband. He carried the child away, and as he climbed the stairs she craned back over his shoulder to look back down at us with her reproachful, black stare.

We stood in the stark room, and displayed interest in one another's lives. The lawyer's wife raised money for refugees. Now that the flood of immigrants had been stemmed, it was easier, she told us, to arouse sympathy: 'So long as all those Russians and Slavs and people could get into Europe by way of Germany, there were the most frightful problems, and of course everything deteriorated over the Hong Kong situation, but thankfully that's all under control now.'

The men from the dress trade camped it up a bit and talked of leaving the country. They told us opportunities beckoned in Malaysia and Singapore, where all that trade union crap was not allowed.

'The garment industry in this country isn't exactly highly unionised, is it?' I snapped. I hated that kind of talk. I hated rich people whose idea of utopia was a dictatorship in a hot climate. I hated their spite towards the armies of unfortunates who seeped all over the land and got blamed for the rot. I suppose I also envied optimists who still believed in some better place, but, ever the cynic, I knew it was only an illusion, and I'd decided long ago to wait out the final sunset in shit city, sit in the Café and build my own dream world there.

When we were seated round the irregularly shaped dinner table the talk moved on to books and films. The collective taste seemed to run to big-budget Hollywood and prize-winning blockbusters.

'Dean,' said Miranda, 'could you see to the wine?' – treating him as if he were the butler.

I remember the cool, greenish wine, and a salad full of sharp, bitter green and red leaves. Miranda carved ducks, the knife flashing in her efficient hands. The Filipino maid stood behind each of us in turn and offered a platter of vegetables.

The lawyer's wife traded clichés with Rusty about the recent controversial Hitler film, but in the end the main focus of conversation was bound to be Myra, and she graciously treated us to nerve-tingling stories of prophecies come true and catastrophes averted. The men, as well as the women leant forward, their eyes eager.

'How do you feel,' Dean – his name had an ecclesiastical rather than a rock 'n' roll feel about it – said in his pulpit voice, 'how do you feel about this return to medieval superstition?'

'Oh Dean – ' Miranda frowned.

I watched him. He towered over us at the top of the table. Now he seemed to dominate, he was no longer Miranda's little lamb.

Myra smiled enigmatically: 'People believe and disbelieve at one and the same time. It's not either/or; it's both/and. You know – they think, well, this isn't serious, not really, *nevertheless* I shall take heed of what is said, I shall draw comfort from it, or, if the outlook is bad, I shall take whatever evasive action is possible.'

Dean smiled, wiped his fingers and said, velvety: 'Ah yes, it's a time of no beliefs and a thousand beliefs – and we all live in a climate of fear. Don't you think that's what the serial killer's all about? If he didn't exist we'd have to create him, just to give ourselves the horrors.'

The other guests looked at him oddly. 'Jolly good thing some people have had the fear of God put in them,' laughed the lawyer. He trembled on the brink of 'bring back hanging', but his wife managed to put a stop to that, and changed the subject by asking Miranda if they would be taking a winter holiday. Myra and Dean looked at each other over the peaches Fujiyama. Miranda made a little face at me and smiled. 'He's such a funny man,' she murmured. Her rose-petal breasts rose in two soft mounds from the mist of blue green. Imagine them making love – his fingers on those breasts, above all his mouth slobbering down on her soft lips – it seemed obscene, but it must have happened because Isobel was there to prove it.

We gave Rusty a lift home. She was about the same age as me, and looked as if she'd been a Goth at some period in her past. In fact she was still a Goth really, with white make-up and beetroot lipstick – and black clothes, of course.

'Aren't they incredible?' she said. 'Utterly random! I've known them since art school. Poor Dean always hung around Miranda, right from the start. She wasn't so . . . confident then. Reserved. But always – what's the word – voluptuous, isn't she?' Rusty sighed. 'Why do women *bother* about dieting. All the men I know like *flesh*.'

'So you've known her for a long time,' said Myra.

'Must be getting on for twelve years. She was different, so shy. She simply never spoke. But boy, did she work. Lot of the girls were just messing around and doing boyfriend stuff, but she really took it seriously. That's where it all began to kick in for Dean. He helped her. Made himself indispensable. All the same, it was a shock when they married. Talk about Beauty and the Beast.'

'So they met at art school and went into business together?'

'S'right,' said Rusty. 'She was the talent, he was the business brain. Flew by the seat of their pants, I suppose, hawking designs around, that sort of thing. I tried for a bit, myself, but – ' She shook her head. 'The rag trade is such a bitch – and it's not getting any easier. I don't mind, though. I discovered a talent for writing.'

'Miranda seems to be doing OK.'

'She's lucky, that girl. And very, very determined.'

'Lucky,' murmured Myra, 'I suppose so . . . there is a price though, isn't there? Beauty and the Beast . . . only her kiss didn't really turn him into a prince, one feels.'

So that was the beginning. Very occasionally Dean came to the Café. You would look up and see him as he hesitated alarmingly just inside the door, and stared round, in search of . . . Miranda, maybe. Then he would launch himself forward into the chic throng, but it was always as if he had nowhere else to go, and no idea what to do once he got inside, always the same uncertainty, forgetfulness, before he finally made it to a vacant table.

I was friends with Miranda, not him. Although you always had the feeling he was looking for her when he appeared in the Café, they were never actually there together, because Miranda only ever turned up on women's night, but she came unfailingly to that, every Tuesday, usually with Rusty in tow.

That wasn't all. She bombarded me with attentions: phone calls, postcards, and invitations to her shop, to lunch, to fittings for free frocks. She gave me a jacket of moss green silk enticingly lined with rose, a grey flannel trouser suit, with inside-out sleeves to show the old-fashioned, striped lining, and a flowing, clinging dress of garnet red.

We discovered a shared love of swimming, and met for early morning dips at the pool below my apartment block near the Café. I owned the penthouse. The building – a miraculous edifice of glass – was only two years old. When I'd first returned from LA some local campaigners – one of them a friend of my father – had gained control of the land, and some social housing and workshops had been built. Then they ran out of money, and the private speculators zoomed back in. In the circumstances, maybe I shouldn't have bought the flat, but I'd fallen in love with the pool.

I loved having it so close. Theoretically open to the public, it charged a price that ensured there was never a crowd. Millennial Moderne in style, like the rest of the building, it was at least fifty metres, but irregular in shape, very deep in parts, tiled with dark blue mosaic and planted all round with giant weeping figs, palms and banana trees. It looked out on a Japanese garden, and natural light played over the pool and was flung in reflected fragments up into the deep blue roof.

After our swim Miranda and I would have breakfast in the poolside café. I drank the coffee and the fruit juice. She ate everything in sight.

One Tuesday evening things went further. She sat at my table and stared into her drink.

'I haven't seen you for centuries. You don't ring me,' she said. Her pink fingers picked at the bowl of salted almonds. 'What's happened to all our plans?'

She licked the salt from her lips, a pink little tongue like a cat's, and looked at me in a charming mime of reproach.

'The Bohemian Collection? But we were talking about it only the day before yesterday.'

Hours passed. Women came and went at my table, and Miranda stayed on. When I closed up she was still there.

'You must be tired darling, but – would you possibly drop me off?'

'Dean's away,' she told me, as I locked the Café door and we walked arm in arm towards the Lagonda, parked by the waterside. 'Away on business.' And she laughed, a drunken little laugh. 'He adores me you know . . . did you know that?'

She *was* drunk. In the Lagonda I thought she went to sleep, but she was awake when we reached her house. It was all in darkness.

'You'll come in for a moment.'

I hesitated.

'Oh do.'

She led me by the hand into the bomb-damaged living room, went over to the asymmetrical tallboy in which they kept the drinks. 'Look – I found these ready-made margaritas, they come in a tin, I bought them just for you.'

'Oh God, I don't think – '

'Just one.'

We sat close together on the crooked wrought-iron sofa. It was not very comfortable. She leant her head against my shoulder. I sat tensely upright as she relaxed against me, pressing her face into my arm. Then she raised it and stared at me, brought her face slowly to mine and kissed me.

I froze. I didn't want this. Although when she was around I couldn't take my eyes off her sunburst of hair and her opal skin, deep down I wasn't interested in an affair. She was too feminine for me, as feminine as fondant almonds. And, I sometimes suspected, as hard.

I'd had a lot to drink myself, though, and I let her go on kissing me, soft, cat-like kisses, no tongues. After a while I touched her breasts. Her skin was like pink pearls. She went rigid. I slid my hand down her body and felt her go tense, close up. What did she want then? I made no further move. I'm not sure how long we lay sprawled on the sofa. Once when I tried to draw back she nuzzled more closely against me. I felt trapped, uncomfortable, confused.

I drew back at last. 'Lovely margaritas – have a sip,' I said.

I helped her to it, almost poured it down her throat. I wasn't drinking mine. I waited, with an arm round her. After a while my patience was rewarded. She was asleep. I withdrew my arm slowly, carefully, but her sleep was as deep as a child's and she only sighed as her head rolled sideways.

I tiptoed away from her across the limed wood floor. By the front door I turned to look back at her. Something felt wrong. My glance drifted upwards.

Dean Mars stood caged near the top of the spiral staircase. 'Leaving so soon?' He spoke softly, unctuously, as always. He stood there looking down at me, smiling.

'I – I just brought Miranda home. She said you were away. I thought . . .'

He put his finger to his wide lips. 'We don't want to wake her.' He came slowly down the stairs. 'I thought I heard a car some time ago.'

'We had a drink.' I wondered how long he'd been there, how much he'd seen.

He reached the bottom of the stairs and stepped softly towards me. When he stood really close I stepped backwards, because I had the feeling he was going to touch me. He didn't. He just stood there.

'Miranda likes you.' He stared soulfully at me, and touched one of the blotchy patches on his face. 'I do hope you're going to be friends – great friends.'

I smiled and hoped it didn't look as phoney as it felt. 'Yes – look, I really have to go – '

'I hope we'll see you again very soon.'

I fled away through the garden. By the gate I stopped. Light flooded out from the uncurtained windows, and reluctant, but compelled, I tiptoed back across the square of lawn and looked into the room. Miranda slept, slumped sideways on the sofa. Dean loomed over her. He was staring down at her, as if transfixed.

Seven

I swear I never mentioned what Francis had told me to anyone, but before long, rumours were rife. The fact was, the Café was a seething cauldron of gossip, and within a short space of time the place was full of it – everyone talking about the mystery of the dead shrink. The media crowd loved it.

Rusty had become a permanent fixture at my table, and it was she who let the cat out of the bag one evening when Francis was there.

'Someone told me,' she said, 'there might be a TV programme, a docudrama or something, about this shrink guy.'

Francis glared at her. 'That's absolute nonsense.' He fidgeted in his chair, and muttered: 'That'd be a disaster.' Myra changed the subject, but Francis sat abstracted. Eventually he brightened up a bit. 'The Cairo family will nip that idea in the bud,' he said.

'But what's the problem?' I couldn't understand his alarm. 'Might be helpful. Flush out what really happened. Get the police to reopen the case, even.'

Francis shook his head and lit a cigarette. He was smoking more than ever these days. 'Why is everyone talking about it?' He looked at me.

I shook my head. 'I haven't mentioned it to anyone.' He looked sceptical. 'I haven't,' I insisted.

Myra backed me up. 'You are being so irrational, Francis. You were the one who started all this. That night we came back from the concert, you couldn't stop talking about Aaron Cairo, and you never told us to shut up then.'

Francis said nothing, just sat there looking self-righteous.

'Anyway,' I said, repeating myself, 'surely a programme couldn't do any harm. At the very least it'd be publicity for your conference.'

'Don't talk about the conference! I'd no idea organising something like that was such a business. Is the venue big enough, do we provide food, how much to charge – it's a nightmare, so many little worries, so time-consuming.'

'Surely you're not doing it on your own?' said Myra.

'No, but the others don't do much. Somehow it's all devolved on me . . . my new secretary's an idiot.'

Francis couldn't delegate at the best of times. Now, when he was in such a fuss about Aaron Cairo he'd have to control the whole thing, couldn't stand it otherwise.

Rusty had wandered off to the bar for another drink, and was talking to Gennady. There were only the three of us now. Francis dragged fiercely on his cigarette. I wished he wouldn't smoke, it annoyed other guests, and after an evening with him my clothes reeked of cigarettes, but I could never bring myself to ask him to stop, especially when he was in one of his anxious, whingeing moods.

'I'm having problems with the paper I'm writing too. His work, what he wrote, I mean, it isn't as coherent as I thought.'

Myra asked: 'What is it you have to write, exactly?'

'There will be a whole day of presentations, obviously, but I'm supposed to give the introduction. I've looked at his published papers – I want to edit those into a book eventually – and then there's the notes he left, the unpublished stuff. I can't make out what some of that means. His notebook is . . . really strange, that's what started me. Some of it isn't about his patients at all, he seemed to be tracking what Leadbetter was doing, it's all so . . . chaotic, somehow, as if . . .' He didn't finish the sentence, seemed to sink into himself, pursuing a silent train of thought, but after a few moments he roused himself again. 'All this silly chat and gossip – I really don't need that. It's deadly serious, the whole thing. Apart from anything else, a lot of speculation about his death will only detract from the impact of his work. I really don't want the media to get hold of it.'

'But it seems they already have,' said Myra.

'Well *exactly*.' And he shot me a nasty look.

'There are two quite separate problems, aren't there,' said Myra, 'and you're getting them mixed up. There's his death, and then there's his work. Shouldn't you try to keep them apart? I mean, his death has nothing to do with how you present his work.'

'That's where you're wrong. It's all connected. Must be.'

'Why d'you say that?'

He shook his head and kicked me under the table, and I saw that Rusty was on her way back to us.

'Gennady says there's been another murder, the serial killer again. That's twice in just a few weeks, you know. It was on the news. They're saying to gay men not to walk alone, not to go home with strangers.' She shuddered. 'I know it's an awful thing to say, but I can't help being glad it's not women, for once.' She sat down, took a long swallow of vodka. 'They say he could strike again at any time.'

It had taken only a few weeks for Aaron Cairo's unfinished work and mysterious death to grow into an obsession with Francis. All the doubts and the guilt that must have seeded themselves long ago, when, cut off in Boston, he first heard about Cairo's suicide, had germinated in some dark corner of his unconscious, and now they were pushing out luxuriant shoots, theories and imaginings as fanciful as they were lurid. That was how I saw it, anyway.

The following week I dragged him off to see the Hitler film, the one they'd all talked about at Miranda's. He insisted we go to the afternoon screening, at a big cinema near Belgrano Square. Afterwards we walked through the crowds up China Road, sat in a window table at the Jade Garden and ate dim sum. It was too early for a proper meal. Francis complained about the slow service. He seemed altogether fidgety – keen to get home to Jim, I supposed. But then:

'What are you doing after this?' he asked.

I shrugged. He knew as well as I did that I spent my evenings at the Café. 'Any suggestions?'

'Come with me to see Françoise Lange.'

'*Françoise Lange?* Is that that ancient Renoir film?' I said stupidly.

He laughed. '*No!* Françoise Lange is one of Aaron's old patients. I visited one of the others already, Valerie Walsh. Which Renoir film are you thinking of? *The Crime of Monsieur Lange?* Was that a Renoir film? Anyway, Françoise Lange . . .'

So he really meant it. I think it was only at that moment that I began to take him seriously, to see it – as a kind of neurotic obsession still, yes, but also as a project about which he was absolutely convinced. 'Sounds interesting,' I said casually, but actually I was full of curiosity.

'She lives in an awful dump out in Garden City. One of the tower blocks. She's only twenty-three years old now.'

'You need a lift, is that it? How else would you get out there? There's no public transport that I'm aware of.'

'That's not it at all. I could have got a taxi . . . well, part of the way. No – but I'd like a second opinion. Hard to keep a grip on reality if you're into something completely on your own.'

A subtle touch of emotional blackmail; how could I resist?

It took a long time to get there. Garden City was further north on the bay, but you had to go a roundabout way to get there. While I drove, he told me about his encounter with Valerie Walsh.

'Not much of an advertisement for Aaron's therapy, I have to say. Still very disturbed. Well . . . she was abused through-out her childhood, it's hardly surprising, I suppose. Actually, she didn't tell me all that much, but what she did say – it was rather odd. She said, at least she gave me the impression, that Aaron and Derek were working *together* in some way. Towards the end.' He sighed. 'Don't know how much she really remembers, of course.'

'You sound a bit down about it.'

'Yes. I do feel depressed. But it's not that. It's his work, his writings. They just don't seem as good as I thought they were. He was so charismatic, I mean, he had this reputation, and somehow it was always assumed that his work was genuinely original, but now – oh, I don't know.' He sighed.

When we reached Garden City I parked the car and we walked through the tunnel that led out to the bleak plaza and the slabs. I remembered it well from the days when Myra had lived here, but as we wandered from tower block to tower block looking for Number 114, I noticed that attempts had been made to smarten up the estate. Cage-like iron gates and an intercom system blocked each entrance hall. I remembered the piles of rubbish, the howling dogs, the half-eaten carcasses of clapped out furniture left on the paving stones to rot as if vultures had been at them – all that had gone. Yet the place still looked bleak, if anything more like a prison.

We found the tower we wanted, and rang the bell for Number 114, but before it was answered we noticed that the iron gate was not properly shut, so we didn't wait for Françoise Lange's reply. The lift worked. It was a claustrophobic coffin seamlessly lined with bright silver metal embossed with a pattern of leather graining so that it was impossible to tell which side was the door. It swayed gently as we rose to the twenty-fifth floor. The door slid back and closed again after us with a metallic clashing noise that echoed round the bleak stone hallway.

Francis banged on the door. After a while the net curtain that masked the glazing trembled. There was a pause. The door opened slightly. A white-faced young woman with cream-coloured hair looked out at us.

'You are Dr Vaughan?' She had the faintest French accent. 'Come in.'

The living room was a pleasant surprise, with clean white paint, pale grey carpet, railway posters on the walls, a black sofa, mass produced but stylish, a low black table, two bright blue wicker chairs. A baby lay asleep in a Moses basket.

While she went away to make tea I stood by the window and watched the lights spread out below. The view was better than from my penthouse.

She returned with a tray. 'You came about Dr Cairo?' She was pouring tea into small white cups. 'At first when I got your letter I didn't want to see you. I don't like to think about that time, you know. It was very horrible.'

'Is it going to be difficult to talk about?' Francis spoke in a soft, soothing voice, unlike his usual sharp, dry tone. 'I don't want to upset you. I don't want you to go into anything painful, but if you could just tell me a bit about that time – when Dr Cairo died.'

'Yes. It's OK.' She looked at her baby, who was beginning to stir. 'I don't mind. But I'm not sure what sort of thing you would want to know.'

'It was a shock when he died? Were you upset?'

She looked at Francis. Her expression was unreadable. She sat on one of the wicker chairs with one leg curled under her. She wore a huge, pale green crunchy chenille sweater, which didn't suit her whey-pale skin, and she seemed to flinch into the garment as if hoping it would hide her.

'I don't remember much about it – it's such a long time ago. And afterwards they gave me the electric shocks, and the sleep treatment. I slept for a long time.' The baby mewed slightly, but its eyes were still tightly closed. She was watching it almost hungrily. Most of her attention was on it, not us. 'Dr Cairo tried to make me talk a lot. With the others. I didn't like that.'

'The other patients?' Francis leant forward slightly.

'With – Maman and Dad and . . . the others. It made him angry when I wouldn't talk.' She smiled wanly, sadly. 'You know, I was actually quite relieved when he went away.'

I glanced at Francis. I didn't think he'd care for that. It hardly contributed to his picture of the charismatic healer.

'Went away?'

She smiled. 'I'm sorry, I mean when he died. But it did feel like that: that he'd gone away. He couldn't pester me any more.'

'*Pester* you?'

'He was always wanting me to talk to the others. I felt he was saying I should spy on them. That was perhaps not it, but it felt like that. When he was there we got no drugs. It was better like that. That was good, I was grateful for that. And we could go anywhere in the grounds. We were never locked up, not even after Beverly tried to run away. Of course, we weren't supposed to go beyond the gates ... Then, after he'd gone, they didn't let us out any more. We were back in prison again. Afterwards – '

Suddenly the baby let out a piercing yell. His arms and legs were going like pistons.

She snatched him up. 'Oh my darling, he's hungry, what a hungry boy, shsh, there – there.' She was hugging him violently, then jiggled him on one arm as she pulled up her sweater, undid her bra and pressed his head to her pale, deflated-looking breast. 'Excuse me – you don't mind?' She stared down at his dark head as he gripped the nipple and started to suck, one little starfish hand on her chest.

Francis watched her. I wondered if he was thinking what I was: that she'd killed her baby sister. I couldn't help feeling tense as I looked at her.

'Anything else?' prompted Francis. 'Anything about the other patients?'

She stroked her baby's head. 'The others? I don't remember much about them.' She paused. Francis let the silence continue, and after a while she spoke again: 'After Dr Cairo was gone they put me in the special ward. F Ward. The nurses called it the five-star ward. You got better food, there were more nurses. Perhaps because the patients were even more ill. Some of them died.'

'Died?' But, gently as Francis spoke, the girl said nothing. She looked across over the head of the baby she was holding so tightly, but her look was glazed, as if she hardly saw us. Then, seeing the baby had paused, she bent over him and pushed her nipple back in his mouth. Francis watched her. Then he said: 'I think we'd better leave you to it. We'll see ourselves out.'

We almost tiptoed from the flat. In the lift Francis lit up. 'So what the hell did that mean? F Ward? There's no F Ward now.'

'It says you shouldn't smoke in the lift.'

'Oh – sorry.' But he went on puffing.

Outside, the dark plaza seemed menacingly empty. Francis took my arm: 'You know, Aaron's notebook had some stuff in it about Derek's patients. I couldn't understand why. Just some names and dates ... I just wonder ... of course, patients do die in mental hospitals, for all sorts of reasons, but – you don't think Aaron stumbled on something, do you?'

'What sort of thing?' We were near the tunnel now, and I was steeling myself to walk through it. When Myra lived here, it had been quite dangerous; but Francis marched nonchalantly towards the mouth of the subway as though we were in the middle of town.

'Derek's treatment programme was as controversial as Aaron's, when you come down to it. Not all the nurses liked it.'

'You mean he was doing something illegal?' I was finding it hard to concentrate as we stumbled through the stinking underpass.

'Maybe Aaron found out something.'

'Then why didn't he tell you at the time?'

We'd reached the Lagonda in safety. I felt something like a rush of affection for the old thing, sitting there undamaged, so reassuring, my bolthole. I unlocked it.

Francis got in beside me. 'That's a very good point. Why didn't he?'

Eight

My ambiguous encounter with Miranda on the sofa was not repeated. Indeed, it was never mentioned, might never have happened. Yet ambiguity tinged our friendship. Miranda turned up every Tuesday for women's night, but it was always as if it were exceptional, as if she'd escaped: Dean doesn't know, she'd say, or: I can't stay long – yet staying, invariably, until we closed. There were also invitations, to lunch, for a drink, but there had to be an excuse. The excuse was usually 'the Bohemian Collection', but although we talked about it, I never saw any drawings.

One Monday in late autumn we did something different: we visited the Zoo. We ate beforehand at an airy glass restaurant at the far end of the Botanical Gardens. She leant close to me as we talked, and I inhaled her familiar scent, a smell of boudoirs, of over-furnished interiors, of feminine intimacies. As I kept telling myself, she was not at all my type. It was like being buried in rose petals, or eating chocolates from a golden box lined with pink satin. Then just when you were feeling stifled she said something sharp in that slightly grating voice of hers, and it was as if you'd bitten on a piece of broken glass instead of strawberry cream.

After lunch, we walked through the gardens to the Zoo. She took my arm and pressed me close. It was not cold, though I'd worn a fur, but this year the fading November days, poised between autumn and winter, were even more melancholy than usual. The city closed in on itself as winter approached.

The Zoo was empty this Monday afternoon. We walked slowly between the cages. We turned a corner, paced down the long vista. A few last yellow leaves hung from their twigs in the opaque grey air, glowing and unreal among so much that was dead. We walked on, and came eventually up against a grey stone pavilion.

'The snake house.' She looked at me: 'Let's go in!'

'I don't like snakes.'

'Nor do I – they give me the horrors, I've got a real snake phobia.'

'Well then, why go in there?'

'For that very reason.' She seemed almost excited.

'I saw a rattlesnake once, in California.'

Her grip on my arm tightened. 'What was it like? Tell me.'

'It was the colour of the desert. You just happened to look down . . . and you saw something, something that wasn't a stone after all, and at first you'd thought the movement was just a pocket of sand subsiding, only then . . . suddenly it moved like a whiplash – '

She drew in her breath, her fingers were really hurting me. I'd often noticed how snake phobics can't leave it alone. I'm a bit of a snake phobic myself, so I should know.

'They say it's phallic,' I said, 'frightened of cocks . . .'

As I said it, I suddenly thought of her husband, of Frankenstein erect, and . . . it was just like thinking about the snakes.

'Is snake phobia a lesbian neurosis?' I mused aloud. But no, that couldn't be right, I knew dykes who even liked snakes, or who couldn't have cared less and were bored when I tried to discuss it.

She laughed softly, and held my arm tighter. 'Is that it?' she echoed, 'men's plonkers. Well, I've never met a dick as long as a snake. Another case of male exaggeration.'

Could it be, I wondered, that only a woman who desired no men at all could bear to be married to that one particular man: to Dean?

'Let's go in,' she said in a low voice.

So we did. We pushed open the door. And we were not so much fearful as excited. Only snake phobics will understand that feeling, and not even all of them. Snake phobia, mine at least, wasn't just terror. It was an absolute compulsion as well. It was fascination, bewitchment: like the proverbial rabbit I was mesmerised. As a child, I'd always had to look at the pictures of snakes in natural history books, although I knew they gave me nightmares. In adult life the closest thing to it was – well . . . pornography. Hardcore: it might be bad, but you couldn't suppress a reaction. And most of all you couldn't not look. Just like I'd had to have the snakeskin jeans.

We pushed open the door. And faced a ten-foot anaconda. Even though it was in a glass case and stuffed, it was as bad or worse than the real thing, paralysed in the act of rippling forward, its glass eyes agleam with brainless malevolence.

I gasped, looked quickly away, then stole another peek. 'Myra likes snakes,' I said. 'She says the other side of snake horror is admiration for their beauty. They're not just killers, they're sacred, magical, mystical. She says there were snake worshippers before the Hebrews came, the Canaanite tribe worshipped the great goddess in the form of a snake, and the stories in the Old Testament are really about the defeat of the Goddess by the patriarchal religion – the Adam and Eve story too.' I babbled on to mask my fascinated repulsion.

'She told you *that*!' Miranda looked pityingly at me. 'She's not one of those mystic feminists, is she?'

'Of course not. I like the idea, though – that there was a time when snakes were seen as a source of life and energy, you know they were magic and powerful. Unlike now, when they're treated as pests.'

'Well, but did you know that they kill between thirty and forty thousand people a year, world wide? That's as many people as get killed in a small war.'

That made me laugh. 'A war between snakes and humans,' I said.

'The snakes come off worst. They've killed so many rattle-snakes in Texas that it's destroying the ecology.' Miranda certainly seemed to know a lot about snakes. She was a mine of information on the subject.

The snake house was deserted. The air was hot, the silence crept round us. Our footsteps echoed as we edged along between the walls of glass, beyond which the unspeakable waited to ambush us. I tried not to look, I wanted not to look, yet my eyes slid round to peer, to peep, to search for the inert, dead-looking something that was knotted round a log, enlaced with itself in the gravel, almost invisible, almost not there.

Only it *was* there. Out of the corner of your eye you saw it, with half a bleeding mouse hanging out of its jaws, or with its great, dun length pressed up flat against the glass, as harmless as a knitted draught excluder.

'They're the undead.'

'Suppose the Zoo was bombed,' said Miranda, 'suppose they all escaped!' And she uttered an hysterical little laugh. In the corner of a cobra's cage a live mouse sat, apparently unaware that it was to be its neighbour's next meal. The snake lay coiled like an old bit of rope, some feet away from it.

'That's what's so horrible, they seem so inert – '

She laughed coarsely. '*Just* like a man.' We walked on. 'Snakes are the most dangerous living creatures – apart from humans. Did you know that?'

'Mmm.' I'd had enough of this place, and of the conversation. I felt trapped. I wanted to get out. 'It's so hot in here . . .'

Miranda said: 'They fascinate people. I saw an article in a colour magazine – in Texas, they have these – you know – trials of strength. Men in glass cages squaring up to rattle-snakes or even cobras, that's the most macho thing, to do it with a cobra, and the women all press up against the glass to look, they're mad to see it, mad to see the snakes, not a dry pair of knickers in the house . . . I suppose they hope they'll see a man bitten, see a man die. And sometimes they do. It takes a man just seven minutes to die from the bite of a Kalahari yellow cobra.'

'It all sounds rather sexual to me,' I said primly, imagining the sweaty bodies pressed against the glass, the shouts coming from gum-chewing mouths, the swaggering, tanked-up musclemen with one hand round the cobra's neck.

'I think I'll go there some day,' she said, 'just to see if I could bear it.'

We walked on. I wanted to leave, more than ever I wanted to leave, but I couldn't. It was getting to me, the silence and all those living, slithering corpses waiting in this reptilian limbo. Hell would be this place: imagine being here for ever. Nothing ever happened. Only out of the corner of your eye, the white mouse fur covered in blood, the hoodless eyes, the writhing.

We turned the last corner. A thin creature waited there, leaning against the wall. She – was it she? – held a broom, but she wasn't sweeping. She was smoking. Strictly *verboten*.

Miranda's grip on my arm tightened. She gasped.

The figure gave a start too. When she saw us she chucked the cigarette down and stamped on it, then began or resumed her work, slowly pushing the brush along the floor.

We came abreast of her. She nodded reluctantly. Seen close to she was arresting. She had that white Celtic colouring – a translucent freckled skin, ginger hair, pale, bluish eyes, pale eyelashes, which, strangely, gave her eyes a lidless look.

Miranda stopped, bringing me up short, and spoke to her:

'D'you work here?'

'Looks like it, doesn't it.'

'Do you like being here, with the snakes?'

'S'okay.'

'It's so quiet – '

'The punters come flocking in – kids can't get enough of it, specially boys. Only empty today because it's Monday.'

Miranda lingered. She asked the girl question after question: was she trained, did she care for the snakes, how many snake keepers were there, did she work long hours? She questioned her the way she'd sometimes questioned me, with a kind of blind thirst for information.

The girl with the cobra eyelids stood taciturn, yet she seemed a little to unbend, even to display enthusiasm for the creatures in her charge. 'Snakes aren't vicious if you know how to handle them,' she said. 'Look at this one here, for instance . . . soft as butter if you treat her right – '

She led us towards the nearest window. Miranda seemed mesmerised. I, though, had suddenly had enough. I broke loose from Miranda's grip.

'I'll wait outside, it's too hot in here, I'm stifling.'

They hardly noticed me go.

A light fog misted the trees outside. Dusk was drawing in. We seemed to be the only visitors to this museum of the living.

I paced up and down outside the snake house. It was a long time before Miranda came out, and I was bored and a little chilly.

'You should have stayed. She's really interesting – she offered to take me behind the scenes: you know, to look at them, touch them even. Maybe you'd like to come too.'

'Are you mad? I thought you hated snakes.'

She giggled and squeezed my arm. 'Don't be cross, darling, it's been such a lovely day. Let's come here again next Monday. You can buy me lunch next time.'

And we did return. It was still mild and damp, the sort of weather that sapped my energy. Miranda, unaffected, skipped into the Lagonda, and chuckled as she belted herself in: 'I love this car. I want one just like it.'

'Sorry to disappoint you, but they don't make them any more. This was just a one-off idea. It isn't a classic car at all, just an imitation. Lagonda was bought up by Aston Martin years ago. Then when Murasaki bought Aston they thought they'd try the market for classic remake models. Engine and all that is state of the art, it's only the style that's pure fifties.

But they found out there wasn't a market for them at all. I must have been the only one. Most customers who can afford a new Murasaki want it to show.'

She settled into the passenger seat like a cat into its basket. I drove fast, too fast, but this seemed to excite her.

'Darling! You're so *daring* when you drive. One never would think it to look at you – Oh, it's wonderful to get away from the factory for a bit. Dean thinks we should work, work, work, he's obsessed with the business.'

Soon the car was filled with the scented intimate atmosphere she created so well – girls' secrets, whispered confidences. And somehow I found I was talking about some of the things that caused me most angst – including, of course, my one real, foolish secret: I wanted a baby.

She didn't react at all as I'd expected. She just hissed: 'Well don't.' She'd put on dark glasses and leant away from me, looking out of the window. I shaved past some bastard hooting his horn at me.

I'd trodden on unknown territory. 'Why not? You have.'

Then words came pouring out. 'Oh *God*, d'you know what it's like – you think you're going to drop it all the time, it's like carrying a dozen eggs around, not in a box, I mean, loose, and they're always crying and you don't know why. Everyone fussing around the bloody baby, I got so depressed, I thought I'd kill myself. Or it. It's slightly better when they're older, but . . . you must be mad. They tie you down like you – you just don't know what it's like – sometimes I'd want to throw it out of the window.'

'But Isobel's so sweet. And you've got a nanny.'

'Yes. I've got a nanny.'

She had Dean too, but perhaps that was part of the problem. She began to fidget about in her seat, dragged her coat round her, stuck a tape in the deck.

After lunch, she said: 'I've got a surprise for you.'

My stomach lurched slightly. I knew at once what it was.

The girl with the cobra eyes was waiting for us.

'You remember Shelley, don't you?'

Shelley gave me a curt nod. 'I got permission,' she said to Miranda. 'I can take you behind the scenes. Your letter did the trick.'

A watery sun came out. I'd have liked to saunter through the Botanic Gardens. Miranda looked at me. 'You'll come?'

The dreadful excitement went through me like a hot flush. I couldn't refuse. The thought of it was horrific, and yet I simply had to go.

'Head keeper's off today,' the sandy woman volunteered. 'Gives me so much grief. Always nagging on, never satisfied, gets on my tits.'

Miranda giggled. 'You should get one of your pets to bite him,' she said.

Shelley took it seriously. 'Can't do that, it'd be put down.'

She led us round the building to a door at the side. I noticed suddenly that I was tensing all the muscles in my body, as you do in the dentist's chair when you're waiting for them to start.

Inside, the heat, and a stale smell – of straw, blood, I wasn't sure quite what – made me queasy. We were in what was obviously the keepers' room, with a table, chairs, the kind of kitchen equipment you normally find in such places.

'Want some coffee?'

Miranda shook her head. But I'd have liked some: anything to put off the moment when we really went 'behind the scenes'. What a gruesome euphemism that was! I felt like I was about to dig up a corpse or visit what they call in the States the 'correctional facility': the room with the electric chair. For some reason I suddenly remembered the hospital, and the room with the men and women pacing round and round.

They'll take you behind the scenes. You'll see things the public never sees. It was always something horrible, something secret, or obscene.

Shelley – I kept thinking of her as Sandy, although that wasn't her name – opened another door, and took us into the wide passage which really was 'behind the scenes', because it ran along behind the cages.

From in front they looked like weird little rooms pretending to be out of doors. Surreal, if you thought about it – how strange, to try to create an illusion like that. Now I saw that the back wall of each enclosure slid back. Shelley had her hand on the first one.

'This one, she's my pet, she's tame.' She reached in.

When she pulled out a long, thin, black snake I couldn't account for my disappointment at first. The creature swayed back and forward, and its thinness made it in an odd way less impressive: none of the thick, coiling horror of the poisonous ones. Then I understood that, of course, it was the fear that excited me. And I had a strange thought: it was the venom that made them potent, the juice that they ejected into you was a kind of life force – only it wasn't, it was the kiss of death.

'Touch her, go on, she won't hurt you. Comes from the Mediterranean. Some of the farmers say, if you have one of these then the poisonous snakes won't come, it'll protect you against them. She was a bit bitey at first, but now she's fine.'

I put my hand out and stroked the narrow head with one finger. The snake felt smooth, dry and almost warm. Silky. It was a nice feeling.

Miranda was leaning against the wall. I'd never seen her look white like that before.

'Are you OK?' A stupid question, because she obviously wasn't, but she nodded.

Shelley slid the cage wall shut and moved on. 'This next one, we've got some pythons in here. They can be a bit naughty, you know. Got quite a sense of humour.'

What a python's sense of humour would be like was hard to imagine, and although Shelley draped one of them round her neck and invited me to do the same, I wasn't brave enough for that, although when I'd touched the black snake I'd crossed some boundary. The gesture, small as it was, had liberated something in me, and I was feeling much less

77

queasy now. It was Miranda who was taking it badly. She still looked as though she might be sick.

'Won't show you the cobras,' said Shelley, 'that wouldn't be a good idea. We can look at some of the smaller venomous ones, they're easier to handle.'

I was beginning to think Shelley was a bit of a showoff, and when she lifted out a green mamba on a forked stick, I was sure; sure, too, that this was slightly dangerous as well. That was what I liked about it, though. The same as with Lennox: a little whiff of danger was exciting, as long as it didn't come too close.

The snake was such a vivid shade of green it was hard to believe it was natural. That made it seem less deadly, as if it wasn't real, but it was hissing and wriggling and I thought it would slither off the stick quite soon.

Shelley laughed. 'I ought to be wearing gloves really.' She flipped the reptile back into its artificial habitat and slid shut the wall of its prison. 'You know what they say? All the great handlers are dead, man. Some of these bastards, *they are dangerous*.' She laughed as she slid back another section of wall.

'That's the gaboon viper – he's best left well alone.' This was a snake as wide as it was long; an obese snake, an obscene sight, beached there, eternally waiting.

All the time Miranda dragged along behind us, but although she looked dreadful she stared and stared at the snakes. Several times she wanted us to linger, when Shelley would have moved on, and there was something urgent and greedy about the way she looked, as if she was desperately trying to get something more out of this expedition. Once or twice she actually stretched out her hand as if to touch the really fatal ones, she, whose head was screwed so tightly on the right way.

At last we came to another door. This led straight out into the open air. The dank, earthy, fresh air smell came as a relief. I cast off the spell. I couldn't think what on earth I'd been doing in there. I promised myself I wouldn't do it again.

'OK?'

'When can I come back?' Miranda asked Shelley. 'You could teach me how to handle them.'

Shelley looked slightly sardonic, as if thinking: rich people's whims. 'Have to be a bit careful. Don't know what the boss'd have to say.'

Miranda stood close to her. Money changed hands. We walked away. Miranda's face was pink again.

'Now, don't you think that was interesting?' she asked, as if daring me to mention how sick she'd looked, how scary it had been. She took my arm and squeezed it. 'I'm so glad you came, darling,' she said. 'Now listen I'm going to take you to a little bar I know, and you're going to tell me all about Lennox.'

My heart jumped in my throat. 'How did you know about Lennox?' I said.

'Oh, Rusty hears everything,' she said.

Nine

Miranda took me to a little place in town, one of those bars destined always to be empty, just as the Café was destined always to be jammed. There was not even a barman at first; we waited for about five minutes before he sloped out from behind the scenes.

'But who told Rusty about Lennox?' I asked.

'Gennady, I think.'

'The shit!' So the Café was a hotbed of gossip, but while it was all right if I, or Gennady for that matter, gossiped about other people, I resented it when the object of interest was *me*. I was especially sensitive about Lennox, for not only had that been a largely unrequited passion on my part, but we were both supposed to be *gay*.

Of course, as Myra didn't hesitate to point out, I could be bisexual, and then it wouldn't matter, but I didn't want to be bisexual, I didn't feel like a bisexual, it seemed so vague and – well, wet. Everyone's a bit bisexual at the end of the day, so where's the identity in that? Anyway, I just felt like a dyke who'd fallen for this guy. I didn't want him to be bisexual either. Every single person in the world would become a potential rival – which was altogether too much to cope with.

When I'd got back from California, I'd made straight for the Café, and Lennox had been there that very first evening. I could still remember the way he came in – as if a gust of wind had blown the door open.

'That was the summer of '95,' I said. 'He used to hang around the Café. We had a kind of one-night stand, but then he disappeared.'

The reason he'd disappeared – lying low in the North Western cemetery and God knows where else – was that he'd blown up a building, an anarchist act of terror, but I didn't tell Miranda about that.

I'd inherited the Café, it all happened around the same time. For a while I'd lived for the Café. Then, just when I'd managed to forget about him, Lennox came back – sauntered back into my life like he'd never been away.

He'd had a skinny teenager in tow. I'd loathed that boy at once. His head was almost, not quite, shaved, with a single thin lock of hair left to hang over his forehead. He had large, bloodshot eyes. His body was so thin he was almost two-dimensional. I found out later his name was Sean. Scrawny Sean I called him. He repelled me.

After that, Lennox was always turning up at the Café. Never spoke to me, but sometimes I'd look up and catch him looking – cat and mouse, I couldn't stand that either, he didn't give a fuck about me, it just pleased his vanity that I was still carrying a torch for him. Every time he came through the door it gave me a pain, a physical sensation as my stomach contracted and shot up into my throat. That must be what they mean by having one's heart in one's mouth. Well, anything was better than wearing it on one's sleeve. Having it in one's mouth meant it could be swallowed back down again, and that was what I was going to do, if it choked me.

It was so shaming. Everyone knew I was hung up on him. 'He's poison for you,' muttered Myra, but Gennady, who'd talked to him, said: 'He's keen to be friends, you know.'

Friends! As if we could ever be friends.

It was Gennady told me Lennox was working in Otto Wegner's secondhand bookshop, Born Again Books. I knew the man. I'd sold my father's library to him. I held off for a few weeks. Then, one afternoon, I had an excuse for going up to the cliff; I'd sold my father's house to the university, and one Monday I needed to go up there to sort out some final details. When I'd signed the papers, instead of going back to the car I wandered away and down the flights of narrow grey steps which wound round the cliff to the centre of the city, broadening out into a square halfway down. It was a quiet little square, encircled with houses and a row of shops, one of which was Otto Wegner's.

I pushed open the door of the shop. An old-fashioned bell jangled as I entered, and I smelt the dusty, sweet smell of old books. And there was Lennox.

'I'm glad you've come. I was afraid you hated me.'

'There's a book I need.'

'Look we have to talk.'

And so on. I clung to my pride, yet let myself be drawn into his web of enigmatic looks and meaningful silences, while the light gradually faded, until I found I'd been there for hours and it was quite dark, and it was all starting again.

By the time we left the shop it was late at night. He put his arm round my waist and held me tightly as we hastened away through the wind, clinging together as if driven by the angel hurling us from paradise.

I drove him through the silent city. The only living things were other drivers swooping past us, vampires of the expressway, as we slipped through the night, and as I drove, looking straight ahead in front of me, his powerful silence, which held everything back, and therefore promised everything, weighed on me painfully: the burden of my desire.

I didn't want to talk to Miranda about those old, conflicting feelings. So all I said was, carelessly: 'I liked having him around. Half my friends loathed him, and the rest were dying of envy.' And it was true that the jealousy and hatred had ionised the air with electric antagonisms. 'He showed me so much of the city,' I said. My life, until I met him, had been an ordered progression through the right parts of town, I'd floated across its surface all my life. Yes, even though my family was left-wing, I'd always stayed on the safe side of the city. Lennox had taught me how little I understood its chaos. He'd taken me deep into worlds I'd never known. By bus or on foot we'd explored odd corners, dismal districts I'd never have dared venture into by myself – outlying suburbs, shabby beach colonies, ethnic enclaves, grim slums.

We'd even taken a bus out to the North Western cemetery, that city of sex and death within the great city.

Her blue eyes opened wide. 'You went *there*?' she said.

'I felt safe with him.' But of course I'd never felt safe with Lennox. That had been part of the thrill. He always worried me. Yet he'd done nothing *to* worry me. Nothing had happened. There'd been no more wild acts, no more forays into the punk hinterland of beach cruising grounds and alternative terrorism. Scrawny Sean was no longer seen. Lennox was quiet in those days, very quiet. He worked at Born Again Books and was going to go to college.

For weeks at a time, ours was just a romantic friendship. Then, when I least expected it, a violent mood would gather like a coming storm. We never talked about it. In the times between, I'd think about screwing Lennox and it was like looking down the wrong end of a telescope at some humourless and fanatical ritual. I'd remember the look on his face as he came towards me, I'd remember sore nipples and a bruise inside my thigh with amazed disbelief, remember the things we did to each other, things I'd never have dreamt of doing before, as if I was hearing about someone else's violent affair – but whether we screwed or whether we didn't I was one-dimensionally hooked on his long, hard thighs, his narrow arse like two clenched fists, his long fingers, his light green eyes.

Miranda stared. Her forget-me-not eyes were opaque. 'So you like men too,' she said.

'Too?' I assumed she meant like her. I thought I was going to hear about Dean.

'I mean, as well as women,' she said in a flat, dead tone.

She looked away, lost in thought. Then she said: 'They say he's beautiful.'

I laughed. 'But of course he wanted to be loved for his mind rather than his body. That was what he liked about Otto Wegner, I suppose. Otto took him seriously. That was a friendship untainted by sex.'

'Who's Otto Wegner?'

'I told you, he runs the bookshop where Lennox worked. He's one of the old socialists, used to be a big power behind the throne before the party split – great factionaliser, machinator, wheeler-dealer. Just a dried-out bit of flotsam on the political beach really – but he runs some sort of semi-underground group.' I could see him as I spoke, a spare, constipated-looking man, with nondescript, shabby clothes and a few wisps of dust-coloured hair.

If there was one thing that didn't interest Miranda it was politics. Her face had closed off the minute I mentioned Wegner. I didn't want to talk about him anyway. I'd never forgiven him for what happened.

Lennox and I had been 'together' again for only a month or so when he begged me to let their so-called study group meet at the Café. There was a mean little apartment on the top floor, in which my predecessor had lived. I had plans to expand the Café up there, but I postponed all that so Otto's group could use it for their meetings. It made me feel good to have a few dissidents lurking behind the smokescreen of amoral chic, it made a piquant contrast to my glamorous clientele living it up like there was no tomorrow, and it made the Café even more of a *Through the Looking Glass* world where nothing was quite as it seemed, and even I could hardly tell the difference any longer between the real and the fake.

Having them meet upstairs also helped me keep tabs on Lennox.

Gennady nearly killed me when I told him. 'You want to get us closed down or something? I always know Lennox will bring more trouble. Now we'll have the three-cornered game everyone love to play – informers, dissidents and shpiks.'

'They're not doing anything illegal, it's only a discussion group, for Christ's sake.'

'Baby – I don't believe you're this naïve. Everything's illegal. Who says it's just discussion group? Lennox. The little petit bourgeois who loves playing with fire.'

'Gennady, look – they won't even come into the Café, they'll use the side entrance.'

'If you do this, I leave.'

I did, and he didn't, although perhaps in the long run it wasn't worth the slight but distinct cooling in our relationship. At that moment, although I didn't notice at the time, battle was joined between him and me for the soul of the Lost Time Café. That battle, however, was far in the future.

'Remember the riots, two years ago?' I said to Miranda.

'Ye-es.'

'Their group had been printing pamphlets, leaflets, it turned out they'd been doing all sorts of stuff over in Garden City, places like that, stirring up trouble. Otto was arrested. But they let him go. I'm really not sure why. It was only Lennox and one or two others who went down.'

So that was how I came to be visiting the prison: every three or four weeks the dreary journey, the smoke-filled waiting room, the twitching, undernourished visitors, almost all of them poor except me. They called us from the waiting room in ones and twos. That was when I started to feel nervous, my heart in my throat. I followed the screw. He was fat and oozed out of his marl grey track suit. It was dirty. He was obscene. He had a card, which he used to open doors, punching in numbers. Then we had to wait while the TV computer screened us. Then there was a big room with tables, like an army canteen – not that I'd ever seen an army canteen.

Every time I felt that knotted up pain in the stomach as

I waited on the other side of the table, and every time I looked up, disappointed, when he came through the door, his eyes looked bloodshot, his face was greenish, he looked ill, slightly unshaven, altogether smaller, less powerful, less beautiful, a pale boy who seemed like someone else, someone I didn't know.

It was only then, when I no longer really wanted him, and anyway he was unreachable, that I'd started to get the secret urge to have his child. I listened as he talked about prisoners' liberation and how he was reading Klages and Nietzsche, but all I was thinking about was how I could bribe the eminently bribable screws to smuggle out some of Lennox's precious sperm.

Ten

It may seem as if I was spending all my time floating around with Miranda, but that would be a false impression. It was true, though, that during those weeks of November Francis had more or less disappeared. I was rather hurt and annoyed, for although I put it down to his new romance, not only did I feel rejected, but I was left with the mystery of Aaron Cairo hanging fire. Perhaps Francis had grown tired of his own suspicions. Perhaps the trail had run into the ground. Perhaps he'd decided he didn't trust me enough to tell me any more, blamed me for all the rumours seething around the Café, had cut me out of his plans. The sudden blackout on information only made me more curious. I wanted to know more, I wanted something to happen. Eventually something did.

At the beginning of December, Francis came back to the Café. He did not look happy. Maybe he'd split up with Jim.

'Everything OK? Haven't seen you for weeks.'

'No. It's not. I've got to talk to you. Can we go upstairs? Too many people down here.'

'Delphine Jordan will be singing later.'

'*Really*? I'd like to meet her . . . but – look, Myra won't mind if we retreat to the *balcon* will she?'

'Course not.'

I asked Chloe the waitress to bring us Manhattans and some grass, and followed him up to the balcony. If he insisted on smoking, at least it should be something I'd enjoy as well. He had flung himself down on the sofa and lay sprawled like an adolescent.

'You haven't seen me because I have been trying to find out what happened. And now I have.'

'Happened?'

'To Aaron, of course. Remember that woman we went to see – the ex-patient?'

'She wasn't very helpful, was she?'

'Not helpful! Justine, she told us everything! Ward F, the patients dying, everything. Well – not everything. But she set me on the right track. It's taken me weeks to work it all out, though.'

He stopped to make a soft, fat cigarette. He stuck the three papers together, obsessively neat as usual. 'There's too many seeds in this stuff.' When he said nothing more, I looked up to find him staring hard at me: 'Aren't you going to ask me about it?'

'I was waiting to hear.'

But, typically, he held back. 'Even now I'm not sure.'

'Sure about what?'

'Whether I've got it right. So I need your help. It's very – sensitive.'

'Sensitive?' Then it was something to do with Leadbetter – the government, even. But in that case, why on earth did he need me?

'I went through all the old files again and I finally saw the pattern. It explained the notes. And in a funny way it was the twins who told me. Well, Michael, the one who talks – you remember the Pike twins?'

'Yes, of course.'

He put them on Ward F after – '

Gennady raced up the stairs: 'Is Ivan again! He insulted me! This time, is the end. You tell him, you're the boss.'

Gennady had it in for Ivan the cook. Their feud had more to do with the situation back home in Russia than it had to do with the Café, but that didn't stop it from poisoning the atmosphere in the kitchen. One of them would have to go, and it obviously wouldn't be Gennady.

'OK, OK,' I said. 'Just hang on a minute.'

'This guy has a knife, Justine!'

Francis stood up.

'Wait,' I said to him, 'I'll be back.'

'No, I have to go. I've got an appointment. I'll tell you some other time. When I'm absolutely sure. And then you can – '

'Look,' I interrupted him, 'I have to talk to Ivan. I can calm him down. I know how to deal with him. I just don't want him to kill someone. I won't be long.'

But Francis wouldn't stay, though I begged him to wait, so we walked down the staircase, and at the bottom he said: 'You know that friend of Myra's, the young one.'

'Marky? What about her?'

'Didn't she say once she does a lot of looking up press cuttings? I wondered if she'd look up the coverage of Aaron's death – you know, when it happened. All the reports in the papers. It's not madly important, but there's something I just wanted to check. It won't take long.'

'OK, I'll ask her.'

'We'll talk soon,' Francis said.

At the last minute I walked out with him on to the jetty. He was stooping slightly these days. He was beginning to look old, I thought, with a surge of anxious affection. On the corner he stopped, turned and gave his hesitant little wave and his humble, hopeful, reluctant smile.

'Francis!' I cried, 'wait a minute!' But he had hailed a passing taxi, climbed into it and was gone.

When I asked Marky to look up the reports of Cairo's murder, she said she was too busy. So was I, but I was fond of Francis, I could do that at least for him. Also, those hints he'd dropped when he came to the Café had niggled away in my mind. I was in danger of becoming obsessed by Aaron Cairo's mysterious death myself.

I called Urban Foster at the *Daily Post*, asked him to have their library look out the files, and next morning set off for the monstrous building that housed their offices. When I got there, the files were waiting for me. I photocopied the relevant reports.

At first the story had been huge on all the front pages. There was the dramatic account of a how a young WPC found the body on a bright summer morning, of how its identity was established, the reactions of his family, the tragedy of his wife's death, the vain attempts of the police to find witnesses, a motive, even clues. Well, there was one clue:

> Detectives investigating the mysterious death of Dr Aaron
> Cairo, have established that the gun found in the car
> beside the body had been stolen. It was a Russian make,
> of the kind circulating in the underworld, and often used
> by drug dealer gangs.

The inquest had been adjourned, and the family had certainly made a big play for suicide. There were lurid speculations from the tabloids, thoughtful pieces about doctors and overwork in the serious papers, but there were really no further developments, nothing tangible, and gradually the reports moved on to the inside pages, until finally a single small paragraph announced the suicide verdict. I left the obituary till last. This was long and boring, but one paragraph caught my attention:

> The last fifteen years of his life were saddened by the
> illness of his wife, Monica, who suffered from multiple
> sclerosis and who predeceased him by only three months.
> Devotedly as he had cared for her, her death, after many
> years of misery and progressive deterioration, would have
> made it possible for him to find new challenges and fields
> of endeavour. Just before he died he was contemplating
> a move to the United States . . .

The obituary was signed by Derek Leadbetter.

The suggestion of a new life, the move to the States – that didn't sound like suicide. The murder theory Francis had developed had only half convinced me. Paradoxically, these words, written by Leadbetter, with – if Francis were to be believed – who knew what ulterior motive, I found compelling.

Urban Foster sent down a message asking me to look into his office. I was surprised, in the first place because Urban was far too important to see me, and in the second because he didn't like me at all, I knew too much about him. That was why he never showed his face at the Café, which was the kind of place where you'd have expected to see him, since he was always desperate to be in the vanguard of style.

Urban's new office was truly the business. It wasn't modern, like the rest of the building, but done in a kind of Hollywood traditional. He must love this – the panelled walls, the portraits of previous proprietors and editors, the parquet floor covered with a Turkish carpet in dull rich reds, blues and browns, the green leather chairs, the vast expanse of space between him and the door. Wasn't that what Mussolini had done, made his visitors walk across an enormous room? Urban didn't look like Mussolini, although he was just as chubby, and his mop of curly hair had been cut and plastered down. He wore a dark suit: this was a very establishment Urban.

'Justine! Good to see you.'

Like hell. He was looking very shifty. He wriggled around in his revolving chair.

'I'm extremely busy – John Carson is due back in a few days – but I felt I had to see you because – '

The man himself. Carson, the great newspaper owner – a fundamentalist, too. I bet he didn't know anything about Urban's seedy adventures with boys.

He was looking so uncomfortable I couldn't resist teasing him: 'How are you these days? Been down to the beach at all? They say it's more cruisy than ever.' That would be enough to give him a nasty little twinge. I sat down on the green leather sofa. 'I haven't congratulated you. You must love it here – this office – power at last. But why don't you ever come to the Café? All the best journalists do. We could chat about old times. I worry about you, Urban. You must get lonely with the wife and kids in the house in the country, and I suppose you have to be so careful now.'

He was married, of course. They so often are.

He looked white. 'Look, Justine, there's something I have to tell you.'

'There was something I wanted to ask you. Aaron Cairo. Remember – he committed suicide? I'm trying to find out more about it. I thought you might be able to help. And then there's the gay murders,' I said. 'The old man in the cemetery ... just shows how dangerous cruising can be – but never mind that, it's really Cairo I'm interested in. Who was around when he died? Any writers who covered it then?'

He put his hand up to his chest and rubbed it across his bespoke lapels. 'Justine, please,' he muttered.

'I suppose you're going to say it's some new publicity stunt for my phoney fortune-telling friend. Isn't that how your TV reviewer described her? You're all so *bitchy*, darling! Anyway, it isn't. It's for another friend, Aaron Cairo's old colleague, Francis Vaughan.'

Urban Foster looked sicker than ever: 'That's what I'm trying to tell you, Justine. Francis Vaughan, the guy at Four Lawns, isn't it? The news just came in. They found his body in the cemetery. Just like the last one.'

I'll never forget his face as he sat there grinning with embarrassment, ill at ease. I didn't believe him at first. I thought he was getting his own back. I stared at him, and he seemed to recede, to get further away from me. I didn't even understand what he said.

'Justine! Are you all right?'

Gradually, I did understand. I suppose it was just as well that my first reaction was to go completely wooden, so I got out of that place without breaking down in front of slimy

Urban Foster. It was only when I got into the street that I started running up and down. I couldn't find the Lagonda, I couldn't remember where I'd left it, and as I darted hysterically here and there across the pavement, like a trapped bird smashing against a window, I heard someone – was it me? – shouting for Myra. Only Myra wasn't there.

After the funeral service Myra and I took Francis's sister back to his flat. It was difficult to know what Margaret Vaughan felt. She was desiccated and reserved like her brother, tall like him, and not much younger. She drew an iron curtain of courteous silence around the murder. Her beautiful, hesitant manners veiled her feelings; you knew at once that she'd never discuss anything that might distress you.

She came from another town and knew no one in the city.

'Oh – that's so kind of you – so enormously kind,' she said when we offered to sort out the flat. 'Are you *sure* that wouldn't be too much trouble?'

'We're co-executors, it's the least we can do,' said Myra, but of course we wanted to find the Aaron Cairo stuff as well. We'd decided we owed it to Francis to carry on with that. The police had been through the flat, of course, but I doubted if the Cairo papers would have interested them. 'Just tell the police you've given us the keys.'

She looked shocked, as if in any circumstances contact with the shpiks would be contaminating. 'I'm going home this evening,' she said, 'this city terrifies me. I couldn't spend a night up here alone – I think you're so brave, I mean the bombs, and all these terrible people. The government said they'd crack down, didn't they, but nothing seems to have changed. Poor Francis, I begged him to come home and live with me when he retired, but . . .' She turned quickly and looked out of the window. 'Such a lovely view – beautiful, isn't it?' She was holding back tears. Then she said: 'I was very fond of my brother, of course, but – we lived very separate lives.'

After that, we none of us knew what to say. I made tea,

93

we sat a little longer and then we left Francis's abandoned eyrie far above the sea to drive Margaret to the station. They were like birds, I thought, the two of them, Francis the lonely, the elegant one, with his beak-like nose, his feathery hair.

'So kind. So terribly kind!' she cried. 'Don't wait for the train – I'll be perfectly all right.' We shook hands and left her.

Back at the flat, I was even more strongly aware of how dusty and abandoned it looked. I sat down, I felt exhausted.

'I wish it hadn't all been so sordid and horrible.'

In the recesses of the city someone was killing gay men. In death Francis had been no more privileged than the rest. Fastidious, even secretive in his bachelor state, in death he'd been humiliated and brutalised, his privacy violated, his whole life laid bare for public scrutiny.

'I wish we knew what we're looking for,' I said, and then, 'Why have we taken this on?'

'We had to, didn't we,' said Myra, 'we didn't have a choice. And then – there must be some connection.'

'How can there be – just a horrible coincidence, that's all.' Two friends, two violent deaths: it was strange, but that was the way it was.

'I don't believe in coincidence,' said Myra.

I looked around. There was something bleak about the sallow, once white paint, and there was a film of dust on the shelves. Good antiques and junk were jumbled together, giving the flat an uncared-for feel. In the study a paisley shawl was flung over a broken sofa, there were piles and shelves of books, a big desk and a small round table also laden with books and papers. Even Francis's more valuable possessions – first editions and eighteenth-century leather-bound books, Korean celadon ware and a set of Samuel Palmer prints – made the room look slightly dingy.

His bedroom windows were shrouded with velvet curtains, once red, now faded like dried blood. A heavy Victorian wardrobe and chest of drawers crowded the room. In a commanding position on the chimneypiece, was a photograph. At once I knew it was Aaron Cairo.

I definitely wouldn't have wanted him staring sombrely out at me like that when I was shagging someone.

'Gloomy, isn't it,' said Myra. 'Let's go back in the study, we ought to start looking through his papers. We can take those, at least.'

Letters and bills were filed in an orderly way in separate pigeonholes of the antique desk.

'They've left it really tidy, haven't they? The police, I mean.'

'Wouldn't know they've been here,' agreed Myra – although we did find some traces of that fingerprint dust they use.

I wondered if they'd even looked at the papers relating to his work. These were not as tidy as the business documents. There were files, papers all over the table he used to write on, folders in drawers, loose sheets, notebooks. We found most of the material on Aaron Cairo's patients. It was all in a box file, with a list of names and addresses – perhaps ex-patients he'd planned to follow up – what looked like Cairo's own notes and manuscripts, and some separate notes in Francis's handwriting.

'Is that everything?' Myra rummaged through the papers. 'There's quite a lot of material, isn't there? You know – suppose Francis being murdered did have something to do with Cairo. Suppose Francis turned over too many stones?'

'But Myra, it's exactly like the other murders – it's the third in the cemetery. The police seem quite certain it's the serial killer again. Don't you think they might have some reason for that, like, you know, there's some signature, something he does.'

Myra looked grim: 'I dread to think what.'

'After all, he was killed in just the same way.'

'Yes,' said Myra, 'but Francis didn't cruise, did he?'

'Oh come on, what about those young men of his? What about Jim? He wasn't introduced to *him* at a dinner party.'

It had been awkward. Jim, whom none of us knew, had turned up at the funeral, he'd been upset, and cried. We felt we had to keep him separate from Margaret Vaughan. Perhaps that was stupid, but it was how we felt at the time. In the end Marky had taken him off somewhere for a cup of tea.

Myra said obstinately: 'But – he wasn't into cruising as such. You know he wasn't.'

And in fact, I did know. I'd always assumed he met his lovers in the usual places: bars, parties, perhaps sometimes through work. But a heavy scene like the cemetery was definitely not for him. That was Myra's only strong point so far. 'But it's still a big jump from that to saying it's connected with Aaron Cairo.'

Myra frowned and stared in front of her. 'We can't just leave it. I mean he really seemed to think he was getting somewhere, didn't he? Didn't he say . . .'

I wished I could remember more of what exactly he had said. But Myra was right. The last time I'd seen him he'd said he *knew*. He'd solved it.

'And a few days later he's dead.'

I was scared. The horror of Francis's death pursued me everywhere. It would have been bad enough if it had happened in some normal way, but this was a double horror. I had to fight back sudden tears in the Café, endure nights when he visited me in dreams and I started up in the hollow loneliness of three o'clock in the morning. I also had to endure the headlines, the reporters, the police, the invisible presence of the serial killer everywhere, and for a while a huge blown-up photograph of Francis staring out of the hoardings to advertise some Sunday paper feature.

It was hard getting through Christmas. I closed the Café for a few days, and spent the holiday quietly with Myra and Marky. Miranda and Dean went on a Caribbean cruise.

Eleven

Soon after they came back Miranda asked me over to her factory. The building itself was more or less what I'd expected, a nondescript, two-storey 1930s affair. Inside – I couldn't believe the place. There was a cramped reception area with plastic seats and a wan receptionist behind a quilted plastic desk like a 1950s cocktail cabinet. That was shabby enough, but behind the scenes was worse. To think that the garments which covered the bodies of Saffron Queen and the fastidious beauties who frequented the Galleria boutique were made in these unbelievably primitive conditions. Greasy black machines clattered like old-fashioned trains, and the women, almost all Asian, juddered slightly with the motion as they sat there. They hardly looked up as we passed, but went on pushing the material through the space beneath the needle where it pumped up and down as if in a race against time, still working at gone six o'clock.

At the far end of the room partitions divided up little cubicles and in one of them sat Dean. He greeted me politely enough, but I thought he was not too pleased to see me. We were all pushed together too closely in the small space. He touched his blotched face. He was dressed as usual like an out-of-work undertaker.

'What about that order, Miranda? They rang again.'

'Later, Dean! Can't you see I'm just showing Justine round.'

He stood in the doorway barring our way. She gently

placed a sugar pink hand on his arm, and he shifted sideways with meek, mute acquiescence.

At the back there was a large hangar, in which partly finished garments hung in long rows on rails on wheels.

'On this side they're part finished, some of them we send out to home workers for completion, this embroidery work, for example, they hire the embroidery machines from us. What you saw back there, that's only the cheaper line. The workroom upstairs is for the originals.'

She led me to a long table to the side laden with rolls of fabric. 'Look, this is interesting, they've finally come up with a silk substitute spun by spiders. For years they tried to develop it – wasn't any good, the thread had no elasticity, too fine, it always broke. Now they've found there's this Australian spider, if you inject it with some substance . . . resin? . . . I'm not sure exactly what it is, it strengthens the filament, it's good for mixing with other fibres. This is mixed with linen, quite expensive, or it can be mixed with viscose – or silk, of course.' She held up the delicate greyish material. 'This is undyed. Doesn't take dye as well as silk, nothing does, but you can get some lovely soft colours.'

'Like *A Midsummer Night's Dream*. Didn't Titania have a dress made of cobwebs?'

'Mmm, did she?'

Poetry, like politics, wasn't Miranda's strong point, but thinking of Shakespeare I remembered his Miranda in *The Tempest*, innocence personified: 'Oh brave new world', and all that.

Dusk had fallen when I left. I drove round the curve of the arterial road and as I took the corner I swerved and almost ran down a cyclist who'd come up beside me and into my blind spot. He swerved too, screeched, wobbled and losing his balance fell tangled with the bike on to the road. I leapt out of the car to see if he was hurt.

'I'm so sorry, that was my fault – are you OK?'

He was clutching himself and rocking to and fro, but

there wasn't any blood and after a while he looked up at me. 'I'm not sure . . . I think so. No thanks to you.'

My heart thumped. It was Sean, the boy Lennox used to bring to the Café: Scrawny Sean. I recognised him at once, and although I hadn't set eyes on him for two years, the old dislike welled up as sharp as if it were yesterday. Its freshness amazed me; I'd had no idea my unconscious still contained that little pocket of poison.

He stared at me. Slowly and painfully he uncurled himself and got to his feet. His eyes were as red as ever, but his hair was long now, long, straight and thin. His anger seemed to fade. He put his hand to his forehead. 'This is – weird.' He shook his head and half laughed. 'I was on my way to see you . . . well, I was going back to the Mission first and then – ' He bent and rubbed his knee. Then he picked up his bike – it wasn't badly damaged after all – and set it against the bricked-up building near where we were standing. 'I was coming to see you,' he repeated. 'The Lord must have intervened.'

'Why don't you get in the car for a minute.'

'Yeah, yeah, OK . . . the Lord has saved me a journey.'

'The Lord nearly blew you away, didn't he?'

He shot me a nasty look, but I held open the car door, and he got in. Then I went back round and climbed in myself.

'Can I drive you anywhere?'

'The Mission's only up the road. Anyway, there's my bike. What's left of it.'

'Why were you coming to see me?' But of course I knew. It would be something about Lennox, couldn't be anything else.

'I'm in shock, d'you mind. Give me a chance to get my breath back at least.' He leant back in the seat. He did look white. I hoped he wasn't hurt.

'I been reborn. 'S nearly two years ago now. I heard a Disciple speak one time – he came down on to the beach, preaching in the open air – and I saw the light. I was reborn.

I came down here to the Mission. Been here ever since. It's changed my life. They said I wouldn't want to go with men any more, that the Lord would strengthen me and cleanse my spirit. And it's true. Only sometimes – ' He stopped and looked at me. 'You mustn't tell anyone about this.'

'I don't know what you're talking about. I've no idea why you want to tell me – whatever it is you want to tell me. You surely weren't coming to see me just in order to tell me about your conversion.'

'Oh I know your sort don't believe in anything, but there's no need to sneer. *He* says we must pray for you and all the people like you.'

'Leave out the religion. Just tell me what you want to tell me. It's to do with Lennox, isn't it?'

His face went blank with surprise. 'No – nothing to do with him.' He fell silent again, and picked at a hole in his jeans with his bitten-down nails. Then he looked up at me, with a cringing expression that made me want to slap his face. 'He doesn't know, *Father* doesn't know, I haven't been able to tell him, I know I must, but I'm afraid he'll be angry if – he'll punish me . . .' and he drew a deep, shuddering breath. 'It still comes over me sometimes, and – well, once or twice I've been to places where – you know – toilets and that, the beach . . . and up the North Western cemetery.'

'Yes?' I was alert now.

'And, you know the one that was murdered?'

'Which one?' I could feel the pulse in my throat, an anxious, slightly sick feeling.

'They said he was your friend.'

'Francis, you mean?' I spoke with a sense of dread.

'Is that his name? They said you knew him.'

'Who said?' I was feeling very jumpy indeed.

'At the Mission.'

I tried to keep the paranoia at bay, reminded myself it had been in all the papers, everyone knew Francis had links with the Café. It didn't help. It still seemed sinister that Tenison-Joliet's lot knew all about me.

'You see,' said Sean, and swallowed, and his voice was shaky, 'I was there, I was there. I was in the cemetery. I wasn't doing anything. I wasn't,' and his hand shot out to claw at my arm. 'I was on my own. I was just . . . watching, sort of thing. I'd left my bike and come in at the back, there's a way in round the top. I was sort of running along and then I stopped. I wanted to go on, I was plucking up my courage, but thinking I ought not to, I was just standing there, couldn't make up my mind, when I heard someone. In the undergrowth. And then I saw this man come out of the trees, he was shuffling and struggling, well not struggling exactly, but he was heaving this other bloke along. Thought he must have been drunk at first – the other one, I mean. The light was just going. And then he just dropped him. Dropped him and ran, well, stumbled away, sort of. Back to where I'd come in myself, where the wall's broken and that. I was scared. I knew something was wrong. After a bit I – I went up and touched him. Stone cold, never felt anything like it, gave me the horrors, I turned and ran back the way I'd come. Just saw the tail lights of a car, that's all.'

He was sobbing. 'I wish I'd never gone there.' He put his head in his hands. 'It's cured me if nothing else has. I won't ever go there again.'

'Didn't you tell anyone?'

'Tell anyone? Who? If I'd have gone to the police it'd've all come out, I'd have had to confess to Father. And you don't know what he'd have done to me. Anyway, I was scared. They might have thought it was me. Course, I didn't know who it was then, but I knew he was dead. So I just biked off back over here. 'S a long way, good two hours. And on the way I got thinking, I thought I should at least call the cops, so I stopped off at a call box, in the centre somewhere. Made an anonymous call.'

I sat and looked at him. 'If he was cold he'd been dead for a while. He wasn't killed in the cemetery. Not in that bit of it, at least. He was brought from somewhere else.'

'Yeah . . . I dunno.' His shoulders shook, and he was

sobbing, great sobs like a cough dragged up from the middle of his chest. 'Then – when it was in the papers, I remembered who you were. I had to tell someone – I thought of nothing else for days and in the end I got this idea, I couldn't seem to think of anything else but coming to see you.'

I stared out into the dimly lit street. The leather-padded cell of the Lagonda insulated us from the world, I felt I'd got into a time warp, I didn't know what I was doing with this stranger in my car.

A cold hand curled itself round my heart, and started to squeeze it – slow . . . slow.

I don't know how long we sat there. I gripped the wheel of the car. Finally I said: 'Are you OK now?'

He nodded, not looking at me. All my old dislike of him flooded back. I leant across him and opened the passenger door again.

'Sean,' I said, 'there's one thing you should remember. You should go and tell Tenison-Joliet to jump in the river, because there's nothing whatsoever wrong with being queer.'

He got out. Then he bent down to grin at me. 'Is that what you told Lennox? How is he, by the way, I heard he wasn't doing so well.'

The little shit. I'd have run him over again, given half the chance.

Twelve

       I drove like hell back to the Café, and raced upstairs to the balcony. Fortunately Myra was alone. I told her what had happened.

'I knew Francis wasn't cruising.'

'Yes.' And that was a relief, a vindication. Yet the memory of Sean as he sat in the car, whimpering and shifting like some cornered animal, gave me the creeps. I wished it hadn't happened. If only I'd driven more carefully. I wished Sean had never existed. 'Why was he coming to see *me*?'

'Everyone knows we knew Francis, and the papers played it up, all that stuff about Francis moving in "artistic circles", mingling with the gay glitterati – wasn't that how they put it?'

'I suppose so.' That also depressed me. Francis hadn't spent his life in the Café any more than in bars and cruising grounds. He had chosen to dedicate it to those damaged minds, those broken personalities in the hospital on the hill. Until he'd died I'd never questioned his dedication. He'd just been a friend who happened to be a psychiatrist. I'd admired him for it, and all the more because it had seemed an alien, depressing world. Now it had become significant and strange, almost perverse. Masochistic. Twenty years in that mausoleum on the hill: how must it have felt to spend your life in that place?

If he hadn't worked there, he wouldn't have died. That was what I felt now – that some contagion of madness had pursued him into the city, had destroyed him, malevolent, implacable. I hated the hospital – the asylum. It hadn't given him asylum. It had taken away his life.

At the same time, the ill-omened place was unreal as I sat in the golden Café. It was the shadow, the opposite of the Café.

'It must have had something to do with the hospital,' I said. I thought of the white-faced young woman, Françoise Lange, and the twins, playing draughts like eight-year-olds.

Myra said, almost dreamily: 'It must have been done deliberately, made to look like the serial killer – they killed him somewhere else and took the body there.'

'But – I know Francis was thin, but even so, what did he weigh? Ten stone? Eleven? Even that would take some lifting, and anyway it's so risky – dragging a body about.'

'This boy says he saw him. And – well, do you really believe it was the serial killer?'

'We don't want to believe that, do we, but maybe it was just him all along, maybe it was him Sean saw, moving the body from somewhere else.'

I hated to think about it, couldn't stand the atmosphere of horror and morbid fascination that had everyone by the guts, and along with the leering tabloid coverage the protests from the gay press had added to the fear and paranoia. Since Francis's death the killings had gained a higher profile, headlines, speculation. After all, unlike the others, Francis hadn't been one of society's rejects. He'd been a professional man, and what the papers had called a 'controversial figure', in other words a critic of the government. That's what they said. It would have rated a bitter laugh from Francis, who was so self-critical and felt he did so little.

Myra said: 'Did you believe this Sean?'

Again the memory of the shivering animal assailed me. Why did I dislike him so much? 'Yes, I do. He was terrified. Shit scared.'

'Well – think about it. Francis started to poke around in an old story: Aaron Cairo's death. There was a renewal of interest in Cairo's work, there was the conference. Francis was tidying up the research work Cairo'd been doing and was writing a paper, but in the course of doing that he came up against something – something that convinced him Cairo had been murdered, something to do with the hospital, or that's what he thought. So if him rooting around got up someone's nose, it really is too convenient the serial killer kindly doing him in.'

'Yes . . . So what do we do?'

'We do what Francis was doing – go through all the material, possibly try to see Cairo's old patients again, go and talk to whatsisname, Derek Leadbetter.'

'Go right back to the beginning.'

Chloe came running upstairs: 'Telephone call for you, Myra.' The instrument was in the back office, a little room behind the balcony. Myra went to take the call. When she came back, she said: 'Guess who that was?'

'Oh God, Myra, I don't know – Saddam Hussein.'

'It was the nurse.'

'What nurse? What are you talking about?'

'She nursed Cairo's wife. She's got something to tell us. I said we'd meet her tomorrow at the Ascot Tea Rooms.'

Myra had told me Rosemary Jones sounded as if she might be Caribbean. This made her choice of rendezvous odd to say the least. The Ascot Tea Rooms had been located in the Galleria since it had been an old-fashioned department store, Maxwell and Gaveston, back in the year dot. Then and now it was quintessentially the home of the polite Far Right, the Patriotic Party, or at least of its female cohorts, many of whom also dated from the Maxwell and Gaveston period. At the round tables with their white damask cloths you saw old ladies who'd been fixtures for nearly fifty years, since the glorious 1950s when everything had been so right with the world of the Right. Why, to hear them talk of that time, you'd think there'd been no crime, no welfare state, no hooligans, no drugs, no violence and no sex. I wouldn't know. I was born in 1960.

When a black woman floated towards our table in the middle of the room we knew at once it was Rosemary Jones. She was light footed and graceful in the way large women sometimes are, and rather beautiful. Her hair in hundreds of thin plaits was caught up in a 1940s roll round the back of her head, and, like most of the customers, she wore a hat. Hers was made of red felt. She was in fact the only non-white person in the place. Even the waitresses were white.

I was dreading this. I had no idea what we were up to.

'We haven't ordered,' said Myra. 'We waited until you came.'

'It's nice of you to meet me,' she began. She looked round. 'Oh, here's the waitress. What shall we have? I fancy Earl Grey myself. They have excellent scones. And their cakes are a dream.'

I glanced at the menu card. 'The full tea, please,' I said to the sour-looking elderly waitress who had veered up by my left elbow.

Rosemary Jones sat back and waited. Something about her serene smile was obscurely disturbing. Myra began a conversation about nursing, and we soon learned that Rosemary Jones was no longer in the profession.

'But you nursed Mrs Cairo.'

The waitress set plates of sandwiches, scones and a tiered cake-stand on the table.

'Oh, that's nice, isn't it! Lovely.'

The waitress made a return visit with a silver pot of tea and a pot of hot water.

'I'll pour, shall I?' said the ex-nurse with a beaming smile.

Myra began again: 'Aaron Cairo's wife was one of your patients, is that right?'

'Mrs Cairo. That was a long time ago. Aren't these sandwiches delicious? I love cucumber.' For some reason she was teasing us, stringing us along. 'Do have another one,' she said and pushed the plate towards me. 'You've eaten nothing.'

What I really wanted was a drink. I mean, a real drink.

Myra picked up one of the petits fours. 'You remember Aaron Cairo and his wife, though. That's why you got in touch with us.'

'It's all been in the papers again I see, with that Dr Vaughan being murdered.'

Myra said: 'Why have you got in touch with us?'

The ex-nurse took another sandwich: 'It takes me back, sitting here, all dressed in my best. You know how I knew about this place? I used to bring her here – Mrs Cairo, Monica. It was a bit different then, not quite so many of these old ladies, there was a time when she used to meet her women friends here. I wouldn't come here normally, couldn't, can't afford it. When I married my husband he was earning good money in the police force. But things started to go wrong. Don't ever let them tell you the police aren't racist any more. He complained – and they got rid of him. It was shameful. Couldn't get a job. And we have three sons. We had some really hard times. But that's not the reason – I mean, something must be wrong, poor Monica should rest in peace.'

She smoothed her green silky bosom. She was still smiling benignly at us. Only I saw now that the blandness was a mask, that all this was hateful to her, and that the smile was one of those dead smiles taped to the face, meaning its opposite.

'You need money, is that it?' I said quickly, feeling ashamed for having not liked her. Now I felt sorry for her. And yet . . . there was something that didn't add up. I looked in my purse, anyway. I had just a single 200 ECU note. It was too much – too much to part with and too much to give her. I folded it and put on the table near my plate. 'That's all I have.'

She made no sign of having heard. I felt like a shit.

Myra said: 'So why have you contacted us?'

'It was Dr Vaughan – he got in touch with me. It seems he got my name from the family. We were to have met, only then – '

'He was murdered.'

'Yes – you see, it seemed an odd coincidence. I know it was this serial killer, that's what they think isn't it, but I couldn't help wondering why he'd wanted to see me, and I felt a need to talk to someone.' She looked at us. She was eating all the while. 'It quite upset me, him – dying like that. You were friends of his, weren't you?' She spread a scone with clotted cream and strawberry jam.

We waited for her to continue, but she just delicately munched her scone.

'What did you want to say to us?' Myra poked at a cucumber sandwich.

Rosemary Jones wiped her fingers, stirred her tea, then seemed to make up her mind, and leant forward: 'Poor Dr Vaughan had some very false ideas about Monica's husband,' she said. 'But then so had everyone, hadn't they? They treated him like a saint. Perhaps he was in his work – but it was different at home. Well – he was never there. I don't think that's right. That's not a saint to me. To neglect someone like that, a sick woman. People said he was wonderful. What they meant was he was wonderful not to have left her, that's what they meant. But he didn't look after her. I did all that. He didn't even see much of her. I was closer to her than he was. They'd all tell you, they'd have to admit that, she adored me. Of course it was very sad, upsetting for him, but he could have – he could have at least been with her, talked to her a bit more. But instead . . .' and she smiled her dreamy, insinuating smile, 'well, he did the other thing, you know. Of course, it's what you'd expect, I suppose, a man with a very disabled wife, that's what happens, isn't it? Well, it's hard for a man, I can see that. But – why couldn't he just have paid for it occasionally, instead of – well, if you want to know, there was another woman.'

Myra stared. 'Everyone said he was devoted to her.'

Rosemary Jones's smile flickered for a second. 'He was very careful. But how could I be so close to Mrs Cairo and not know everything? *She* knew. She guessed, I'm sure.'

'Have you any proof?'

Rosemary Jones smiled and shook her head. 'Like I said, he was very careful.'

'This isn't much, is it?' Myra was looking baffled.

The ex-nurse looked indignant. 'Why should I lie? I guessed, I knew. When a man starts to spruce himself up – he never bothered about how he looked, always wore the same old suit, expensive, mind, but . . . you know. Then one day it all changes. New shirts, new shoes, new ties. Don't tell me a man does that unless he's courting.'

'It's all very nebulous. Weren't there any letters? Nothing?'

'Oh no. But I'll tell you something else. The other doctor came to see him once. It was on a Sunday, a rare occasion, the whole family was there, a big lunch, it was his birthday, the last time they were all together before Monica died – in the middle of it all this other doctor came round. They went into the study. The study was next to Monica's bedroom, on the ground floor you see, it was easier for her, she was in a wheelchair but she could use the whole ground floor. Anyway, I happened to go in to get something for her, and just as I was about to come back out into the hall they came out too, and Dr Cairo was saying something like: "It musn't come out", but then they saw me. Dr Cairo saw him out to his car – they went on talking in the drive.'

'You know who this doctor was? Dr Vaughan? Another doctor?'

She shook her head.

'What did he look like?'

She looked across the tea room, as if into the lost past. She shook her head again. 'I really can't remember . . . tall?' Then she smiled, it was placating, she was wanting to please. She sat back: 'And I suppose you knew about the money?'

'Money?' Myra said, 'what money?'

'That's what was bothering them – the money, what had happened to it all. There was a tremendous row about that. They couldn't keep that from me. You see, he didn't leave nearly as much as he ought to have done. They didn't like any of what had happened, of course, but that's what they didn't like most of all.'

I glanced at Myra. She wore her blank Buddha look.

Rosemary Jones's expression made me feel certain that there was still something more, something she was holding back. But now the manageress came up looking as if she had a prune in her mouth.

'I'm so sorry, madam,' and she addressed me exclusively, 'but there's been a complaint about the noise at this table.'

'Noise?' We'd been muttering conspirators. I looked round the room. 'You must be out of your mind. We've been practically whispering.'

'I'm sorry madam, but there has been a complaint.'

'I can't see how we can talk any softer.'

Myra kicked my foot. 'I think we're being asked to leave, sweetie.'

The manageress reddened, but stood her ground. 'I'm sorry, madam.'

'We haven't finished our tea,' I said.

Rosemary Jones stood up. 'I have to go anyway, I have to get home.'

There was nothing for it. I felt as if every one of those old women in the room were staring at us. Actually, no one was looking at us, not even the manageress, but that made it all the more embarrassing. It was all so trivial, but I could have murdered the lot of them. And in fact it wasn't trivial, it was sinister.

'I hope you don't expect us to pay for the tea,' I said as a parting shot.

We made a flamboyant exit in good order, escorted by the manageress, but nothing could hide the fact that we, above all that Rosemary Jones, had been humiliated.

We stepped on to the open escalator and descended to the ground floor, mistresses of all we surveyed and completely impotent.

'Since when have they been doing that sort of thing?'

It was naïve to be shocked, but I was. It had happened so quickly I hadn't adjusted.

'Those patriotic ladies get so spiteful as they get old,' said Rosemary Jones. In the Galleria she stopped. 'I do have to go now, that was true, so I'll say goodbye. But this is my number – if you want to get in touch with me again.' She smiled and handed Myra a piece of paper. Then she slipped away into the strolling afternoon crowd of shoppers before we could stop her.

'Shit,' said Myra. 'The bloody Ascot Tea Rooms.'

'I'll write to the management to complain.'

Myra laughed: 'Always so middle class, Justine. What the hell good will that do?'

I felt horrible – in shock, soiled, and also somehow guilty. We walked slowly back to the Café at the far end of the front.

'That was depressing, wasn't it?' I said after we'd paced along for a while. The whole incident had confused me. It seemed wrong to be critical of Rosemary Jones, as if that would make us complicit with what had happened. Yet I felt deeply ambivalent about her. 'Was it worth 200 ECUs? I never even saw if she took it off the table.'

'She did,' said Myra. 'Strange woman.'

'She didn't tell us much.'

'She told us quite a lot.' Myra paced along. As we came abreast of the bric-à-brac stalls set up along one section of the front, she said: 'The money, for example.'

'Yes. What was that about? We never heard about that before.'

'We did, actually. Ruth, his sister mentioned it, that evening at the concert. Didn't you notice? She just started to let something slip, but then her brother appeared at the crucial moment. Almost as if he was trying to stop her talking about it.'

'But what could money have to do with all this?'

'Perhaps Aaron Cairo was a gambler. Too late to go round the gambling joints now, though. I wonder if the police followed that up. Money doesn't just disappear. If he was a secret gambler, say, he'd have been seen, *someone* would have known . . .'

'There was nothing about the will in the press cuttings.'

'No . . . odd in a way. And what about the woman angle?'

'Myra – did you believe that?'

'I don't know. You know, though, she's the first person who hasn't thought the sun shone out of his arse. Cairo's, I mean. Up till now he's been everyone's Dr Wonderful. But she didn't like him, did she? First whiff we've had of anything other than wholehearted hero worship.'

'That's not true. Françoise Lange didn't like him either. Francis wasn't too pleased about that.'

'Really? You never told me . . . anyway why should it all lead to murder? Suicide makes more sense. What about the incident with the other doctor? Suppose he'd done something wrong. Perhaps terribly wrong. He was a bit close to the edge. His wife had just died. He was depressed. He shot himself. Are Jews against suicide? I mean would it have seemed less shameful to the family if someone had killed him as opposed to him killing himself?'

'That's Roman Catholics, Myra. I don't think Jews have a hell. Anyway, they were the ones who were so keen for it to be suicide.'

'I tend to assume this other doctor who came round to see him was Leadbetter . . . Might not have been, of course.'

'Francis perhaps?' I said.

Myra shook her head: 'He'd have told us.'

A gust of wind came off the sea. It was mild for February, but not that mild. I pulled my fake fur tightly round me; it was one Miranda had given me.

'You know,' I said, 'I wonder if Francis had turned up something about Cairo he didn't really want to know – you know, like he wasn't the great hero after all. Could he have been trying to preserve Cairo's memory, keep up the legend of Dr Wonderful, prevent anything from coming out?' But that didn't make sense either. Apart from anything else, it did nothing to explain why Francis himself had been killed.

'Let's say,' said Myra, 'that Rosemary Jones was telling the truth, and that this other doctor did come round to see Cairo. Let's assume it was Leadbetter. We really ought to talk to him.'

I wished she hadn't said that. The last thing I wanted to do was go back to the hospital. It loomed up in my thoughts as a place of horror, worse than the prison, as bad as the snake house. Yet I knew she was right: 'That's what Francis thought. He thought it had something to do with Leadbetter.'

'A murderous doctor?' murmured Myra. 'I suppose doctors commit murder as often as the rest of the population. More, maybe – they have access to all sorts of methods.'

'I didn't exactly mean murder . . .' I thought about why not. 'For one thing, he could have done it in a lot easier way than that.'

'Yes, both Francis and Cairo were his colleagues. He could have got rid of them inconspicuously. Less conspicuously than that, anyway . . . although I imagine murder is never easy. Not if it's premeditated.'

Thirteen

Impossible in the feverish Café atmosphere to discuss our plans, decide what to do next. There was never any privacy there. We went up to Myra's balcony, but the minute we showed Gennady came up and started to bitch about Ivan again.

'This guy is big crook, Justine. OK, he's wonderful chef, I agree, but how you know what else he's doing? He's maybe an informer. Yes – ' he warmed to this new theme: 'Maybe our little Ivan is the man from the Ministry.'

'Oh come on – '

'It's very likely. His kind are all doing anything they can to make money. Is as many Russian mafia in this city as pebbles on the beach.'

'They're not working as cooks, though, are they, darling, they're living up in St Anselm Heights in two-million-ECU mansions.'

'Oh, they have their Ivans, the bottom-level boys. Yeah, I think maybe he's a plant, why he should come here anyway – '

'Oh Christ, Gennady – take a tranq. and you won't feel so paranoid.'

Myra said: 'It's hopeless here – I'm going back to the flat. Join me when you can.'

'Yes, I'd better stay for a while. I'll come over later this evening. We must get something sorted out.'

As soon as she'd left, Gennady was at me again. He came over to my table and hissed: 'You know what he just did?'

'Who?' I enquired innocently. 'What are you talking about?'

'You know, Justine. You *know*. And what you think he did now? He groped Chloe, the pig. Is an animal, this man – she's threatening to leave. And she's not the only one. I tell you, baby, is not going to last like this. Very soon – finish.' He made a karate gesture with his hand. As always when he was angry his Russian Ls grew more pronounced and seemed to roll forward from the back of his throat.

'Oh Christ, where is she – I better talk to her.'

'She left. She walk out. Whether she come back, I don't know.'

'She will,' I said, 'she's a tough cookie. She can take care of herself.'

He didn't like that. He leant towards me. His face was pale and his blue eyes, like marbles, seemed to be bulging from his head: 'He goes, Justine. He goes. He give you perfect excuse now, sexual harassment, that was stupid of him. But he did it. So tell him to go.'

'OK, OK, I'll deal with it.' If things went on like this I soon wouldn't have any staff except Ivan. But I wasn't looking forward to sacking him, particularly after that earlier knife-throwing episode.

'Get rid of him,' said Gennady, 'I think we don't have similar cook any more. Is too much hassle, millenial cooking, *haute cuisine*, that's all out of fashion now. What people like is good, old-fashioned home cooking. No more elaborate stuff, instead we have short order, like in the French café, the *choucroute*, the *boudin noir*, omelettes, pâté, fast food, but not American, French fast food is brilliant idea. No more Ivan, anyone can cook this stuff. Save on wages, save on hassle. We even can do the little English things from way back, mushrooms on toast, cheese on toast. We could have little period menu. Teashop food from 1930s. Chloe dressed in period as well. Is wonderful.'

'I'll mull it over. Give me time. There's quite a lot of work involved in things like mushrooms on toast.'

Gennady sat back and folded his arms. He looked pleased with himself, but a lot of what he said wouldn't do: Chloe would never agree to wear a little apron and frilly cap, for starters. Or perhaps she would if he wanted her to. Then he leant forward again and renewed the attack: 'At least you sack Ivan. Now. I bring you a drink and then you sack him.'

'OK. OK.' He brought me a gigantic margarita, and I finally sacked Ivan. Then I felt terrible about that, as well as about everything else, for instead of trying to murder me, Ivan broke down in tears and told me all about his destitute family back home.

These days Myra might be living in a luxury millennial flat, but she'd recreated all the old Garden City atmosphere: hardly any furniture and a surfeit of drapery – paisley shawls that turned the living room into a tent, cushions, joss sticks, shades of deep purple and bitter chocolate, all very early-seventies. As was the rosehip tea and the cannabis R.

When I arrived the cannabis wasn't in evidence, and Myra wasn't alone.

'This is Detective Sergeant Rennie, Justine.'

Detective Sergeant Rennie was no chic dresser; she wore an anorak with a flannel skirt, had short hair and looked rather dykey, but I noticed a broad gold ring on her wedding finger. That sort of thing annoys me. Married women shouldn't try to look lesbian, and lesbians shouldn't get married – although I'm hardly one to lay down rules like that. But then I've never let consistency interfere with my prejudices.

'We're still making enquiries about Dr Vaughan's death,' she said, 'trying to build up a picture of his movements.'

'We hadn't seen him for several days,' I said. 'I went through all that with your colleague.' I couldn't remember the other cop's name.

The woman detective looked at me with bland, blank eyes: 'I understand Dr Vaughan was under some sort of strain.'

I glanced sideways at Myra, who raised her eyebrows very slightly. 'Miss Rennie and I have already been over it all again,' she murmured, sending an unequivocal message that she was finding this rather tedious. She might have co-operated with them on occasion, but basically she despised the shpiks, perhaps because of those attempts at co-operation. They've no intuition, she would say.

Detective Sergeant Rennie ignored her interruption. 'When did you actually last see Dr Vaughan?'

I tried to remember. 'At the Café?' I hesitated. That was a pretty safe bet.

'You understand there's a very strong presumption he was killed by the same man who has murdered several other victims?' Ms. Rennie was still resolutely expressionless. 'We found traces of semen, as in the other cases, and the method was the same – stabbing.'

Traces of semen . . . the abyss of horror opened up as I imagined – tried not to imagine – what had happened to Francis, before or after he died, tried not to read the rumours in the press, as the harmless phrase 'traces of semen' became a euphemism, a minefield for the imagination, concealing unspeakable acts and hideous mutilations. There'd been a lot of knowing stuff about the special signatures serial killers liked to leave on their victims. One murderer had gouged out his victims' eyes, another – it was all too horrible. No matter how hard I'd tried to shut them out of my imagination, those images were always lurking just below the surface, threatening to float up like a bloated corpse.

The police had said nothing about a signature in this particular case. Myra said, though, that that might be because they were always afraid of copycat crimes.

The policeman who'd interviewed us soon after Francis had died had asked a number of questions about Francis's sex life, but it had all been fairly routine, related to visits to clubs and pubs, cruising, on the beach or in the cemetery, was he 'promiscuous' and so on. Detective Sergeant Rennie took it all a bit further. She wanted names.

'Surely it was some stranger? What's it got to do with his friends?' I objected.

But she ignored this. She went on asking about his last hours, his last days. I only wished I knew what he'd been up to.

'What about a regular boyfriend?' I shook my head. I was determined to say nothing about Jim. I didn't want them to harass Jim. We'd only met him at the funeral, but he'd certainly seemed vulnerable then, and he'd trailed round to the Café several times since in a pathetic search for comfort. 'You say you don't know – yet you were a close friend of Dr Vaughan. That's right, isn't it?'

'He was a very private person,' said Myra in her most pious cliché-ese.

Detective Sergeant Rennie remained unmoved. 'Don't try to shield anyone. That won't help, it'll make things worse.'

'Why should we? We don't know anyone to shield.'

She just looked at me with those grey eyes that were neither friendly nor unfriendly, but which made me feel as if I were hiding something, as if I were somehow to blame.

'Any problems up at the hospital?' she said, unexpectedly changing tack. 'Dr Vaughan have any difficulties in that department?'

We looked at her warily. 'The hospital?' murmured Myra.

'Any problems at work?' she repeated.

I looked quickly at Myra, who shook her head so minimally that the pseudo-dyke didn't notice. We stalled and stone-walled, and eventually she gave up.

'Thanks for your help, anyway.' She looked around. 'Oh, there is just one more thing,' she said. 'He had a friend with a record – burglary mostly – Jim Patterson. Name ring a bell?'

I swallowed. It was like she'd slipped a knife between my ribs.

Myra kept her head: 'No . . . someone he met in a club or something? I suppose you got the name from someone on the scene?'

Rennie wasn't going to tell us where she got it from.

'Francis wasn't really on the scene,' I said after the silence had gone on too long.

'Well, if anything occurs to you – I'll be in touch in any case, we'll need a formal statement.'

After she'd gone, I raged. 'All they can think of is pick on his boyfriend.'

Myra wandered slowly up and down the room. She'd begun to smoke some particularly fragrant grass. She offered it to me, but I refused. In my present mood it might make me feel worse, as I knew from experience.

'Oh *God*,' I groaned.

'Look, we know it isn't the serial guy. If Scrawny Sean told you the truth. And there's no reason he wouldn't.'

'He was scared. He might have misremembered. It isn't that conclusive. Anyway, she wasn't going to tell us, was she? That bitch Rennie, I mean.'

'They've no imagination,' said Myra. 'Still – a bit unfortunate about Jim. D'you think Francis knew he had a record?'

'Probably. He'd be too loyal to tell us. Anyway, so what, so he did some break-ins. That doesn't make him a multiple murderer.'

I hated Detective Sergeant Rennie for coming back and making us go over it all all over again. I hated her for having a right to poke her nose into Francis's life, I didn't want her brisk personality, her no-nonsense attitude, her blunt fingers to be touching my memories, rifling through his sex life, reducing him to another lonely gay or kinky pervert, and then homing in on pathetic Jim just to improve her clear-up rate and appease the tabloid press. The worst thing about the shpiks was they made you suspect everyone. Now I was even suspicious of Jim.

'Forget about her,' said Myra soothingly. 'She's not important. Our problem is, deciding what to do next.'

'Mm – yes.' I wasn't a hundred per cent listening. Even if Francis hadn't been murdered by a sex maniac, he was still dead, he'd still been strangled, someone had come all over him . . . and nothing was sure, nothing was certain, the ground kept giving way beneath one's feet. We could be sinking into quicksands. It still *could* be the serial killer. He might have moved the body, he might have . . . who knew what he might or might not have done. It was still lurid and horrible, we were still no closer to understanding it.

Myra fetched a pad of lined paper, and began to write.

'What do we know so far? Francis suspected Leadbetter. Was Leadbetter up to something? Did either Francis or Aaron Cairo have something on Leadbetter? The answer's probably yes. So Leadbetter's one possibility. Then there's the patients. Francis seems to have been thinking more about them just before he was killed. Why would any of them have wanted to get rid of Francis? If he'd discovered one of them murdered Cairo. But could they have? And if so, why? Then there's the money: why did Cairo leave so little money? Another possibility: Rosemary Jones says Cairo had a mistress. Francis never mentioned either of those things. That's at least – what – four possible explanations – leads, at least. And now we hear the filth think it might be Jim.' She sighed and put the writing pad aside. She said: 'There's something else. I forgot. You know the notes and stuff we brought back from the flat – the stuff Francis was working on? Well, I've been looking through it – and it's incomplete.'

'What d'you mean?'

'When Francis was telling us about it, that last evening, he talked about how there was one notebook Cairo had kept that seemed to be – I can't remember exactly, but it was different from the other notes, something about notes he kept about Leadbetter's cases . . . anyway, it's not there. D'you think we overlooked it somehow in the flat?'

'I don't know.'

'You'll have to go up there and have another look.'

'Me? Why me? I don't want to go back there.'

'It's important, I'm sure. You remember when I read the cards? That other time – when Francis asked me to? Remember what that showed? That *Cairo* was up to something – something weird, something crazy, rash.' She paused, mellow now from the grass. There was a long silence. She said: 'I think I'll read them again.'

My heart sank. I didn't feel like it this evening. She always had to create an atmosphere, it all took so long, and I was feeling particularly impatient and irritable.

'I don't think I'm really in the mood.'

'Have some of this.' She passed me the cigarette.

She dealt a pyramid spread. She looked at it for a moment, then slowly turned up the card at the apex.

'Ah.' The card showed a person sitting up in bed, weeping, head in hands. Behind him or her, nine swords shot bars across black space.

Myra turned over a card in the bottom row of the pyramid. The card, which was upside down, depicted a half-clothed figure who danced against a blue sky inside a laurel wreath.

Myra turned over a card in the row above and a card in the row above that. I recognised the Hanged Man – upside down like the rest. I knew reversed cards were bad.

'All these wrong paths,' Myra muttered.

Slowly she turned up all the remaining cards, pausing at each one. Most were reversed, but not the Sun nor the skeleton in armour on a horse, which was placed directly above the Sun.

'It's so rich,' murmured Myra. She stared at the spread and said nothing for a while. I remained silent too, I knew it was unwise to interrupt during a reading. Sometimes, I thought, when the negative cards were upside down that made them less bad, but Myra didn't seem to think so:

'There's such a very strong message, it's so consistent . . . such terrible pain . . . and then . . . it hasn't been dealt with – look, those two together – ' and she pointed to the three and five of Swords, upside down again. The three swords plunged through a red heart. A soldier grabbed the five swords as his defeated adversaries slunk away.

'Something hanging around, an aftermath. And then there are these two women.' She pointed to two cards at the left side of the pyramid. At first glance they looked similar: each showed a richly dressed woman in a garden against a glowing yellow background.

'But even those cards in this context – I don't know, sex and ambition all mixed up together . . . and above them you have the lovers reversed, so whatever it refers to is all wrong somehow as well. Of course, for a time there was some benefit to someone . . . success, a moment of liberation.'

She brooded over the cards. 'There's someone who carries on, bearing a tremendous burden of suffering or conflict.'

'Could that be Francis?' I ventured.

No . . . no . . . they're behaving as if it didn't exist. Perhaps that was his marriage, Aaron Cairo's I mean, or perhaps . . . and then there's the Queen of Cups reversed. See? The Queen reversed, then the Hanged Man reversed, then the Empress, who signifies female sexuality and emotion. Misused love – perhaps that marriage was a very destructive relationship . . . that's what Rosemary Jones said in a way . . . and at the top, the Fool upside down, and the Moon . . . it couldn't be stronger, there's something so deeply malignant about it all.'

Unfortunately it didn't seem to tell us anything concrete. Myra went over the cards, she talked about every card, and there were twenty-one of them. She said: 'There was a crime – a terrible crime, a betrayal.'

'Well, we know *that*. Francis was murdered, wasn't he?' I was almost in tears, my nerves were in tatters, and all she could do was waffle on like this.

'No. Going back, before that. To do with Cairo.'

'You mean it wasn't suicide. We *know* that, Myra.'

'You shouldn't have smoked, it always makes you worse when you're upset.'

'You suggested it, remember?'

'Some terribly destructive relationship . . .'

'But Myra, we need something concrete. It's no good just speculating indefinitely.'

'No – no. Of course not.' Offended, she swept up the cards and returned them to their box. 'I'm exhausted. Can't look at them any more tonight.'

'What do we do next?'

'I don't know. See Leadbetter perhaps.' She sounded absent-minded now, no longer piqued and sulking, almost as if she'd lost interest.

'Can't we be a bit systematic? Deal with one angle at a time?'

'Sure, good idea.'

'Myra, you're stoned.'

'Have some. Good stuff.'

'You just told me not to.' However, I took the spliff from her fingers, lay back on the cushion, stared into the shadows. The trouble was there was this Chinese boxes quality about what we were trying to do. We were looking into Aaron Cairo's murder in order to find out what had happened to Francis – or was it the other way around? I wasn't sure any longer. I'd no idea what the order of things should be.

Myra sat very still with her hands planted on her knees. After a while she said: 'We'll go and see Leadbetter tomorrow morning. And you must go back to the flat.'

'I can't at the moment, I'm too busy. Gennady and I have a meeting with some suppliers.'

'This is more important,' she said.

Fourteen

Scaffolding stockaded the Four Lawns façade. A builder's lorry was parked to the side.

In the entrance hall the receptionist was seated beneath her notice.

'We've come to see Dr Leadbetter.'

'What name?' She looked down her list. 'There's nothing here.'

'He is expecting us.' Myra looked down her nose at the surly receptionist and her voice took on a booming, compelling quality as she lied. The receptionist was unmoved.

'I'm sorry. Without authorisation – '

'We can go up to his room, can't we? I know the way,' I said.

'I'm sorry, that's not – '

'Can you put us through to him? Can we speak to his secretary?'

'Secretary's on leave.'

'Please at least tell him we're here.'

I wondered if there was much mileage in all this. After all, we hadn't got an appointment, Leadbetter wasn't expecting us. As I'd suggested all along, we should have telephoned first.

'We'll wait.' Myra paced up and down the baronial hall in her hunting green skirt and jacket.

I turned away, and stepped out into the soft air. Spring was coming. We could have a look around at least. I thought I could find my way back to the side entrance through which Francis had taken me all those months ago.

As I came slowly down the steps I almost collided with a tall man who came out of nowhere. We both stepped back, winded.

'Good heavens, I'm so sorry.' He put his hand on my arm. 'You look a bit lost. Can I help?'

He hadn't recognised me – always a blow to one's confidence. Also, one tends to dislike the people who forget one: 'We've met before, Dr Leadbetter.'

He looked at me more closely. The pale, flinty eyes took on a slightly furtive expression. 'I'm afraid I don't think . . .'

'Don't you remember, at the concert, with Francis Vaughan – at the Cairos' little drinks thing?'

'Yes. Yes, of course,' he said slowly. A cautious smile dawned on his face.

'We were coming to see you – actually, it's about Francis, in a way. He was a great friend of ours – mine.'

'Ah.' His manner changed from benevolence to high seriousness. He held out his hand and took mine in a crushing grip. Then his gaze shifted. He looked past and above me.

'Dr Leadbetter? You remember me, don't you.' Sweeping down the steps in her garment like a riding habit, Myra was at her most regal. At some level the two of them were weirdly alike, both so booming, so relentlessly *there*. 'How lucky we've run into you. They weren't going to let us in. I'm sure you're very busy, but it is important, we do need to talk to you – just ten minutes, it won't take long.'

Dr Leadbetter looked furtively at his watch, but his smile stayed put. He had recognised Myra. 'Of course. I'll show you round. Come and see what we're doing to the place! Whole new building programme – the next phase.' He marched us round the side of the building. He and Myra strode along. I almost had to run to keep up with them.

The ruin had become a building site. 'New wing,' boomed Leadbetter, 'thanks to DCI – Drugs International. And Lord Cairo's been very helpful. In any case the state can't cast us off completely,' and his laugh barked out, 'we're looking after too many people nobody else can deal with. The criminally insane, they'll always be with us.' His laughter boomed out. He seemed in a good humour with the world.

I wondered what it meant to be criminally insane. Did it mean you were mad because you'd committed a crime, or a criminal because you'd had a nervous breakdown?

Leadbetter stopped at a strategic point in order to describe how the new wing would work. I wasn't really listening to what he was saying, I just wanted to get indoors so that we could talk to him. At last he led us away, and eventually we found ourselves back on the first floor, in an office like the one Francis had used, but furnished differently, with black leather armchairs and a modern Formica desk.

Leadbetter sat down behind it, facing us. That made me feel obscurely at a disadvantage, like the relative or parent of a patient perhaps.

'Francis's death must have been a great shock.' He watched us. As he had his back to the light it was difficult to make out his expression. He made no attempt at a conventional speech of sadness or horror.

Myra shifted in her chair. The low-slung chairs were not comfortable, especially for someone of Myra's size: 'Francis seemed worried,' she said. 'The last few times we saw him he seemed quite preoccupied about Dr Cairo – as if the memorial service had brought it all back. I don't know if you felt he was depressed . . . preoccupied?'

Dr Leadbetter swivelled round in his chair so that he could see out of the window. Finally he said: 'I think you may be right. I should probably have taken more notice myself at the time, but then Francis always had an anxious personality. Tendency to depression as well. Yes – I think you may be right. But his mood can't have had much to do with what happened.'

Myra spoke softly: 'Did you know he was trying to dig up a whole lot of things about Aaron Cairo?'

Leadbetter swivelled back. 'Dig up? He told me about the conference, naturally. Is that what you mean?'

'He didn't say anything else?'

'Not really. He was – very worked up about the Cairo conference, of course. Yes, I suppose he was quite keyed up, I'd say. But he wouldn't really have talked to me about it, he knew I saw the treatment picture rather differently. We've always agreed to differ.'

Myra leant forward. 'So he never told you he thought that Cairo had been murdered?'

Leadbetter seemed to tense up, and swivelled away from us so that his face was in shadow once more. 'No,' he said slowly, 'I didn't know that. He didn't tell me anything about that.' Then he swung slowly round again, and stroked and smoothed the Formica in front of him. His hands were slightly swollen, ageing hands; perhaps he was older than fifty.

'He was convinced Dr Cairo was murdered,' repeated Myra.

Leadbetter looked down at the desk, then up.

'You knew Francis pretty well, didn't you? You know he used to get the odd bee in his bonnet, to put it mildly. About the sponsorships, for example, didn't like that at all. I dare say he talked to you about that. He could be very obstinate.'

'Sponsorships? What sponsorships?' I asked brightly.

Myra kicked me surreptitiously. It was too late. Leadbetter was looking more cheerful. He knew, or thought he knew, that we didn't know something he didn't want us to know. He leant towards us now, doing a good imitation of confiding frankness. His fingers caressed the edge of his desk: 'When I say Dr Vaughan was a depressive I wonder if you're aware of the full implications of that. Someone who's depressed can develop a fixed idea – what is sometimes termed an overvalued idea, bordering on the psychotic: a delusion. I have to say honestly that what you tell me makes me feel that this theory about Aaron's death you say he developed was almost of that nature. You shouldn't take it too seriously, you know.'

Myra's voice was smoother than ever: 'Of course not. But I still wonder why such an idea should have taken that particular form. Why should he have been so convinced that Cairo had been murdered?' Myra smiled, gazing at Leadbetter with an air of bovine naïvety.

Leadbetter's face seemed heavier and more flushed than it had before and he was frowning. He seemed to brood. Then suddenly he looked at his watch: 'Good heavens, is that the time – you know I really musn't keep you any longer.' He stood up.

I stood up too, but Myra stayed where she was. 'Before you go – there were just one or two more things,' she said.

'Well I – all right.' He sat down again, with a bad grace. Now he was visibly in a hurry.

'How did you rate Dr Cairo? Francis tremendously admired him, as you probably know, and I just wondered – I mean, was that part of Francis's obsession as well? Or was Cairo really outstanding – original – brilliant, I don't know how to put it.'

Leadbetter considered the question. 'Cairo *was* brilliant,' he said after a bit. 'We had our disagreements. I'm more of a pills man myself. Psychotherapy . . . well, I don't know how much you know about it – does seem to help some patients, but I'm very sceptical about its scientific basis, don't go for the theory behind it all. In a way, though, that made for a good partnership, the government liked it anyway. Basically, they prefer drugs, because therapy's too expensive, but Aaron was the icing on the cake, the international reputation.'

'Were you surprised when he killed himself?' asked Myra, silky smooth.

Again it took a while for Leadbetter to answer. 'I thought he'd lost his bottle,' he said at last, slowly.

Myra fidgeted in her chair. 'I'm sorry . . . ?'

Leadbetter shoved his hair back from his face, but I still couldn't decipher his expression. 'What do I mean by that? I mean he was losing his grip. Both of us were in for the post of medical director. Old Dr French was about to retire. I'm not even sure Aaron wanted the job to begin with, but all his psychoanalyst buddies were pushing him like crazy. You know, they've been losing ground all the time, and it would have been such a boost for them – for what they believed in. Well – I got the job, and Aaron . . . didn't exactly crack up, but – ' He paused. 'Let's just say he wasn't a very good loser.'

We waited for more, but there was silence. Finally he added: 'You know eight years is a long time. I don't think it can help anyone to rake over it all now.'

'But at any rate you never thought of it being murder?' insisted Myra.

'No, no. Ms. Zone, it's a very far-fetched idea. You really mustn't let it start worrying you now. Poor Francis, I'm afraid – and it had nothing to do with *his* death, I'm sure.'

'You don't think one of the patients could have had anything to do with either of their deaths?'

He seemed relieved. 'I doubt that very much. I suppose there is always a small risk, but . . .' He shook his head with a slightly pitying smile, suggesting that lay persons had foolish ideas about the mentally disturbed.

'There are some dangerous patients in here,' I began.

'Whose death are we discussing, my dear? We know how Francis died, and Aaron Cairo too, after all.' He looked at us, significant, paternal, humouring. 'Whatever Francis had come to believe.'

'You and he – you and Dr Cairo, I mean – did have some disagreements about what kind of treatment they should have, though, didn't you?' Myra was not giving up.

Leadbetter stared at her. 'As I said, I've never made any secret of my views about treatment. That wasn't an issue. And look, I'm afraid you'll have to excuse me, I have a meeting, I must get off to the Ministry.'

As he led us downstairs and out into the garden again, Myra asked: 'Doesn't it sometimes depress you, dealing with all these dangerous patients? I mean, do any of them ever get better – some of them leave, do they, or are most of them here for good?'

Dr Leadbetter smiled back over his shoulder. 'Some conditions are more intractable than others,' he said, 'but you know we medical men must never give up hope.'

I drove along the expressway at about ninety, cutting in and sheering past the men in their steel penises. They hooted their horns and shouted that I was a castrating bitch. I didn't care. Life on the expressway isn't worth living unless you take it at a hundred miles an hour.

We sat in the Café balcony. It was rather slack downstairs for once, so Gennady joined us.

'If you think about it,' said Myra, 'he had a motive to get rid of Cairo.'

'What?'

'Both after the same job.'

'Oh Myra, come on. I don't think he was a murderer. That sort of situation happens every day. People don't kill their colleagues to get the job. Anyway, he *got* the job.'

'Rivalries can linger on. I must say I didn't take to Dr Leadbetter. I'd love to know more about what's going on at that hospital.'

'You didn't manage to get much out of him.'

'Why must you always be so critical and so negative? It isn't as if you'd taken the initiative.'

'You said you wanted to.'

'It's the life you lead, it's unhealthy. In any case, we did discover something, quite a few things: he hoped we didn't know about what he called sponsorship – something to do with the drugs programme, I imagine. He was quite tense about that. And he was very keen to play the whole Aaron Cairo thing down. He wasn't a bit pleased about that, and he did his best to discredit Francis by saying he was depressed.'

'What gives about drugs?' Gennady perked up. 'Something illegal?'

'I never said that, Gennady.' Myra looked shocked.

'I ask around,' said Gennady. 'You see – my Russian contacts . . .' referring to that expanded underworld which had such close links with certain terrorist groups that it was difficult to know where one ended and the other began.

'What would be the use of that?'

'Did he act edgy, act like he didn't like you nosing around?'

'No,' I said. I was almost disappointed to have to say it.

'Well – ' Myra demurred. 'It was sort of a clever kind of holding operation. 'He seemed friendly enough, but . . . you know, he had this professional façade.'

Gennady laughed. 'What you say, Myra, I do a little investigation. Is time Justine stop neglecting the Café and I have some time off. Anything dodgy about the drugs scene – I find out. And maybe there's nothing.' He paused. 'But you know what I really think, I think it's blackmail. Why else should all the money disappear?'

Blackmail. I hadn't thought of that. 'If *Cairo* had something to hide, you mean? Someone blackmailing him?'

Myra looked loftily sceptical. 'How would that tie in with Leadbetter, though? And the cards said nothing about blackmail . . .'

'What about the nurse?' I said. 'I reckon she'd be up for a bit of blackmail.'

Myra looked down her nose at me. 'Oh! Do you think so?' she said.

She never liked it when anyone else had the bright ideas.

Fifteen

As I took the lift down to the bowels of the building next morning for my early swim I was still feeling annoyed with Myra. She was full of ideas that didn't hang together, and so far as I could see, the Tarot had told us nothing.

When I came out of the dressing room, Miranda's compact, sturdy body was poised on the diving board. I called. She arrested her action, waved, prepared herself again to spring. The dive was mediocre, but her crawl was alarming; she ploughed through the water like a tank. These early morning swims were one of the best things about our friendship. Afterwards, in the showers, I said:

'I've been taking too much time out from the Café – but I simply must go up today and start sorting out the flat. I can do a couple of hours' work on it before the Café opens.' I was talking to myself as much as to her.

'The flat?' Her blue, blank stare.

'Francis.'

'Oh . . . yes. Poor you.' Somehow I felt she wasn't really listening, found it hard to respond. Like me, she did her best to steer clear of disturbing emotion.

After we'd had coffee together I drove up to the cliff. The rooms in the flat were dustier than ever, but otherwise just as we'd left them.

They made me feel guilty. We'd promised his sister we'd sort everything out, but so far we'd done nothing, and now I was only here to have another look for the missing notebook.

I decided I had to make at least a token beginning on the flat as a whole, so I had a preliminary look round before going through all his papers again. I was half afraid of uncovering some unknown, unexpected aspect of Francis's life, some secret he'd hidden from us, wouldn't have wanted us to know. In an odd way I was also half afraid of finding the notebook, as if its secrets, if that's what they were, would be dangerous – but I needn't have worried about that, the notebook definitely wasn't there.

I found it hard to keep going once I felt certain of that. I kept finding I was slowing down, stopping altogether and staring into space, as though the atmosphere of life suspended, of silence and sleep, was a narcotic. At the same time I was edgy, I didn't like being alone in the empty flat. The smell of cigarette smoke and dust brought Francis back so powerfully. Reminded me of clearing out my father's house, too. And I hated the silence.

The telephone rang. It startled me as much as a live intruder. After four rings, however, there was a click, a silence, a further click, a third. Then there was more silence, followed by a shrill pip, indicating the end of the message time.

I was shaking. I don't know how long I sat motionless. I'd just calmed down and told myself how silly I was being when it happened again: the four rings, the click, the silence, the click. This time, however, stifled laughter exploded out into the room where I stood as if turned to stone.

It must be children, messing around. But no sooner had I forced myself to settle back to my task than the telephone rang a third time. No laughter this time, no message either; just silence – but now the silence itself seemed like a message I couldn't decode. I stood blankly in the middle of the room for I don't know how long. Then I rang the telephone exchange and told them to disconnect the line. Stupid of us to have forgotten to do that as soon as he'd died. After I'd replaced the instrument, I carefully removed the incoming message tape from the answering machine. I didn't know quite why, but I just thought it might be a good idea. Then a thought occurred to me. I stuck the tape back into the answering machine, wound it to the beginning, set it to play.

The first voice I heard gave me a jolt. It was my own. I heard myself arranging with Francis to go to the movies to see the Hitler film. If I hated hearing my own voice, it was worse when Francis replied, but almost at once there was another click, another message began: it must have recorded over the old one. This was a man's voice, someone with a flat accent and an ingratiating sort of tone:

'Is that Francis Vaughan? There's something I wanted to talk to you about. Not on the phone. You'll be – '

Francis's voice interrupted: 'I'm sorry, who is this?'

'Y'know about Dr Cairo, well, I've some information might interest you.'

'Who are you? Is this some kind of joke?'

The anonymous caller sounded as if he were smiling. 'On the level. Lennox said I should get in touch.'

That was a shock – but maddeningly another message cut through the smiling voice of the unknown man. I let the tape play on, hoping for more. There were a few fragments of messages – from Jim, from another doctor, from his secretary. After that there was only the slight hiss of silence as the tape continued to wind from one spool to the other.

I played it through again, hoping I'd missed something the first time around, hoping, too, that it would be possible to date the stranger's mystery conversation. But the only clue was the fragment of conversation about our arrangements for seeing the Hitler film; it had to be since then. I couldn't remember exactly when that had been, but I could look up my diary, the date was probably in there.

I wondered how come the conversations had been recorded. I looked carefully at the machine. It was an old one. Presumably it must have been plugged in, he must have answered the call on his extension in the study, and the machine didn't automatically cut out, but just recorded everything. I dropped the tape in my bag, left the sorting and packing and locked up the flat. Then I made my way on foot to Wegner's bookshop.

It looked even shabbier than I remembered. I walked between the shelves to the back. Otto was seated at a narrow table. He didn't seem to have an assistant these days.

He was as colourless as ever – he had certainly perfected the art of buying dust-coloured clothes. I hadn't seen him since the riots. After Lennox had been arrested I'd stopped Otto's group meeting at the Café. Otto had accused me of political cowardice. I'd screamed at him.

Now I was calm and polite: 'Lennox asked me to come and see you.' This was not true – I couldn't think why I'd said it, but telling lies has never been a problem for me, in fact I cultivate the art; at the very least I *always* embellish the truth. It's so much more creative.

Otto Wegner smiled minimally. 'That's a coincidence. I heard from him last week.'

'I didn't know he wrote to you.' I didn't like it, but I tried not to let it show.

'At first he used to, but I had to tell him to stop. I thought it was unwise. Since then we've devised another method of communication.'

'Oh?' I wasn't going to ask what it was, although I was dying to know.

'So it's rather odd, isn't it, that he asked you to come and see me.'

He didn't trust me – of course not. The rich dilettante who fucked Lennox, and a woman at that: of course he didn't like me, but he didn't admit it. He persuaded himself, I'm sure, that his contempt was purely political.

'He wanted to know what's happening, you know, the group and all that,' I said.

Otto's sour half-smile flickered. 'I gather one of these Celtic terrorists has turned up inside. That seems to have rekindled his revolutionary ardour.'

I ignored the cheap innuendo.

'Well – better than drugs, I suppose,' said Otto. 'There seem to be more drugs in the prisons than ever these days.'

'Lennox was never into drugs,' I said. And hadn't that been part of the fascination: Lennox the corrupt, but also the sea green incorruptible, who hated drink and drugs, and really, I suspected, hated sex for the loss of control it involved, yet who was also so reckless, uncontrollable.

'No, not into *drugs*.' Otto smiled thinly. The silence was growing awkward when he said: 'Alasdair Roxburgh ... heard of him, have you? Rather a hell raiser, of course. But a clever man. Lawyer originally – broke away from the Nats. Took to the hills. But he's got a big following in the North. I don't think any of these armed groups have the strategy, but he's better than most. Charismatic too. He's impressed Lennox no end.'

'Of course I've heard of him.' But not from Lennox. I leant against the door frame, and wished I hadn't come. Then I pulled myself together and explained about the tape. I even offered to play it to him, but he didn't have a machine.

'It's a bit odd, don't you think? Why should anyone mention Lennox to Francis?'

'Someone from the prison, I suppose,' murmured Wegner. 'A way of identifying himself, possibly? Other than that, I've no idea.' He shook his head. 'You will have to ask him, won't you, next time you visit – you do still visit, do you, in spite of everything?'

'Why shouldn't I? I've always visited Lennox. No one else does.'

'I just thought you might have grown ... tired of it all.'

'He's only got another few months to go,' I said as coolly as I could.

'And what is he going to do when he comes out?' enquired Otto.

'I've no idea. Why – are you hoping he'll be working with you again?'

'That might not be a good idea, after what happened,' he

said primly, as though Lennox had committed some rather nasty kind of offence.

'Oh great,' I said. 'He carried the can for you and now you don't want to know.'

'Now don't jump to conclusions. It's just that things are getting rather difficult – we may have to move into another mode.'

Later, much later, the Café was crowded with early evening drinkers, while others lingered over their tea. It was that transition time, a mist veiled the sea, dusk, two times at once, late afternoon and early evening, all merging together. Gennady was looking very good, and Chloe too. I ran upstairs to see Myra, but she was with a client, so I had Chloe mix me a margarita and talked to Gennady instead. We were on good terms again, and looked out over our domain, making plans for the summer.

It was women's night at the Café, and Gennady went off duty. As I waited for friends to join me at my table, Otto's hints went on taunting me. How much I didn't want to know if Lennox had sex with men in the prison, but the images were going in my head, images that hurt but which also aroused. How painful that I, a woman, could never be part of that. I saw it so vividly – Lennox surrendering to some faceless man, Lennox fucking and being fucked by a hard, compelling stranger.

I'd fucked him too, but I'd never be part of that all-male couple. The most my presence would do would be to convert it into some silly kind of permissive threesome. I didn't even like threesomes.

Men – straight men – seemed to have no difficulty with the idea of joining a female couple. It was as if two women made the perfect, inviting excuse for male intervention; indeed I had regularly encountered men who seemed entirely unaware that the prospect of their active presence might not be unreservedly welcome to me and my girlfriend of the moment.

The masculine couple by contrast clenched in on itself, a rock against which a woman would beat in vain. I had a mental image of it as a smooth, abstract piece of sculpture, turning a blind flank to my entreaties.

But I shook off these morbid thoughts. Myra had often said I romanticised gay men.

A couple seated on high stools at the bar caught my attention. *She* twined long legs in tight black and white check leggings round the bar-stool legs and rested one suede-clad foot on the crossbar. The other stilettoed foot swung to and fro. The long sleeves as much as the low neck of her tight white Lycra top signalled her breasts, which rose, erect, as she leant towards her girlfriend. She courted her with her large brown eyes, her painted, parted lips, her long, wavy brown hair, an adoring film starlet insinuating herself into the force field of butch power that so subtly surrounded her companion.

She smoothed back her short black hair. She held a cigarette in her other hand. I couldn't see her face, only her leather jacket and the edge of a hard profile. As a couple they perfectly pantomimed the ritual of masculine control and feminine seduction.

I watched them. I couldn't take my eyes off them. I devoured them with my eyes. The starlet looked up and caught me, looked away and murmured to her lover. I knew she was telling her girlfriend that I fancied her, but that wasn't it at all. She wasn't my type, the dark boyish one was far more for me, yet I didn't fancy her either. It was them, together, the two of them, their perfect enactment of lesbian desire. That was what I wanted: what I desired was their mutual desire. I longed to be inside that magic circle. I felt painfully my exclusion from desire. To be looked at and to look as that woman looked at her lover, that was what I wanted. I wanted to look at someone in that way, conquered and conquering, submissive and demanding, insatiable, in thrall, swept up in the whirlpool of: 'Take me – I'm yours, you're all I ever wanted.' Instead I was exiled, banished, because I desired no one. There was only this emptiness where Lennox had been.

I watched the couple at the bar until my glass was empty. Then I got up to refill it. I had no wish to speak to them. I simply wanted to *be* them: both of them – to be suffocating in that bell jar of obsessive desire.

Now, a third woman joined them, but she seemed unaware of their magic aura. She laughed and chatted away to them, but she was visually cruising the room at the same time with dark, narrow eyes. She was sort of a flying ace type, not S/M gear, but a distressed brown leather bomber jacket, slicked-back hair, an odd, crooked, lean face.

I caught her eye and she half smiled and half lifted her hand in a greeting. Did I know her then? I couldn't remember who I knew or didn't know any more: fatal, I was losing my grip as a hostess.

She came over: 'You don't remember, do you?' Flirtatious too. 'I'm Vic – Vic Randall. You came to my first private view – a long time ago.'

'Of course I remember you.' That was a lie, but why didn't I remember? Could I really have been so hung up on Lennox then that this woman's cynical smile had failed to turn my entrails to jelly?

Unfortunately Myra came downstairs just then. I grabbed her. 'We have to talk,' I said, and to the flying ace: 'I'll be down again later.'

I hustled Myra back upstairs and told her about the tape. We went into the office and played it on the answering machine in there.

'That might have been the voice of the murderer,' I said, as the horrible thought struck me.

'I suppose so . . .'

'I dropped in on Otto Wegner,' I told her. 'He thought it might be someone from the prison.'

'Well, that's obvious,' said Myra tartly, 'any idiot can see that. But what could this guy – the voice – have known about Francis?' She sighed. Then she said: 'Find anything else in the flat? The notebook? We absolutely have to have it. Where can it be? The police didn't take it – they gave us an inventory of what they took. Could it possibly still be at the hospital? Listen – I have an idea.'

I listened. I thought it was a terrible idea – but it was always difficult to refuse to do anything Myra really wanted you to.

It was just my luck, of course, that someone as glam as the flying ace should turn up when I had to spend half the evening running Gennady to earth (he wasn't home – *of course* – and his girlfriend, Jacqui, had thought he was at the Café, so there was trouble in store at that end). When I finally reached him, it took hours to persuade him to do what Myra wanted.

Still, when I got back to my table Vic Randall was still there.

Sixteen

Gennady drove his old Citroën past the hospital gates, and drew up in a layby a hundred or so yards further on.

'Hey, you've passed the gate – you've driven past it.'

'Yes – we go in a different way. See – you ruin my night out, Jacqui nearly kill me, but still I find time to work out a better way of getting in.'

'Sorry – I'm sorry, Gennady.' I didn't feel too bright myself. The flying ace and I had drunk a jug of margaritas. 'All right to leave the car here?'

'They'll think we just hopped off in the undergrowth for a quickie.' Gennady laughed. 'Mind you – I never say this before, but might not be bad idea.'

'Give us a break.' Gennady would make a pass at anything that moved; anything female, that is. Mind you, he was attractive, in an ugly sort of way, very Slav with high cheekbones, protruding blue eyes, a long, inquisitive nose, full lips.

Cars were shooting past, and we had to wait and then take our lives in our hands to get across the road. On this side, barbed wire separated the soft verge from a copse. I followed Gennady a few yards along, until we came to an old-fashioned stile. From there the path wound away into a little wood.

'I thought this was high security hospital – '

'There's a big fence round the special wing,' I told him. At the same time, it was strange. We climbed up through the bare trees with new leaves just beginning to spurt all over the branches. After about five minutes we came out on to a sloping lawn. We trudged up it, skirted the lake at the top, turned a corner, and to our horror saw a little group of men crouched over a herbaceous border, but they seemed to be weeding or planting, and took no notice of us. We walked on across the vast open space of the lawn.

'This was a terrible idea,' I muttered. 'What time is it anyway?'

'Eight o'clock.'

'It's too late already, Gennady, too many people about. We should have got here an hour ago. Two hours. At six.'

'You were too drunk. Come on! You were still in the Café at three.'

We walked round the side of the main building. I was looking for the door through which Francis had taken me all those months – how many months was it? – ago. In front of us the special wing, encased in its wire mesh, came into view. The whole place seemed like one of those folk-tale castles, cast under a spell to sleep for a hundred years.

The door was where I remembered it. Then it had been open; now it was locked, but I'd brought Francis's bunch of keys.

'I'm not sure which key it is.'

'Just take your time.' Gennady stood in such a way as to shield me – although no one was around – while I tried one key after another. The third worked.

'See – is not difficult. No problem.'

Inside, Gennady followed me up the stone stairs. I wished we'd never come, but it was just the sort of escapade Gennady enjoyed. On the landing we paused. The silence here was even more profound. It unnerved me. I stepped forward as if treading on eggs, my feet noiseless on the carpet. The four white-painted doors leading off the landing were shut. I couldn't remember which door led into whose room. I tried the nearest. It opened on to the secretary's empty office. Gennady followed me. The desktop was immaculate, trays marked 'In' and 'Out' were empty, and in the desk drawers we found only writing paper and other stationery. There was a cupboard built into the chimney recess, but all it contained was coffee and tea making equipment. There was also a filing cabinet. Gennady pulled at the top drawer, but it refused to budge.

'Is locked,' he said unnecessarily. He examined the lock, then selected a paper clip from the saucer on the desk, unbent it and started to jiggle it into the keyhole.

'No, leave it for now – '

'Only take a minute.'

I opened the door into the adjoining office, the one that had belonged to Francis. I began with the desk drawers again, but they had been completely cleared. On the book-shelves were a few medical texts and journals. Another built-in cupboard was empty. I looked desperately round: 'Oh shit, shit shit.'

Gennady was still tampering with the lock.

'There's nothing in his room. I'm going to try Leadbetter's office. Why don't you leave that? Gennady – leave it, there's no point. I expect it's only patients' files and stuff.'

I opened another door; this one led into a store room. There were more filing cabinets, boxes of papers, packets of photocopying paper and black plastic sacks of what turned out to be old clothes. Perhaps there might be some-thing here, but it seemed more important to investigate Leadbetter's room, so I left the store room and tried the adjacent door. It was locked.

The fourth and last door opened into Leadbetter's office. There was the Formica-topped desk, the easy chairs, and a further row of filing cabinets along the wall opposite to the door. I tried the desk drawers, but they were all locked. I left them for the moment, and turned to the cabinets. I was surprised when the first drawer I tried opened easily. It was filled with a mass of disordered letters and papers stuck in hanging folders. As I began to shuffle through it all, I could hear Gennady moving about in the passage. I called his name. He didn't answer. I looked round.

It was Leadbetter. Not Gennady. Leadbetter loomed up in the doorway, and his face, slabbier than ever, managed to look both threatening and expressionless – he neither smiled nor frowned, but his whole face seemed swollen with repressed rage. His physique was massive. We stared at each other. He recovered first.

'What the hell are you doing?' He spoke tonelessly, taking it in. 'This is outrageous.'

The only defence was attack. 'Some things belonging to Francis have disappeared. I'm very worried about it. I came up here to search his office, but it's been cleared. I thought just possibly some of his papers might have been brought in here.'

Leadbetter was still looking hard at me. Suddenly he turned and peered out into the landing.

'Who's with you?'

'No one.'

'My dear girl, don't be stupid. You thought I was someone else, you spoke to someone.'

Where *was* Gennady? I was trying to think fast: 'No, no,' I babbled, 'I just thought I heard someone – but obviously it was you.'

'This hospital is private property. You have no right to be here.'

'I don't know about that,' I said. 'I'm Francis's executor. There are things of his that are missing. It's my responsibility to – to sort it out, to find them if I can.'

'Not to the extent of breaking and entering.'

I stood my ground. 'How dare you say that. That's not it at all.'

'I doubt if the police would agree with you.'

The police: oh *shit*. Where was Gennady? Yet there was a curious uncertainty about Leadbetter. His anger lacked conviction.

'You don't want the police nosing round up here,' I said,

with what I hoped was a poisonously sweet smile. Now he looked distinctly shifty. I followed up my attack. 'I know it looks a little strange,' I said. 'And I'm sorry. Of course I shouldn't be searching your office like this. But Francis was really desperate for Aaron Cairo's work to be published, and if some of it's missing – well, I shall feel it's all my fault.'

'You do realise Francis was paranoid; he had a bee in his bonnet about the whole thing. It's not as if Aaron's work was even original.'

'Oh? Francis thought it was.'

He flapped his hand in an irritable gesture. 'Oh, never mind,' he cried. 'We'll say no more about it – but now you'd better leave.'

'Yes, but will you look – I mean, if you find anything, *anything* belonging to Francis, you will let me have it, won't you? The secretary must have cleared out his room. I do hope she didn't throw it all away.'

'Have you looked in her office?'

I shook my head. He relaxed a little. 'I'll have a look round later. Let me just take you back to the front entrance – so easy to get lost in this place.'

He shepherded me back on to the landing. All the doors were shut again now. Gennady had completely disappeared.

Leadbetter unlocked the fourth door. Beyond it the corridor stretched away interminably, its floor covered with shabby coconut matting. A telephone rang distantly.

'This way, after you,' and Leadbetter almost pushed me through ahead of him. We walked down the endless corridor. Leadbetter walked very close to me, which felt threatening, but at the same time he began to talk about his work. It was extraordinary. His whole manner changed, and it was as if I was some visitor he had to show round.

'You see, people don't understand about mental disorder, you all think we're sinister, don't you, you don't like us at all. And I'm afraid Aaron and Francis didn't do anything to help. It's not a question of kindness, or therapy, family breakdown, all those explanations are out of the window. It's chemicals in the brain. Most of our patients don't come from broken homes. You can't put mental illness all down to social causes.'

We walked and walked – further and further into the depths of the asylum, just like the time I'd come here to see Francis, but in the opposite direction. We didn't meet a soul.

At last the corridor broadened out into another landing. Main stairs, a double flight, stone, with a broad balustrade of polished wood led down to the entrance hall. He steered me out towards the front.

'Where did you leave your car?'

Oh God. 'I didn't bring it.' We'd thought it would be too conspicuous.

He looked at me. I started to move. 'It's OK, I'll be all right, there's a bus,' I called with a backward wave as I retreated as fast as I could without actually running.

'No – wait!' he called, and raised his arm. I looked back. I thought he was going to follow me, but again he was indecisive, although he must have worked out now that I definitely hadn't come on my own. He just stood there as if arrested in mid-stride. I waved again, walking more quickly, and then I saw him turn and almost run back into the hospital. Once I was out of sight round the first bend in the drive, I ran too. I struck off to the right across the lawn, making for the path I'd climbed earlier with Gennady. The grounds were as empty as ever. I sped nervously down the hill and through the copse, tripped over a tree root and nearly fell, reached the stile and climbed over. There was so much traffic on the road now that it was actually less difficult to get across, although I was nearly mown down by a motorbike weaving through the nose-to-bumper jam.

I was afraid Gennady's car would have disappeared along with Gennady, but as I stumbled along the soft verge I could see it in the layby, but no Gennady. Then, when I came alongside it, I saw he was seated in the driving seat.

'Thank God you're here. What happened to you?'

'Sorry I leave you in the lurch. When you've gone I shut

the door. Is better if it looks like normal, how we found it. I get the filing cabinet open – then I hear voices. So I open the door very softly and slip away.'

'You might have come to my rescue.'

He grinned. 'Can't do that, I have to get away without him seeing me, because look what I found.' He whipped out from behind his back a marbled hardbacked notebook, A4 size.

'Oh, you got it. Oh Gennady, that's brilliant. Where was it? Let's see.'

'In the filing cabinet. Let's get away from here first though.' He held the book away from me, then dropped it in my lap as he screeched away from the verge.

The traffic jam was all the way into town. Instead of joining it Gennady drove in the opposite direction, turning right at the first opportunity. 'We join the expressway further up, I know a way,' he said.

As we drove along I opened the exercise book, but Gennady wanted to talk.

'I was in psychiatric hospital once, I was very young boy – you know, in Brezhnev time, ultra-leftist dissident,' he said cheerfully. This was news to me. 'If I go back now is probably the same.' He laughed. 'Four Lawns looks much more comfortable, I think.'

I left Gennady at the Café, to get the place ready for the day, and also to guard the notebook, rang Myra to tell her the news, and went home for my swim. I was later than usual, and missed Miranda, but a swim's the best cure for a hangover, and I felt about 200 per cent better when I left the pool.

When I got back to the Café, Myra had turned up and was already reading Cairo's notes. I took coffee, herbal tea and croissants and joined her on the balcony.

'How did Leadbetter get hold of this?'

'You know, I thought about that,' I said. 'That time I met Francis up there and he showed me round – he was rummaging around for the spare set of keys to his flat. He kept a spare set at work. That's the only thing I can think of – that Leadbetter nicked them and went to the flat.'

'Yes . . . there's only the one set of keys now.' Myra tapped the notebook. 'You know, this isn't what I thought at all,' she said. 'What awful writing he had.'

'I know, I had a look on the way back here in the car. I'd assumed it would be all about Cairo's patients.'

'There is something about them at the back, but this stuff at the front . . .'

I sat beside her at the table and we looked at it together. There was not even all that much. It was just a diary, after all. He'd written dates, and beside them there were names and abbreviations I didn't understand, also brief comments.

'I think I've worked out what these are,' said Myra, 'but we'll have to check the dates somehow. These dates are over a period, look, 89, 90, about a year, from 3.89 to 5.90. It could be names of patients who died, and the drugs they were given, and the comments must refer to their behaviour. Look – that word, it's "manic" isn't it, and that: "extreme elation", then "comatose" – I mean his writing is difficult, but I think I'm right. And these aren't the patients he was treating, none of the names are the same.'

The notes we were looking at spread over a page and a half. That was all. Most of the following pages were blank, but then he'd started again at the back.

'These notes *are* about his patients.' Myra frowned as she read out his writing, which was in black ink with minute letters all looking the same. 'It's the same sort of thing – just little notes about their behaviour, only with them there are no drugs, it's a record of when he saw them. 9.40 to 10.30. 11.00 to 11.45. And so on.'

'How disappointing,' I said. I thought of the risks we'd taken. At this moment Leadbetter was probably phoning the police, in fact he'd probably got on the blower the minute we left Four Lawns. I was expecting them to come through the door of the Café any moment.

'Oh, it's not disappointing at all,' said Myra. 'Can't you see? He was keeping tabs on Leadbetter, must have been. Francis mentioned that, remember? That a lot of patients died.'

She was still looking at the notes at the back of the book, following the tiny writing with her finger. 'It looks like some sort of comparison. His patients get therapy, not drugs like the others . . .' She read on down to the last entry. 'But then Beverly Smith dies. There's nothing more after that.'

'So where does that leave us? I just can't see why this was important.'

'Francis talked to some of them, didn't he,' said Myra. 'D'you think we should as well?'

'Well I did visit one woman with him, you know that – what's her name, Lange. He said she started him on the right track, but she didn't seem very helpful to me. And anyway, what are the two of us going to look like, traipsing around like we were social workers? Get real. Do we *look* like social workers?'

'We have to find out more, though. What was going on at the hospital? We need to know.'

'Anna – I'll go and see Anna. I'm sure she'll be able to help.'

Seventeen

I'd first met Anna when I came back from California; she was all part of that strange period after my father died. She'd rented a room in my father's house in order to hide from her violent husband. He'd killed someone else, thinking it was her, but he only got six years, so she'd continued to keep a low profile, running a drop-in youth centre over in Marshtown. About six months into his sentence he committed suicide, but she stayed where she was, she said she liked the job.

The Lagonda had developed some vaguely worrying symptoms and had gone into hospital for tests, so I had a tortuous journey across the city on public transport. I took a bus, then a local train, then another bus, and there was still a lonely twenty-minute walk at the end. Marshtown always had that deserted, threatening feel, as if its population had gone indoors, expecting an air raid or a shoot-up. I passed the Tenison-Joliet mission. They were singing gospel songs inside. I hoped I wouldn't see Scrawny Sean.

Anna's centre, sponsored by some voluntary body, was housed in a disused cinema at the edge of what had once been a municipal housing estate. I had been there before, but not for some time, and I wandered around the outskirts of the blocks of flats for quite a while before stumbling upon it.

The door was locked and protected by a grille. It wasn't very inviting – you could hardly 'drop in' to somewhere protected like Fort Knox. I rang the bell and waited.

'You! This is a surprise.' She was looking bright and healthy, her black hair was shining and glossy, her Mediterranean colouring set off by a red sweater. I'd never seen her looking so well. The centre, on the other hand, was as drab as ever. We were in a dingy foyer lined with dark brown wood veneer and carpeted in swirling tangerine. Off to the right I heard the clack of billiard balls, a triumphant shout and boys' laughter. Anna took me into her office to the left.

'So what are you doing in this part of the world? Slumming?'

'I was just passing by.' It didn't sound convincing. 'It's been so long.'

'Let's have some coffee.'

The coffee came in a mug with a message, and it wasn't real coffee, but the stuff they make from acorns, no doubt ecologically pure, and although it might keep you awake at nights that would be from stomach cramps not caffeine.

We sat down on the 1960s vintage armless purple plastic sofa and stared at the charity calendar on the wall opposite.

'How are you, Anna? I've been meaning to ring – but you know how it is.'

'We struggle along.' She looked at me. 'You didn't come to hear about me. What's the real reason?'

'I need your help. We need your help, Myra and I.'

'Oh yes?' She looked sceptical.

'We're trying to trace some ex-mental patients, and their families.'

'The Café gone bust, then?'

I had to laugh, she was such a crusty old thing. 'Don't be like that. You do your job, I do mine. We both keep the punters happy and out of mischief – well, off the streets anyway.'

'Except you run a day centre for the rich, and mine's for the poor.'

'Mine's more fun.'

'But mine's more useful.' She always came the moral high ground.

'I've never claimed to be useful. In fact as Charles Baudelaire once said, I find the idea of usefulness quite horrible.'

'Divinely decadent, I suppose.'

'D'you get any mental patients in here?'

'Not many. To tell you the truth we don't get a lot of interest at all. I suppose we haven't got that much to offer these days. The kids prefer guilt and flagellation set to music by T-J, and then there's the People's Army and Albion and the drug dusters . . . not to mention bootleg videos and gang rape and all the other sideshows.'

'Funnily enough I know someone who lives round here – Miranda Mars, the dress designer? Their factory's further along the road.'

'There are sweatshops by the score. Sweatshops and knocking shops and crank religions. And drugs of course. It's a great district. We're even beginning to have religious wars. The Tenison-Joliet crowd decided they didn't like that Hindu offshoot, Behold the Child, tried to set fire to their temple the other day. Nearly killed someone.'

'Didn't hear anything about that.'

'Tenison-Joliet got it hushed up. Anyway things like that don't make the national papers.'

'Tenison-Joliet goes in for fire bombing?'

'Oh of course he disowned the attack. Disciplined the perpetrators. They were well punished I expect – I think he's big into corporal punishment.'

'Oh, how nauseating!' I thought with distaste of scrawny Sean cringing and whimpering in my Lagonda.

'Suppose he has to get his kicks somehow.'

'I heard on good authority they're going to legalise drugs next year.'

'They say that every year. I can tell you, it won't go down too well around here when they do. The community's main source of income.'

'But Tenison-Joliet campaigns against drugs. How come they haven't put a bomb under his car?'

'They need each other. He acts as mediator between gangs and the police – he may be an informer as well, I wouldn't be surprised – but the parents like him and he does get a few kids off junk.'

'He seems to like persecuting poufs as well.'

'Oh yes, he gets off on that too. You hear all sorts of things about T-J around here. Starting to campaign against the sweatshops as well. I've more sympathy with that. But it's all for his own greater glory.'

'Where does his money come from?'

'Good question. From little old ladies who send him their life savings? As a tax loss from the banks? Maybe the drugs boys slip him a bit. While we've got practically nothing – and so few volunteers. We used to get students coming here for work experience, but that's dried up completely. We don't offer the right kind of training, and anyway, there aren't the jobs. But there – enough about me. What about you? What's this about psychiatric patients?'

'You knew about Francis Vaughan?'

'Yes. I should have written – I'm sorry. Even I've heard about the serial killer, everyone talks about it – the kids love it. I don't read newspapers – except the local one. Or watch TV,' she said, 'but you can't get away from it.'

'Only we don't think it was the serial killer.' And I went over the story again. When I'd finished, she said: 'People certainly are talking about Cairo's work. There's a kind of disillusionment with drugs and behaviour modification creeping in. Psychotherapy is usually too expensive, but his method is seen as a sort of short cut.'

'Was his work really original, was it as important as Francis thought it was?'

'He had a theory about family interaction. In itself nothing special – although he placed more emphasis on relations between brothers and sisters than most. Had a very dim view of only children, by the way.' She smiled at me. 'You're all narcissists,' she said.

'Oh, thanks!'

'It was his therapeutic method that was new. He mixed up family therapy and co-counselling.'

'What's that?'

'Co-counselling? Well – say you and I are doing it. First of all one of us tells the other her problems etcetera – I'm telling you, for instance, and you listen, react and maybe interpret, maybe confront me with how I'm affecting you, how I make you feel. Then we switch roles and do it the other way round. It's supposed to be more egalitarian than the usual patient–therapist relationship. I've always thought it was a bit dodgy myself. And the way Cairo adapted it was rather controversial, because he used it within families. I mean, mix up that sort of confrontational approach with family relationships and it all becomes potentially explosive.'

'I thought therapy was supposed to be explosive. Frankly, I've always run a mile from it, myself.'

'You would. But where do I come into all this?'

'We need to find out more about what was going on at the hospital. Not just recently, but around the time Cairo died as well. We thought maybe you could help us. You are a social worker, after all. You must have contacts.'

She stared at the floor. Eventually she said: 'Are you sure Francis wasn't a serial killer victim? Or is that just what you want to believe?'

I swallowed. 'We can't be absolutely sure.'

'Is it sensible to go rooting around like this? It could be dangerous.'

'It just seems like we have to go on. And you wouldn't be in danger – just some discreet enquiries . . .'

She sat there, silent, thinking. After a bit she said: 'I tell you what I will do. I know someone who used to be a social worker up there. I'll ask him what he remembers.'

'You're an angel.'

'When I've seen him, I'll get in touch.'

'How long will that take?'

I thought she blushed slightly. Maybe this was a romance. 'Not long.'

I stood up to leave. Then I remembered. 'One of Cairo's ex-patients lives at the Tenison-Joliet place.'

'Oh? Who's that?'

'A woman – Mary Mahoney.'

'Really? Mad Mary?' Anna laughed. 'Poor thing. She's not much of an advertisement for any doctor.'

'I'll be in touch,' she said, as she saw me out. I traipsed back the way I'd come. The pavement was narrow and every time a vehicle passed it blew up the dust and flung grit in my eyes. The distance to the roundabout seemed to increase as I walked towards it. Even after fifteen minutes' walk it hadn't come into view. Still hardly anyone was about. The streets and the little houses seemed to shrink as the light faded. Then I realised I was walking in the wrong direction, and the roundabout – and the bus stop – were miles back. I crossed the road and retraced my steps, feeling tired and dispirited. When I reached the bus stop no one else was waiting, and it felt worse to be standing still than walking along. I waited. No bus appeared. I waited, losing all sense of time. I seemed to have been there for ever. I felt cold and conspicuous in the deserted street in my expensive grey flannel suit.

A group of three young white men loped along towards me. I looked the other way, but that didn't deflect the whistles. They seemed to slow down as they drew abreast, and the one nearest to me said: 'You look as sick as a seaside donkey.' He grinned and his eyes glittered with hostility.

Without thinking, I'd looked straight at him when he spoke. Now I quickly looked away again, humiliated, stupid. They walked on, but I was left seething with rage, and furious with myself for having let them see I was scared.

Still no bus. Then, as I began to wonder what I was going to do – no chance of a cruising taxi out here – a black Murasaki flashed past. It was slowing down. It stopped.

'Justine!' Miranda's head craned round from the passenger seat. 'Get in!' she called.

I ran along the road, jerked open the rear door and

settled in: 'Thank God you turned up. I thought the bus was never going to come.'

'What on *earth* are you doing round here?'

I told them all about Anna and how we needed her help.

'So you don't go for the serial killer idea?' said Dean. We were waiting at some traffic lights. Dean lifted one fat hand from the steering wheel and caressed Miranda's neck.

Did she edge away just fractionally? 'You do want to be careful, Justine,' she said. 'Those crazy people – they let far too many of them out these days. They're roaming all over Marshtown. Ugh.' She shuddered, then glanced at her husband. 'You know darling, we really ought to move.'

Dean said: 'We've often toyed with the idea of Latin America.'

'You know I didn't mean that. Just another part of town.'

'The workforce wouldn't move. We need to be near the source of labour, you know we've ruled that out,' he said, and they talked on about business matters until we drew up outside the Café.

I left Miranda there, and went home to change into the clinging, dull-red dress she'd given me. I loved it. It had been made from a number of secondhand garments taken to pieces, dyed and re-sewn up together, so that the clinging skirt was composed of godet sections in different shades of garnet, rust, dried blood. The bodice was tight, cut high at the front and low at the back, and each long, tight sleeve was fastened with six small buttons. Then, just as I was about to leave, I looked one last time in the room-high looking glass, and thought it was wrong, too on-her-high-horse hostess, too glamorous, not approachable enough. So I started again from scratch, and ended up in a striped silk grandad shirt and a waistcoat.

Miranda and Rusty were seated at my table, and that evening it was like we were greater friends than ever, Miranda and I. She *was* seductive – but it was Vic I'd had in mind when I changed out of the garnet dress. Yet I didn't want to lose Miranda either.

'You're not really going to Latin America, are you?'

'What? Oh . . . *that*.' She laughed. 'Dean's always talking that way. Doesn't mean a thing.' She drew her chair closer to mine. 'I want to hear all you've been doing. Tell me more about the – investigation. That was fascinating – what you were saying in the car.' She made it all sound like a joke, and although she listened, intent and sympathetic, when I paused, she said:

'Darling, don't get too hung up on it, it's all so gloomy, you're looking quite depressed. Let's think about something more cheerful.'

'How's Isobel?' I asked. 'Dean brought her in here the other day, you know.' Gennady, a recent first-time father himself, had sat the child on the bar and, dainty and solemn, tremendously pleased with herself, she'd been persuaded to sing a little song. When the guests seated nearest to her applauded, she'd burst into tears. She was sweet.

'He brought her here? Whatever for? He's mad.' She seemed agitated, appalled for a moment.

'Why not? What's the problem?'

'Oh, nothing, really. I don't know. I suppose I feel this is my territory. I don't see why he comes here at all. He doesn't enjoy it.' She added in a lower voice: 'Doesn't enjoy anything as far as I can see.' She shrugged. 'Oh well, don't let's talk about Dean. But . . . I wonder if you'd do me a big favour. I have to get something from a shop way out beyond China Road somewhere. In the next few days. D'you think you could possibly drive me there? I know it's a bore.' She smiled winningly.

How like a child – funny she couldn't drive and always had to depend on other people.

'What about Dean?'

'He's so busy at the factory these days. Anyway, it's kind of a surprise for him.'

'Sunday morning, maybe?'

'They won't be open on Sunday.'

'What about Tuesday afternoon? Gennady's here then.'

'Why can't you manage Monday when this place is shut?'

'We're interviewing for the new cook on Monday. Have to be Tuesday, I'm afraid. I'll collect you from the factory.'

'Don't do that. Let's meet in the Ascot Tea Rooms. Have something to eat before we go.'

'I'm never going there again. Got chucked out the last time I was there.'

Her eyes looked bluer than ever. 'Chucked out? What on earth do you mean?'

Well, that wasn't quite true, of course. I wasn't the one who'd been chucked out. Like I so often do, I was just trying to turn it into a funny story – but it wasn't funny and I wished I hadn't mentioned it.

'They asked us to leave. We were having tea with the woman who nursed Cairo's wife. It was disgusting, actually.'

'Because she was black, you mean?'

'Of course. Whites only. Strictly illegal, but – well . . . I don't expect they exactly took to Myra either. In fact, when you think about it, I was the only one who *wasn't* chucked out. We'll meet here, that's the simplest,' I said.

'It's sweet of you, angel.' She looked at me and her mood seemed to change, the smile faded and a sad look replaced it. She scraped her chair back and stood up clumsily. 'I have to go. You coming, Rusty?' It was more of a command than a question, but Rusty shook her head.

'I'll stay for a while.'

Miranda had gone. Rusty ran her hand through her hennaed locks: 'I've got a deadline, I ought to go too. I have to finish a piece for *Fascination*.' But she didn't leave. 'Miranda was in a weird mood, I think she's going through one of her funny phases.'

'Funny phases?'

'Every so often she gets some fixed idea, some obsession

about something or someone. When we were at college there was this girl . . . oh well, it was so long ago, and anyway Dean came along.' She was looking at me, half curious, half concerned. 'For a while I thought it was you, but you're not really interested, are you? You're another enigma, are you or aren't you, do you or don't you, what do you really want?' She laughed. 'Anyway, Miranda's all caught up with this snake woman now.'

'Snake woman?'

'You know, at the Zoo – snake trainer, minder, curator. I don't know. Rather creepy, anyway, and nothing really definite.'

'Christ!'

Rusty shrugged. 'It'll pass. It always does. Though if I were Dean . . . he'll put up with anything. *Anything*.' She looked over to the bar. 'At least I know what I want,' she added, half to herself.

What she wanted, it turned out later, was Gennady, and I believe they did have an affair. I don't know if Jacqui ever found out, but Chloe, with whom he was also on at the time, most certainly did, and . . . but that's another story.

I felt someone's hands on my shoulders. 'How's Justine tonight?'

It was Vic: 'You're coming to my private view I hope? You got your invitation?'

She sat down in the chair Miranda had vacated. Her thin face fascinated me. Her skin was pale eggshell brown, and speckled with some rather dark freckles. We drank champagne, she stuck around, it was all going to work. Even I sometimes had to get lucky.

Moonlight irradiated the room. It was like a wedding cake, a room made of plaster icing. Vic, like a marble ghost, got up and went looking for a glass of water. I lay on the white sheet and stared at the shadowed ceiling. It was so high I could hardly see the plaster coving or the sculptured rose from which a bulb was suspended on a flex.

I drank the water. Water was all you would ever drink in this room, and it was exciting to fuck in such a cavern of purity. Vic stood unsteadily beside me on the mattress. Her silver nipple-rings gleamed like two drops of water. She looked down at me and held out her hand. I passed the glass back. She was holding the bottle in her other hand and filled the glass again. A cold drop fell on my stomach.

I knelt in front of her and put my hands on her thighs. I stroked her thighs and moved my hands slowly round to her buttocks as I kissed her cunt. I'd almost forgotten the feel of that crinkly, mossy substance as my tongue stabbed in and felt it harsh against my lips. I'd forgotten how exciting it was.

Especially in this tomb-like room, in which we struggled and writhed as if giving birth to something, bringing it back to life.

I don't think I went to sleep, but for a while was suspended in a dream-like waking state in the gloom, the dusk of the room, caught in its web, but I must have slept in the end, for now the cruel light of day woke me. I could hear the seagulls mournfully shrieking in the great open sky above the ocean outside. The feathered hounds of heaven yelped as they wheeled round the rooftops and I drank water from the bottle to ease my parched mouth.

She'd gone; not even a note. I gathered my last night's finery from the floor. Few things are less dignified than walking into the street in what you wore the night before. Thank God at least it wasn't the red dress, but in the cruel morning light even the silk shirt and snakeskin trousers looked somehow tacky. I opened the door and listened. This was one of those squatted houses far along West End beach, stucco palaces built for Regency lords and now housing a colony of artists. Vic had told me the squatting laws were a dead letter and these days you just paid the cops to stay away, because no one wanted these great white elephants, damaged by last year's bomb and probably structurally unsafe.

I sidled into the passage and looked down the stone staircase with its iron balustrade. I should have liked to find a bathroom, a kitchen with something to eat, or at least a lavatory, but I dreaded meeting any of Vic's friends. I heard distant voices, and although I needed to piss, I scuttled down the stairs, out on to the Front and hailed a passing taxi.

Eighteen

I went straight back to the Café, deciding that, after all, my bedraggled finery and generally beat-up look was rather cool. We weren't due to open for another hour, and Chloe had already prepared all the components of the traditional – and I had to admit not very original – Lost Time breakfast: pastries, fruit and so on, so I had time to spare, and while I waited for Gennady to come on duty I read the morning papers.

There was a new burst of headlines about the latest murder. I'd almost forgotten about it. It was odd, and horrible, but the most recent victim, another poor old dosser, had aroused less outrage, certainly less than Francis had. It was almost as if we were all getting used to it. Gay men escorted one another home, there were notices which read 'Don't walk alone!' in all the bars, it was almost routinised.

Now, however, there was something new to write about: a psychologist who specialised in profiling serial killers. The police had flown him over from Florida to help them with their enquiries.

'Professor Dwayne Passaic's subtle reconstruction of the murderer's mind,' intoned the *Daily Post*, 'suggests that he hates his father. His victims have all been older men, and it may be that the attacker cannot forgive his father for making him homosexual. Each time his obsession draws him to one of the gay cruising haunts he feels compelled to seek out a victim who represents the father he must violate and kill. Professor Passaic emphasises, however, the irony that the killer "may not even be gay. The sexual component in the killings," the Professor told us in his hotel suite at the Central Hilton this morning, "is expressive of hatred not arousal as such. Revenge is the underlying motive. We are dealing with a very sick mind here." '

A suite at the Hilton and no doubt a fat fee seemed a high price for Professor Dwayne Passaic's less than dazzling insights. My glance travelled down the page, to another, smaller headline, CLAIRVOYANT SHOWS HER CARDS:

> In an apparent effort to assist in the solution of one of the murders, that of her friend, Francis Vaughan, Myra Zone, the well known Tarot reader, launched an appeal for help on last night's edition of her chart-topping slot, hinting at a cover-up. Ms Zone was embroiled in controversy several months ago as a result of her forceful accusations of government and police indifference when the serial killings were first being treated as such.

CRYSTAL BALLS was the comment on this by one of the tabloids, which nevertheless used the same report to recycle with excitable credulity an old story about a case Myra had 'solved'.

I wondered what Myra was up to, and felt annoyed she'd said nothing to me. I pushed the papers aside. I hated reading the stuff about Francis. Yet this morning even that couldn't entirely quench my benevolent mood. The memory of Vic lingered, and as I waited in this agreeable state of suspended animation my memories were already melting into anticipation.

Gennady was late. He'd recently shaved his head, but now the stubble was growing back in an unattractive sort of way. He brought his cup of coffee to my table. He sat down opposite me, grinning: 'You had good time last night, I think, Justine.' And he winked.

'Was OK,' I said repressively. I supposed my fling with Vic would be all round the Café now if I wasn't careful.

'Nice girl.'

'Thanks.' He was spoiling my romantic memories.

'What are you talking about?' It was Myra. Usually red faced, she looked pale this morning.

'*Nothing*. Are you OK?'

She sat down. 'There's been another big row at work. Tenison-Joliet's made a complaint about *Tarot Zone*. Says it's the work of Satan, satanic necromancy he called it. Do you believe that? He actually wants to get my TV programme banned. Next thing, he'll be trying to have me burned as a witch.'

I started to laugh, but then I saw she was really upset and angry.

'I bring you some tea.'

I said: 'Why did you say that about a cover-up? What did you mean?' I was hoping for some news of a breakthrough, but all she said was: 'Oh, I don't know. Thought it might flush someone out, I suppose. The thing is, I'm fed up with the bloody programme anyway.'

'I know. You said.'

'People's problems, their terrible lives, abuse, tragedy, crime. Then yesterday some guy rang the channel to confess to the serial killings. He wasn't the first, either. Sometimes I feel like setting up as a rival to Tenison-Joliet. Everyone wants absolution for their sins, they want to be saved.'

'That's probably what he resents.'

'But now I'll have to go on, I can't let myself be banned by a fundamentalist. Too naff.' Myra lifted the tea bag from the cup Gennady had placed in front of her, and plopped it messily on the table. 'Then he said he'd withdraw his complaint in return for free air time. What a cheek, he wants his own fucking programme.'

'I thought he already had a programme.'

'That's only on the radio. I actually think they might do it, you know. Give him a slot, I mean.'

'Anna said he's a real pain down in Marshtown.'

'You saw her, then. Any luck?'

'You weren't here last night, I'd have told you, and I was going to phone but something came up.' I rushed on, not wanting to talk about Vic just yet. 'She said she'd contact some friend who used to work up at the hospital.'

'But we need someone *now*.'

'OK, well she's going to get back to us as soon as she can.'

Gennady was opening the Café. Myra stared moodily at the floor. She'd spoilt my mood. My erotic dreams of Vic were fading fast.

'I did my best,' I said. 'What's the matter? You look terrible.'

'*Don't ever say that to a hypochondriac*. I'm fine, just fine. But what are we going to do next? When can we talk to Anna's friend?'

'I told you, she said she'd be in touch.'

'Don't wait, ring her,' Myra snapped. 'And when are you seeing Lennox? You must talk to him.'

Chloe arrived and slotted in her favourite tape of golden oldies, the one I hated. Madonna's 'Like a Virgin' breathed its jaded lyrics across the room. I must have heard it so often in public places without consciously listening to it that its moody chords seemed the very essence of nostalgia – but nostalgia without a memory, a longing for something that had never been. It was just a vague mood, an image slipping by you couldn't grasp, feelings turning to dust, nothing to hold on to – just like our conversation, with the wraith of Francis lost in half hints and fragments and nothing adding up or making sense at all.

All that day I felt strange. Myra's mood was contagious. I sat in the Café, hoping Vic would call. I wondered if she'd come into the Café, if I'd ever see her again, and the thought of going up to see Lennox in prison was depressing too.

Vic didn't show, but late in the evening Miranda turned up. She was in such high spirits it grated on my nerves. She talked about everything under the sun, but I felt sure there was something else. At last it came. As she swept the froth off her third cappuccino and almost sucked the spoon into her mouth, she leant forward.

'Shelley's given me a present.'

'Shelley?'

'You *know*. At the Zoo. How could you have forgotten? I've been back – several times – you know I have.'

'Yes.' She'd begged me to go with her, but I'd refused. The compulsion mingled with horror was not something to indulge, I'd decided. Better not to think about it – my policy with so many aspects of my life. In this case, though, I was sure I was right. The whole thing was a bit too weird, and certainly too risky.

'I'm not afraid of snakes any more. She's so gentle with them, so sweet. She's taught me how to handle them.'

In my wildest nightmares I could not imagine being sweet with a snake. 'You mean you . . . touch them and all that?' I recalled Miranda's horror that afternoon. I simply couldn't imagine her toying with a snake, letting it wrap itself round her neck, and push its head at her lips the way strippers do.

'She's given me a black mamba.'

'A black mamba!' I nearly fell off my chair. 'Are you serious? What about Isobel?'

'Isobel?' A puzzled frown grazed her brows. 'Oh – but it's quite safe, Shelley's drawn its fangs. It isn't poisonous now.'

'All the same . . .' I shuddered, but I felt the usual creepy feeling of can't-leave-it-alone, that awful porno feeling, like it's bad but you want to have a peep – I felt all that stealing through me.

'I suppose she shouldn't have let me have it but – they have far too many at the Zoo. They're not exactly rare any more.'

'Well, don't start playing with it when I'm around.'

'I'll keep it in a special tank.' She laughed. She was excited, flushed, her eyes bluer than ever. 'It'll keep the burglars away.'

But the whole thing bothered me. If you wanted a snake as a pet you got a python or a grass snake or some other non-poisonous variety. This was really taking things too far.

Francis had told me once about the way they treated phobics at the hospital, a technique called 'flooding'. The patient was put in a room filled with the object of dread, in this case, snakes, they'd have snakes all around them, crawling on them. It sounded terrible, cruel, but Francis had told me that the panic would reach a crescendo and then it would tip over, the patient would cut out and wouldn't be afraid any more. If you were forced into a snakepit it would stop you being frightened of snakes. I imagined Shelley pushing Miranda into a cage that was full of sliding, slithering, writhing snakes, snakes coiled round her arms and neck and waist, their dead eyes, their rippling bodies . . .

I said: 'I thought black mambas were what you sent the head of a rival gang as a friendly warning.'

Miranda was slightly mad when you came down to it. She had these fixed ideas, she was so determined. She hadn't rested until she'd got me to agree to have a fashion show in the Café; entirely against my better judgement, and despite Gennady's furious outburst.

Now she laughed, and said: 'Darling, you are silly. It's so exciting. I see now how beautiful snakes are. Dean doesn't like it, of course.'

'Oh, it's just a Dean-tease is it. So what's with you and Dean anyway?'

She looked at me flirtatiously. 'Oh, darling, you know how it is with old married couples . . .'

That was one thing I precisely didn't know. My marriage had been of quite another kind.

'Don't let's talk about Dean,' she said. 'I must tell you about Shelley and the snake house. The things she does with them, you wouldn't believe. You must come with me again, you really must.'

No, no, I musn't.

'No one else understands, but I know you do.'

If I hadn't understood, I'd have maybe done something about it. I've often wondered about that; whether, had I not been slightly tinged myself with that snake obsession, I'd have been able to stop her. But we were interrupted. Chloe called me to the telephone.

The voice was familiar, but I couldn't quite place it. 'Mrs Hillyard? It's Rosemary Jones. I'd like to meet with you and the other lady again. We never finished our conversation in the Galleria, did we? I was expecting you to call. We must arrange another meeting.'

Back at the table, Miranda asked with her usual upfront nosiness: 'Who was that?'

'Monica Cairo's nurse.'

'Oh – the Ascot Tea Rooms woman.'

Something was wrong. Something was bothering me. But I couldn't work out what it was – although I was thinking about it all the way to the garage to fetch the Lagonda.

Nineteen

We rendezvoused in the Botanical Gardens Palm House. Our footsteps clanked on the wrought-iron walkways like we were in a cathedral. The steamy heat seeped into my nostrils and lungs and at every step I felt as if the writhing creepers and tropical trees were about to move in on me, suffocating, and wreathe and twine themselves around me.

To say that we were overdressed was an understatement. Rosemary Jones was wearing the same red hat as before, and was wrapped in a black coat. I had on my new herringbone tweed trench and a Dashiell Hammett trilby. Myra wore a heavy grey cloak lined with paisley.

The place was empty. We found a secluded bench.

Myra sat between Rosemary Jones and me, so that I had to crane forward to hear the nurse's muttered words. 'Someone rang – they threatened me. It was a man – soft sort of voice. Told me to stay out of it.'

Myra said: 'Have you been to the police?'

Rosemary Jones shook her head. 'My husband says they won't do much, there's nothing to go on. Someone must have followed me. Someone knows I met with you. I'm telling you, I'm scared. If I had the money I could get away for a while, I've a cousin up North, I could stay with.'

'You need some money?' I said.

'I don't really understand this,' said Myra. 'Why should anyone follow you? Even if they did . . .' But she didn't finish, looked away, smoothed her hand up and down her knee. Then she went on: 'You see, you had so little to tell us, it's rather hard to see why anyone should be frightened of you.'

'You remember when we met before, I had more to tell you, but there wasn't time.'

So she'd been holding out on us all along. I feebly fanned myself with my hat: 'Well you'd better tell us now,' I said.

'There were some photographs. Look, after my husband left the police, things were difficult. I thought it might not be a bad idea to see what Dr. Cairo was up to. I was more and more convinced it was like I said. I persuaded my husband to follow him. Well, there wasn't much to go on. I began to think I was wrong. It was mostly just one-off visits. Sometimes, you know, he saw patients at home – to see if they needed to go into hospital. Domiciliaries. But there was one address he went back to, a flat in a small block built between two older houses, it wasn't difficult to watch and see who came out. My husband took some photographs.'

'And what was the purpose of that?' Myra sounded grim.

'I was angry for Monica – believe me, I was. It wasn't for money. We were going to confront him.'

'Let's just get this straight,' said Myra: 'You mean you had a photograph of him with someone?'

'No. Just of the people living in the flats – anyone who went in and out on a regular basis.'

'That wouldn't prove anything,' I said. 'If they weren't with him it means nothing.'

Her face, usually pleasant and bland, was suddenly distorted with anger. 'I told him what I thought of him. It was disgusting.'

'And you made some money out of it.'

'If you'd have seen Monica, you'd have understood.'

'I think we do understand,' said Myra smoothly.

'You don't, you don't at all. It wasn't long before Monica died. When she did die, I had to look for another job, didn't I, and my husband was unemployed. We needed the money.'

'Well, can we see them then?' I snapped. I was fed up with her.

'I haven't brought them with me . . .' and she cast us a sly, yet nervous sideways glance.

This was too much. I stood up, feeling a wave of heat and sweat with every movement. 'You're wasting our time. I'm going.'

Myra put out a hand to hold me back. 'Why don't we drive you home, Rosemary, and you can get them while we wait. We don't mind paying, but we have to have them upfront.'

She stood up. 'No . . . no. I'd rather you didn't do that. Look, can you come round sometime next week? I'm going away for a few days, but I'll be back by – Tuesday.'

She was leaving. I put out a hand to stop her, but she was edging towards the exit. 'I have to be going now. I'm sorry.'

We stood up too, but she slipped away from us down the humid pathways and disappeared among the palms.

All the way back to the Café, Myra spat fire: 'She held out on us! Why did she do that! We should have gone back with her now, we should have insisted.'

'I think she's a waste of time.' Yet now I began to feel sorry for the woman. There was something genuine somewhere – mixed up with the need for money was something sad, shamed, some good impulse thwarted or distorted, some genuine passion. She really had cared about Monica Cairo.

'What use will the photographs be? Even if her bloke snapped Cairo with someone – how would we trace that person? And she said he didn't, so we can't possibly have any way of knowing which of the women he photographed is *the* woman – if indeed there really was a mistress at all.'

Myra hadn't thought of that, I could tell. To hide it, she assumed a lofty expression, and changed the subject.

In the Café a stranger was leaning across the bar in conversation with Gennady.

'This is Ivan.' Whenever Gennady introduced one of his mates as Ivan, you knew that wasn't his real name, that he was part of the floating population of Rotties (rotten to the core, as they'd been described by the Prime Minister), made up of dodgy immigrants, unemployables, petty crims and lunatics who lived in that hidden underworld which lay just below the familiar, everyday city surface.

Ivan wore a black leather bomber jacket so old that it was colourless at the seams and on the shoulders. He had sought to disguise his Slavic features by growing his hair – sparse on top – long and it hung round his face in tobacco-stained locks. His drooping moustache was also stained yellow, as were the fingers of his left hand. He was rolling a cigarette.

Gennady said: 'Mind if we go upstairs.' It wasn't a question. 'Ivan and I we just do a bit of business, OK?'

Myra did mind. She glanced at her watch. I knew she was expecting a client soon; she didn't want the Russians on her balcony, especially exhaling bad-karma nicotine smoke.

I sat with them. They sat at the table Myra used for reading the cards, and conversed in Russian. Ivan made gestures with his large, long-fingered hands. When he smiled you could actually see where decay had corroded his yellow teeth.

I sat there a while. I resented Gennady scheming with his cronies in Café time – but it was so obviously pointless for me to sit there fuming and listening to a language I didn't understand that I gave in, went downstairs and got them the thick black double-strength ristrettos – the coffees Gennady and his Russian friends knocked back like it was vodka.

When Ivan left he passed me a small card. 'Any time you getting rid of any machines, Gaggia, you name it, give me a call.' He winked and gave me an informal salute before striding nonchalantly for the door. Lennox would have loved him.

'What did he say?' I asked Gennady.

'Oh – is nothing much. Trying to make money. Hustling. Usual things. Was in Bentham until just now. Says everything's very bad at the prison. He says soon there's big breakout.'

'Oh Christ!'

I didn't need that on top of everything else. What I needed was to think. I cast a quick glance round the Café. The voices, the music, the hiss of the coffee machine – it was all proceeding smoothly on its own. Myra was upstairs with her client now.

I stepped outside and walked down on to the beach. The shingle stretched emptily away from me. The sea stretched flat and calm towards the horizon.

Everything in my life was confused and muddled: Lennox, Vic, Miranda – all overshadowed by the death of Francis and the mystery of Aaron Cairo. How could I have a focused, orderly life when all these ambiguous figures – Rosemary Jones, Otto Wegner, Leadbetter – insisted on intruding? All with their stories to tell, perhaps none of them true. Had Cairo really had a love affair? Did Leadbetter know more than he'd admitted? What was Gennady up to with his Russian friend? All these stories, sinister, plausible, implausible, baffling, wove in and out of my life, interfered with my desires until I no longer knew what I needed or wanted. Where did any of it fit in, if at all? It probably didn't. Nicotine Ivan was just a con, Otto Wegner was a clapped-out conspirator, Rosemary Jones was on to a good thing – leading us up the garden path for a few hundred Es.

I gazed out to sea for a long time, watching the soothing, dull grey horizon, the line between bluer and greyer grey. It didn't help. Eventually I turned back, hobbling painfully in my heels over the stones. The gulls called as they wheeled round far above me, the sound hanging there in the sky. I climbed the steps to the jetty.

A youngish man was lounging against the wall alongside the Café. He looked at me quite hard, then turned away: jeans, a jean jacket, lanky brown hair, three or four-day stubble, bright blue eyes. I didn't think anything of it. People often hung around on the jetty. I was just relieved he didn't tell me I looked as sick as a seaside donkey.

I suddenly couldn't cope with the Café, couldn't be my

bright, hostessy self. An impulse that didn't bear close examination was pushing me in another direction, towards Born Again Books. I couldn't delay my visit to the prison much longer, yet – unrealistic though this was – I somehow hoped Otto might have some news of Lennox, something that would mean I didn't have to visit. Otto did know about the voice on the tape, after all, I'd told him myself, and I managed to persuade myself that he might have found out more about it.

I drove through the old town and up the hill towards the university, circling the big square with the palms and banana trees and thick creepers like boa constrictors, and finally reached the top of the cliff. I parked there, and walked down the stone stairs to the little square and Otto's shop.

Something about the shop looked different. The books that had filled the window were gone. I reached it and peered in. Everything had gone. There was only an empty room with nothing in it but some bits of paper and cardboard on the floor, and a disconnected telephone.

I stood there. Pure anxiety – unformed, too primitive to transform itself into thoughts – flooded me. Confusedly I groped towards a language for my terror, to bring it down, to look it in the face. I turned slowly away and walked across the little square. I walked all the way back to the car in a dulled, blank state. It was sheer formless apprehension, a kind of panic just, only just, held at bay.

Otto had been arrested or gone underground. Maybe Lennox was in trouble too. I was afraid of something unknown about to happen. Things had staggered on, stagnant and unchanging, for so long, but the future had always been waiting in the wings. Now it would unleash itself upon us, events would roll over and over us, bearing us away, scattering us all like the gulls hurled shrieking out to sea.

I made for the nearest distraction I could think of. The front door of Vic's squat was open. I pushed it and stepped inside. She had hidden herself away at the back of the house, and

I found her working in the empty ground-floor room she called her studio. I liked the smell as she cleaned her hands with some kind of spirit. It lingered on her, sharp, benzoid, erotic. Upstairs, the room was freezing. She wound her arms round me. I was shuddering, goose-pimpled.

'I'm so cold!'

'You'll soon be hot.'

It worked. I forgot the fear. And after a while it seemed as if a great bird had spread its wings, covering me. I forgot the tidal wave of the future, rolling over me, filling my mouth with choking, salty water; the salt on my mouth was only from her.

I felt safe. I could talk to her about Francis, about Lennox, even about my fantasy baby.

She laughed. 'Oh, shit, there's always *something*.'

'What d'you mean?'

'It's never just plain dykes, is it, it always has to be dykes with something, you know, there's always a fashion. Like there was a time when everyone had dogs, and then it was fetish gear, and then there was a vogue for boyfriends. Babies too. But I don't think I want to share you with a baby.'

Ah! She liked me. Possessive, even. Or was she just flirting?

'It doesn't look likely now, if it ever did. I don't want to talk about it.'

'You just did. Talk about it.'

Yes – in that soft, deep moment when she spread her wings and I felt safe. Perhaps I should have kept quiet.

It was dark and drowning in the room. The twilight came. We lay there for ever. But when she switched on the bleak electric bulb the illusion was shattered and the last of the softness drained away, and I knew that in the morning I had to go to the prison.

The first thing Lennox said to me was: 'Alasdair Roxburgh's been transferred in here, y'know.'

Since Roxburgh had arrived things were hotting up.

Roxburgh – Lennox muttered all this at me through almost closed lips – Roxburgh was getting them organised. The men were angry. The screws were scared. The whole thing was going to blow.

'For God's sake, Lennox, don't get involved. You'll be out in a few months. Just take it easy.'

'I know you don't like it, Justine, but he's the one we've been waiting for. And then,' he added, descending into bathos, 'it's so fucking boring in here.'

'You'll be out soon.' I repeated myself rather desperately. I didn't want my potential sperm bank to go on the run. 'And how can you join up with him? He's organising the Scots.'

'My mother came from Glasgow,' he said defiantly.

'First I heard of it.'

'Anyway, it's broader than that now. But *don't worry*, I won't do anything crazy. But I do have to think about what I am going to do. When I get out, I mean.'

'Yes, of course.' And in a way I couldn't help admiring him. He didn't give up or sink into cynicism.

'So what are you going to do?' I felt I'd been selfish, hadn't thought about him, only about myself in relation to him. All the same, I was determined to talk about the baby before the end of the visit, and worked round to it eventually.

We'd discussed it before, and then he'd seemed willing, but today he wasn't encouraging. It would be really difficult to smuggle out any sperm: 'It's not that the screws wouldn't do it,' he said, 'but they'd probably spit in it, or give you some of theirs instead. And take the money anyway.'

The idea that one of the screws instead of Lennox might father my child was so frightful that I began to feel hopeless. The one thing neither of us ever considered was waiting until he got paroled, as if we knew, though it was never mentioned, that then he wouldn't stick around.

I was so preoccupied, so discouraged, that I forgot about the voice on the tape. The visit was almost over when Lennox gripped my hand: 'I nearly forgot to tell you. Oh shit, I'm sorry. Listen, there's something you have to know, I feel bad about this, I knew about it the last time you came, I should have told you then.' He leant forward and spoke even more quietly. 'Guy in here, paroled a couple of months ago. Just before he went out he heard something on the radio. There was something about that psychiatrist you told me about, the one your friend Francis was looking into before he was offed.'

'I didn't know there'd been a radio programme.'

'It was some concert repeat. There'd been some concert in his honour, yeah? And this mate of mine – well, he's not a mate, really – you see there was quite a lot of drink around, before Christmas, you know, the screws don't give a fuck, the place was awash, anyway, he got drunk and started to say things – like he knew all about it.'

Why the fuck hadn't Lennox told me this sooner? I wanted to scream. Just around the time Francis was murdered. If Lennox had told me sooner, maybe it wouldn't have been too late, maybe Francis wouldn't have died . . .

'He said he supplied the gun.'

'End the visit now please,' came the bellow from the fat screw, a different fat screw this time.

'*Lennox!* You should have written. You could have phoned.'

'They look at the letters, not supposed to, but they do. And they ran out of phone cards. There was nothing I could do. And then I forgot. I'm sorry. But at the time, I told him you might be interested. Hope that was OK. Thought he might have been in touch with you, but I suppose he was too drunk, he probably didn't remember.'

'Oh Lennox – I think he did get in touch with Francis. There was this message on his answering machine. He mentioned your name.'

'Sounds like him.'

I was so shaken I didn't know what to say. Chairs scraped back as visitors got up to go. I was in tears as I put my arms around him for the ritual hug.

'Take it easy. It's OK. I'll be out soon.' He thought I was upset about him. But it wasn't that, it wasn't that at all.

'End the visit *please*.'

Outside we, the visitors, wandered round the shed-like buildings in a disconsolate troupe. As we approached the high wire gates a line of four kilted men followed by two screws marched out from a path to the left and towards us. The first of the four Scots had a black beard and broad shoulders, a swarthy face like Charles II, thick hair, keen eyes. He glanced at our ragged procession scornfully: Alasdair Roxburgh, I presumed.

Twenty

On Tuesday morning we looked for Rosemary Jones's house in the suburb that trickled out from the China Road in the direction of Harvey St Anselm. The district had been shabby and decayed for years, but these days it was beginning – slowly – to 'come up' as 1930s semis became fashionable. I could understand that. I liked the ocean liner look, the way the steel-framed windows curved round the corners, the porthole windows, the sunray fanlights which matched the low garden gates. There were flowers in the gardens, cars all along the kerb, and some of the houses had recently been painted.

The Jones's house was not one of these, but someone was looking after the garden. We rang the bell.

I felt at once that the tall man who opened the door would have been a good policeman, good at talking to people, good at helping old ladies cross the road, too good a policeman in the wrong way, maybe, too genuine a Christian. Because undoubtedly they were Christians. In the hall a three-dimensional reproduction of Dali's Christ on the Cross lunged aggressively out at us.

'You must be the ladies Rosemary talked to.'

'Is she in?' Myra stepped forward.

'She asked me to tell you she's gone away for a while. But come in anyway.'

He ushered us into a sitting room crowded with furniture. 'A cup of tea perhaps?'

'No thank you.' Myra smoothed the offer away with a grand gesture. 'We won't trouble you for long.'

We sat down on the art deco three-piece suite. I faced a glass-fronted cabinet filled with reproduction William Morris coffee cups, which I recognised as a colour supplement special offer. There were also some mass-produced bookshelves, an upright piano, and da Vinci's *Last Supper* and *Holy Family* on the walls.

'This is rather difficult for me,' he said. He sat there, legs apart, hands clasped between them, looking at the floor. 'Rosemary didn't start this up again, you know. We'd put it all behind us, years ago. Then, last autumn, the psychiatrist got in touch with her.'

'I thought it was the other way round,' I said.

Mr Jones looked up. 'No. He'd got her name and the telephone number from the family – the Cairos, you know. He wanted to know what she knew about Dr Cairo.' He stopped again, gazing at the floor. We waited, and after a short pause he continued: 'This is all quite painful – to have it all dragged up again. You see, I shouldn't have taken those photographs. Only Rosemary got so . . . upset. I'd just left the force, we'd been a bit greedy, run up debts, and there were expenses, we wanted to send our sons to a decent school, things like that cost money. I was desperate at the time, out of a job. I'd done nothing wrong, but I was dismissed from the force. Left under a cloud. No big redundancy deal, nothing. Rosemary persuaded me. Said the doctor was up to something. I succumbed to temptation.' He paused again. 'He used to visit some strange parts of town.'

Myra said: 'Rosemary told us about the photos.'

'Sure. She said you'd want those.' He got up and fished out an envelope from behind a book. 'Just negatives. That's all there is. They're old, of course. But I expect they'll print up again. I thought she'd got rid of them. I told her to. If I'd known she was hanging on to them . . . You see we did make a bit of money out of it, I'm afraid.' He handed Myra the envelope.

Myra opened it, but only glanced at the strips of negative.

He went on: 'It's all – more complicated than you think. Rosemary told you he was having an affair, right? Well – ' He swallowed. 'If you must know, it was Rosemary. She got involved with him. I knew nothing about it. Not to begin with. But after a while she was acting strange, got very upset. He broke off with her, you see, and she was convinced it had to do with something going on at the hospital.'

'*She* was the woman? She told us about *herself*?' Myra sounded incredulous, as well she might. 'And she never said anything about things going on at the hospital.'

That wasn't quite true, there was what she'd told us about Leadbetter coming round to see Cairo on his birthday, but I let that pass.

'You have to understand. My wife has a vivid imagination. And over the years she's convinced herself it didn't happen that way. That's how she sees herself now – Monica's friend, Mrs Cairo's devoted companion. She's bitter about Cairo. So far as she was concerned we had every right to the money.'

I stared at the William Morris coffee cups. There was a vivid blue and yellow one, a pastel pink and green, an orange and brown . . .

'She can't admit it was wrong. I'm training for the Ministry now, I've had spiritual help, and I've prayed for her of course, but she's too proud.' He sighed. 'I don't feel guilty about the money as such. It wasn't even all that much, £5,000. It was still sterling then, of course, not ECUS. What's £5,000 to the Cairos? I wouldn't pay it back to them. I give a sum to the Church each month instead. I'm about halfway there.'

The inside of the Lagonda was like a perfect padded cell to protect you from all the pollution swirling around on the expressway. Awash with Wagner and my own scent, Amazone, we floated along above the city. We touched ninety miles an hour.

Myra said grimly: 'I guess you were right. She's just a

complete red herring. Still – we'd better get the negs developed, I suppose.' She pressed her seat back viciously into a reclining position and lay there with her eyes closed. 'Oh God, what does it all mean . . . I must read the cards again. And then there's Lennox's friend with the gun.'

At first, she'd dismissed that story out of hand. They tell lies all the time, these guys, she'd said, they boast, they brag, they can't even tell what's true from what isn't. And Lennox was always naïve, romanticised the crim. scene, he'd believe anything he heard from a con, he thinks they're all so marvellous. That's what she'd said. How do you know so much about the criminal personality? I'd asked. I just do, she'd said. In the end I'd persuaded her to take it a bit more seriously, but we didn't know what to do about it. We had no way of getting in touch with the mysterious parolee.

We dropped the negs off at a chemist and cruised back to the Café. We talked some more, and then Myra left for Channel Nine.

'What about the photographs?'

'Can you collect them?' She handed me the voucher. I put it in my bag.

In the Café it was lunchtime as usual. There was laughter. There was music. The guests drank, gossiped, waited to be amused, passed the time, frittered their lives away.

Miranda turned up, wearing black again. She always looked her best in black. This time it was a robe like a cassock with hundreds of buttons down to the floor. But she had left it unbuttoned so that you glimpsed the flesh of her leg. She swept her Spanish hat from her blonde hair and sank on to the chair opposite me.

'Sorry I'm so late, darling. Are you ready?'

Oh Christ. I remembered. I was supposed to be driving her somewhere. I'd messed up. I'd forgotten. And I didn't want to go. I just didn't want to chauffeur her around town this afternoon. I wanted to get back to the chemist's shop and collect the photos. He'd said they'd be done in an hour.

Even if it was a long shot, they might provide some clue, and I was curious to see them.

'You haven't forgotten our date?' Miranda's smile was sweet and caressing, but I couldn't conceal my annoyance.

I gritted my teeth. 'It's slightly difficult . . .'

'Oh please! Don't let me down.' She looked distraught.

'No, no, it's OK. Of course. Can you just hang on for – say, twenty minutes.' I was toying with the idea of rushing back to the shop. Or maybe we could stop on the way.

She smiled. 'Fine. Oh, while I remember, we wanted to invite you round again – you will come, won't you? It's been ages. Just the four of us this time – next week, maybe?'

The four of us? Which four – was I supposed to bring Myra, or was Vic on the hit list now?

Vic showed up and it plainly wasn't her Miranda had in mind. It dawned on me she didn't like Vic. She barely said hello, just a curt nod, when Vic planted herself at my table. It's true she looked like a tramp, in a greasy old raincoat and paint-stained jeans and T-shirt.

Miranda stood up. 'Justine – I think we should go.'

Vic raised her eyebrows. 'Have I interrupted something?' she drawled. I felt embarrassed. Why had she said *that*? Then I had a brainwave.

'Vic, you wouldn't do me a huge favour – collect some photos for me – its quite important. This nurse who looked after Aaron Cairo's wife – she had some photos taken. Look, the ticket's in my bag, take it out, I have to make a phone call.'

'Sure. Just have a quick one first.' She got up and mooched languidly over to the bar.

I called Anna's office, but there was no reply. When I got back to my table Miranda was clearly fidgety. 'Are you going to be much longer?'

I gave in. 'No – let's go.'

Miranda curled up on the passenger seat as we coasted along the expressway.

'You should have brought Isobel,' I said.

'Are you mad? She's with the nanny.'

'D'you mind seeing so little of her?'

She laughed. 'I can't believe you really want a child.'

'I know you think it's a terrible idea. And I don't know quite how I'm going to do it, I don't think Lennox is going to come through.'

She didn't take me up on that, just looked out of the window, and didn't say any more until she took out the street map and directed me off the expressway. We slipped down into a decayed section of the city, its dead heart, wedged between Avenue West and the smart central sections. It was a vacuum where a nerve centre should have been, once stuffed with factories, workshops, working-class streets, now alien, abandoned, nothing there but a new university, half built, boarded-up buildings, the odd junk shop, a tattooing parlour, some offbeat entertainment joints.

'Turn left. That's right. Now slow down, it's along here somewhere. Here – no – yes, that one, Number 16.' She was fumbling with the door before I'd stopped. 'Don't bother to come in, I'll be OK. Just wait for me outside.'

'I'll have to find somewhere to park. I'll wait in the car.'

She stomped towards a shop which looked abandoned. A faded raspberry curtain was drawn across the window, and its dull green glass-panelled door was firmly shut. She rang the bell. I watched until someone I couldn't see opened it and she disappeared inside.

She soon returned, carrying a box of the kind shoe shops sell long boots in. It was elaborately tied round with string. 'Let's get out of here.'

'What's that?'

'Oh nothing – just something for Dean. Something he wanted. Some boots. That's a wonderful shoemaker. You should go there some time.'

'Oh – why didn't you tell me? Can't we go back in now?'

Her hand was on my arm. 'I have to get back. Actually – can you possibly take me home? I'm not going back to the factory.'

184

'Of course,' I said, although it was inconvenient, and she sat beside me and made business calls while I steered through the softly grey streets, taking an idiosyncratic route north of Avenue West and over to Marshtown.

'I won't ask you into the house if you don't mind. I'm just nipping in and out again.'

'I could wait and take you where you're going.'

'Oh no, please – don't bother – sweet of you, but I'd rather you didn't.' She kissed my cheek and trotted up the path, holding the box containing the boots in front of her.

I drove back to the Café. No Myra. Worse – no Vic. I'd hoped she'd have the photos by now.

'Where's Vic?' I asked Chloe. But Chloe just shrugged. 'She left soon after you, boss. Said she had to get back to work. Someone else waiting for you in the back though.'

I peered round. Anna was there, seated at the back of the back room. I sank down beside her.

'Well, I've got hold of my social worker friend.' She sat back and looked at me.

'Great – so tell me.'

'I couldn't have a sandwich, could I? I'm starving.'

'Sure.' I gritted my teeth, swallowed my impatience. Everything was frustrating me today. 'Anything in particular?'

'Whatever you've got.'

Of course we had everything, but I wasn't going to prolong the conversation. I went and made it myself: ciabatta and goat's cheese; tomato and black olive salad. 'So?' I placed the plate in front of her and sat down.

Anna delicately picked up one of the sandwich slabs. The trouble with ciabatta is that the flour with which it is dusted gets on your clothes and your face. And it doesn't make for a dignified mouthful when bits of cheese and salad squirt out from the sides.

She smiled. 'If you can come to the centre tomorrow lunchtime, William, my friend, will be there.'

'You came all the way over here to tell me that?'

'You don't mind, do you? I thought I'd like to see the

place again. And – I hope it was OK – I pumped Tenison-Joliet a bit about Mad Mary. I don't suppose there's anything in it, but it seems she does go roaming round at night. T-J said they tried to stop her at first, but that caused more trouble, she got very agitated. So now they let her. Really, the Mission is just a base for her. She comes and goes. I mean, I suppose theoretically *she* could have murdered your friend, she might not have been at the Mission the night he died, but probably no one remembers and they don't sign her in and out. Still, that's really unlikely, isn't it? She's so tiny. She couldn't possibly have moved Francis once he was dead.'

'Oh, that's out of the question, it was a man Scrawny Sean saw.'

'And she'd never get as far as the cemetery, she just wanders around in Marshtown, people know her, they leave her alone. T-J seemed to think she was pretty harmless. Though he said she does get into rages now and again.'

I didn't say anything. I was beginning to feel very tired, and I didn't know what to think about anything.

'Don't look so worried. I have a feeling William may be able to help.'

'That's great. You are marvellous. Thank you so much.'

But inwardly I almost groaned. More time out from the Café, more exhausting journeys; and it probably wasn't worth while. Maybe Myra could go.

The worst frustration was Vic. Chloe had told me she'd gone back to work – that probably meant she hadn't collected the photos.

Then I remembered it didn't matter. They always took a name and phone number and if you could give them that, you could have your prints. Having worked that out, I couldn't wait to get back to the chemist's.

I left the Café with Anna. She gave me a wave as she wobbled away on her bike across the rough stone paving of the jetty. I decided to walk to the chemist's – it wasn't far.

I could have saved myself the effort. The Asian guy behind

the counter looked at me: 'Oh, but they've already been collected.' He showed me the register he kept and the tick beside my name. 'A lady came earlier.'

I cursed. I should have rung Vic first. Another wasted journey. I tore back through crowded streets, past the swimming complex and into the Café.

Chloe flicked her golden curls off her face. 'Myra's upstairs. Wanted to know where you were.'

I was glad. I ran up the curving staircase.

Myra stared. 'You've got the photos?'

'Well actually – no.' I explained about Vic. 'She must have collected them,' I said, 'but when I phoned she was out. Shall I try again?' But the thought of the amount of effort involved appalled me. On my way back from my abortive trip to the chemist's I'd been filled with an insane kind of energy, born of frustration, had surged through the crowds, shoving people aside, crazy to get back to the Café in the hope that Vic would have showed. Now I suddenly slumped. I felt absolutely exhausted, totally drained.

'Never mind,' said Myra. 'I've been reading Cairo's notebook. Should have done that before. I think I'm really beginning to know what happened. It's all beginning to come clear.'

I waited: 'Well – aren't you going to tell me?'

Chloe came galloping upstairs, a newspaper in her hand: 'Thought you'd want to see this.'

The headline was huge: CEMETERY MURDERS: MAN CHARGED. I was shaking as I read the front page:

A man who has been helping the police with their enquiries since yesterday afternoon has been charged with the murder of Albert Arthur Wicksteed. James George Morton, of 3 Cataline Avenue, will appear in court . . .

The worst thing about it, the thing that hollowed out my inside, was that Francis was still included in the list of murders.

Some nifty journalist had already visited number 3 Cataline Avenue, and on an inside page I found his interview with the couple who had rented a room to the accused man:

'He was what you'd call moody,' Kevin Bond told me, 'and on one occasion he threw away some bloodstained clothing, saying he'd had an accident at work. Looking back, he did seem to be a bit obsessed with the murders, used to buy up all the papers every time, and once he even sort of half suggested he'd done it. But I thought it was a joke – he had a bit of a funny sense of humour.'

In spite of my shock and dismay, that made me laugh: 'Christ, listen to this, I don't *believe* this, he came home bloodstained, he was obsessed with the crimes, and he half confessed. And they didn't take a blind bit of notice.'

Myra frowned. 'He may have confessed to murdering Francis ... even if he didn't ... or it might be just a convenient way of improving the clear-up rates. Cops won't want to have to think there's another killer out there somewhere.'

'What are we going to do?'

She just stared into space. After a while she said: 'This is brilliant, actually. Now they'll feel they're off the hook, that everything's OK.'

Twenty-one

Myra said: 'It's better this way. Believe me. Don't be upset.'

She had clients to see. I went downstairs. I felt sick and strange, but it was better to carry on, and maybe she was right. I hoped so. Meanwhile, I had to smile, had to talk to guests, had to plan for tomorrow, make sure other people were happy. I was kept busy, I could drink coffee and margaritas until I passed out, if I wanted, I could push the thought of Francis in the cemetery to the back of my mind.

I rang Vic again. She was still out.

Maybe Myra was right – but suppose the man they'd arrested had, after all, killed Francis? Maybe we'd been wrong all the time, and it was just our obstinacy to refuse to accept – against the evidence – the obvious, the simple explanation. That still left the mystery surrounding Aaron Cairo. I was weary, thinking about it all. I sat at my table in the back room, and friends and acquaintances came and went. Only Gennady noticed that I looked tired and sad. By this time some of his favourite customers had arrived and the evening developed into a mellow, sentimental party in which old enemies became friends, former friends fell out, flirtations were suddenly transformed into life-and-death passions and everyone drank a lot. I drowned my sorrows along with the rest of them.

Rusty was there, coming on strong to Gennady. He put up a good defence, although I could see he was weakening, but not soon enough for Rusty, who left in a huff.

After we'd closed Gennady and I sat on among the dirty glasses and cups. Nicotine Ivan had stayed behind too. Gennady made a face. 'Everyone is getting upset, depressed these days.'

'Are you surprised?'

'With you, baby, no, I understand.' He put his arm round me. 'But why is everyone sad? Chloe, me, Rusty.'

I feared he was about to tell me about his complicated love life, but he said: 'Justine, I have little confession to make.' He smiled ingratiatingly. At his stage of drunkenness, it was more of a leer, but at my stage of drunkenness that didn't matter.

'Gennady,' I said, 'you know what Winston Churchill said? He said: "Never apologise. Never explain." Well, he was right.' I wagged my finger at Gennady, to show I meant it too.

'Winston Churchill say this? I don't think so.' We almost had an argument, but Gennady's brain was still sufficiently clear to get him back on to the main track. 'Never mind about Winston Churchill, I don't care what he say. Listen to this. Ivan here, he's heard something will interest you. And also he has little proposition for us.'

They exchanged a few words in Russian. Nicotine Ivan was smiling. He looked even more wolfish than usual this evening. He leant towards me: 'Gennady tells me about your little problem, your friend who died, so I thought, why don't I ask around, ask a few questions here and there, like to give a lovely lady all the help I can. Well, I met someone – guy used to work at that hospital. Harry Theophilou. Used to be psychiatric nurse at Four Lawns, yes? Job was awful, pay was lousy, he developed a little sideline – siphoning off a few drugs into, er, other channels. The underground is always needing penicillin, everything like that, when terrorists are wounded – you know, they have underground hospital these days, you knew that, didn't you?'

'Actually, I didn't,' I said.

'Oh yes, baby, very well organised these days. Anyway,

Theophilou built up the business, saved up the money he made, then when things looked as though they might get a bit tricky at the hospital he quit the nursing, and went into business full time. Got lots of contacts by then, lots of irons in the fire. And you know what he told me? He said his old boss, Dr Leadbetter, sails a bit close to the wind. Patients die, inquests, nurses complained. Has gone on for a long time. These patients got the benefit of all kinds of new drugs – very useful. Since the Greens blew up so many labs and killed those zoologists, testing is more and more difficult, that makes problems for the drugs industry. Along comes Leadbetter. And everyone knows DCI is part of the Cairo empire, so Leadbetter gets government protection, Lord Cairo's in there helping him along, OK, so maybe questions get asked, but nothing happens.'

My mind was not working well, but I slowly worked out what he was saying: 'You mean – they test new drugs on the patients at Four Lawns? Experiments? Is that what you're saying?'

Ivan nodded. 'Human guinea pigs, baby.'

'And no one's realised, no one's done anything?'

'Well ... there was some enquiry once, but it was a whitewash of course. You see, they choose the patients who don't have no relatives, no one to make any fuss. Well, patients in psychiatric hospitals do die, of course. We knew that in Soviet Union, right? But this, it's worse than back home, baby.' He drank off the last of his whisky, and stood up. 'And now – I have to go.'

'You're getting very friendly with Nicotine Ivan,' I said after he'd left. I was already beginning to sober up.

'Why not? He's good contact, useful guy – I maybe do deal with him.'

'Nothing to do with the Café, I hope.'

'Justine! Baby! You know me better than that!' The liar. But I let it go. Gennady took another slug of whisky. Chloe had been clearing up around us. Now she sat down beside Gennady with a proprietorial flounce. I wished she'd go away, but could hardly ask her to when I suspected she and he were an item.

Gennady had no such scruples. 'Chloe – is private, darling. You tidy up some more, then I take you home.'

Bloody hell. Now I resented him for ordering her about. 'I'll drop her off,' I said nastily. 'You'll be wanting to get back home to your common-law wife and kiddywink, won't you.'

He gave me a long look, but left it at that. Then his expression changed. With an awful, wheedling look, he said: 'What Ivan say is helpful, I hope.' He played with his glass. 'You know, Justine, I could maybe do little deal with this guy. All my Russian contacts, is lot of things we can do together. He show his gratitude in the usual way and then we have more money to invest in the Café.'

He stopped. He looked crafty, but I could tell he knew I wasn't going to like it.

Not like it: I was appalled. What he meant was that *he* would have more money to invest in the Café. I didn't need more money; I had plenty of that. I needed him; and he knew it, and he was planning to capitalise on it.

'What sort of thing exactly did you have in mind?'

Gennady played with his glass: 'Well . . . sometimes I think you flirt a little bit with danger. We don't pay protection here, right? But how much longer are we going to last like that?'

'No one's asked me. I haven't had any threats.' As well he knew – but the thought was a chilling one.

'Sooner or later they ask. And might be good if we do pre-emptive strike with someone like Ivan – otherwise these underworld guys, they're everywhere.' He drew in his breath through his teeth and shook his hand violently as if he'd burnt his fingers. 'And these are real tough guys. Hong Kong, no kidding. But Ivan, he's doing well, he's my friend.'

'How come you know so much about the underworld? I thought you were supposed to be a socialist.'

'Socialist! Get real.' He laughed, but angrily. He was

a smart operator, wasn't he, that's what mattered now. That's what he'd been in the resistance back in Russia, now the only place he could use the same talents was in the mushrooming grey world of illegalities.

From underground to underworld. It was far, yet not so far.

'I'm just trying to survive,' he said through clenched teeth.

'You're surviving pretty well, or hadn't you noticed?' I shouldn't have said that. There was a big issue here, only I couldn't deal with it now. It was dawning on me he didn't want the salary I paid him, no more dependence on Lady Bountiful, he wanted in on the whole deal. Partnership. Something like that. 'We'll talk about it,' I said.

'Yes, Justine, yes, I think we do.' He poured himself another trickle of whisky, knocked it back. Then he laughed. 'You know, Justine, business is OK, I like for us to expand, I like to do deals. But you know, at the end of the day, we never make money like these informal economy guys.'

For three reasons – I didn't want to be alone, I didn't want to have to think about the serial killer arrest or Gennady's designs on the Café, and I did want to see the photographs – I drove by Vic's place.

I parked on the front and ran across the empty road in the moonlight. Yes, you could be murdered between your car and the front door.

The front was a moonscape. The stillness was eerie. Even a suspicious character, someone loitering with intent, would have been better than this absolute emptiness, as if I were the last person on earth.

I rang Vic's doorbell – didn't hear it ring – wasn't even sure the bell worked. I rang again. Just as I was about to give up, I heard shuffling footsteps. Vic opened the door. She was blinking and squinting at me, holding her greasy raincoat round her with what looked like nothing underneath.

'Ugh . . . oh – Christ, it's you.'

Her horror was so evident, I knew in a flash what I should have thought of before. I had no claims, after all, I'd only known her for five minutes.

'Look, I'm sorry, I'll go, I didn't think.'

'No, come in, it's OK. There's someone here, but – just an old friend . . .'

'Some other time.'

'Please.' She grabbed my arm. 'It's all right, it really is. Anyway you can't leave now. It's the middle of the night.'

'I didn't come on foot, y'know.'

'Oh, come *in*.' And she started to laugh.

In the white room, Marky was sitting up on the mattress, with the white quilt dragged up to her chin.

'Oh dear,' she said when she saw me.

If I hadn't had such a splitting headache I expect I'd have freaked.

'You know we really are old friends,' gabbled Vic.

I found I was sitting down on the floor. 'Oh God!' I said, 'do I have a headache.'

'Let's have a smoke,' said Vic, slithering out from under the social dilemma.

That was actually a good idea. Before long everything seemed amazingly amusing and some time after that we were all lying in the bed and I didn't remember taking my clothes off.

I woke up because the light was pouring through the enormous uncurtained window. No one was there. I still had a headache.

After a while Vic came into the room. 'I made you some coffee,' she said.

She lay down beside me. 'You look sweet,' she said, 'all white and fragile. As if I'd touch you and you'd bruise.' As she said 'bruise' she drew her finger down my arm.

'I feel like death on wheels.'

For some reason she found this incredibly funny. After a bit I grasped that she was still rather stoned.

'Marky really is just an old friend, you know,' she murmured. Her fingers touched my left nipple and she was staring very hard into my eyes.

I wasn't up for this. I might be feeling sick.

'And now she seems to be my old friend too,' I managed, faintly.

'Mmm – exciting. She said she always fancied you. Said you were her type.' She put her hand between my legs.

'That's rude,' I said.

'We both seemed to be *your* type anyway. It was your lucky night, darling.'

'I don't remember nothing, guv.'

'I'll remind you then.'

'No, don't!'

She did, anyway, and it was like times when I've made love feeling ill, a peculiar, feverish experience, the sheets were hot, her body was hot, her brown nipples with their heavy rings looked very large, I gasped and grasped for something that might remain for ever beyond my reach, and a thread of thought stayed in my brain, nagged like a bad tooth.

I remembered as we lay panting.

'You got the photos for me. That was sweet of you. I partly came for them.'

'What photos? What are you talking about?'

'You know, I asked you to take the receipt from my bag and get them for me, because I had to go off with Miranda.'

'Oh right, yeah. But I couldn't find the ticket, it wasn't in your bag.'

Twenty-two

I now had a problem. I had to see Myra – I *ought* to see her. But if I saw Myra I should not only have to confess to the loss of the photos, I should also have *not* to confess to last night's threesome. Of course what had happened 'wasn't important' (as people always say). Yet I would feel just a little guilty and embarrassed. I probably didn't need to, but I would.

I therefore evaded the problem. The main thing, I told myself, was to get over to Anna's Outreach Centre and meet her social worker friend. After all, the hospital was the most important thing, if what Nicotine Ivan had said was true.

In the Lagonda I thought about inquests; they would be reported in the local press at least. That meant another trip to the *Daily Post*, or maybe to the National Library. Yes, that would be better. I'd no wish to return to the *Daily Post* offices, where I'd first heard the news about Francis. I felt quite phobic about that place.

I drove to the National Library. The newspaper index told me there was a *St Anselms Gazette* and a *North Western City Times*. I began with the *Gazette*, working backwards from December 1990. I found nothing until I reached May. Then I came upon what I was looking for – only it was not quite what I'd been expecting. Just one small paragraph and it reported the death of Beverly Smith, Cairo's sixth patient: a verdict of accidental death, exoneration of the consultant in charge (that was Cairo), exoneration of the hospital, exoneration all round. The *North Western City Times* had a slightly longer report:

Giving evidence, Dr Derek Leadbetter, medical director, blamed shortages of staff for any lack of supervision that might have occurred. 'In any case, some of our staff cannot speak English, and it is arguable that even had the patient's state given cause for alarm at the time when the accident occurred, the presence of non-communicating staff members might have caused further agitation. The alternative of confinement did not seem appropriate,' he pointed out. 'Of course we endeavour to ensure that all our patients are looked after. I must emphasise again that there was no reason to suppose that this particular patient was a danger either to herself or to others.'

Dr Leadbetter spoke strongly of his colleague's conscientiousness, integrity and empathy with patients. Dr Aaron Cairo was a psychiatrist of international repute, and there was no evidence of a lack of judgement on this occasion.

On an inside page I found a commentary on the incident: ACCIDENT PRONE HOSPITAL: DEATH STRIKES AGAIN.

Why was a seriously anorexic and possibly suicidal patient allowed near the lake on her own? Returning a verdict of suicide, the coroner conceded that in an institution for the care of the mentally disturbed, such occurrences could not always be foreseen or prevented, and absolved the hospital of blame, except to say that the grounds of a mental hospital was no place for a deep and dangerously weed-infested lake, and that the lake should be drained and turfed over.

We say: not good enough. This is the fourth death of a young, apparently physically healthy patient this year. Surely patients are placed in psychiatric hospitals to prevent them from injuring themselves?

I continued to work through the newspapers backwards, but I could find no reference to the other deaths mentioned in the report. It sounded as though they had been suicides too, which was not what I was looking for. Still, the fact that

Leadbetter had stuck up for his enemy on this occasion gave me food for thought, and as I walked back to the Lagonda I was wondering why.

Now that I'd had all this expensive work done on the Lagonda I didn't like parking it near Anna's centre, so I decided to leave it in the Mars Factory forecourt. There were always spaces there. It wasn't such a long walk back to the centre.

I was walking away when I heard my name called. I turned. Dean: on this bright day his black suit looked more undertakerly than ever. He came up behind me.

'Hope you don't mind,' I gabbled. 'Just left the car in the forecourt, seeing a friend, must rush.'

'You have *friends* round here?' He put his hand on my arm. 'Who can you know round here?'

'The worker at the community centre.'

'Why don't I walk up there with you?'

I could hardly refuse, but his offer wasn't welcome. We trudged along the road. I couldn't think of a topic of conversation, my mind was too full of what I'd been reading in the newspaper files. I was also plain exhausted from lack of sleep.

'I've been wanting to talk to you,' said Dean. He looked down at me as we walked along. His face, always out of alignment, actually looked worse when he smiled. I know body fascism is all wrong, but I can't help judging people by their looks. Hate my own, of course. Anyway, it wasn't just Dean's disintegrating mouth and disfigured skin, his hunched shoulders and enormous hands, it was something more intangible, a miasma of self-hatred which at the same time silently dared you to admit you were repelled. It was the way he kept touching you, and himself: his hand on your arm, on the small of your back, his fingers picking at spots, pulling the slack lip. He had all these tics and twitches and sly touchings which were at odds with his pulpit voice and grandeur of height.

I thought of James George Morton, the serial killer. I wondered if, like so many murderers, he'd look ordinary and inoffensive. Dean's horror-film looks, by contrast, were too bad to be true.

'It's about Miranda.' He attempted a laugh. 'Who else would I talk to you about? She's not too well. Something happened.' He smiled again, but the ingratiating smile conveyed anxiety, unease, and I suddenly felt sorry for him. 'She'd like it so much if you went to see her. She'd love a visit from you. Take her mind off things. Actually, she's not exactly ill, it's her friend Shelley.'

'Shelley?'

'At the Zoo. Been bitten by a snake. Discovered she had an allergy to the antidote. They think she'll pull through, but it's touch and go.'

'How horrible! How on earth did that happen? Surely they're very careful?'

'I wish Miranda could get it in proportion.' He was speaking more to himself than to me.

Personally I thought it would be difficult to get an accident like that *out* of proportion, but I didn't like to say so.

'Promise you'll go and see her. She's at home – perhaps you could look in after you've seen . . . your friend?'

'I'll try,' I lied. 'If I have time. Problem is I'm terribly busy, you know. Maybe I could look in tomorrow, or the next day . . .'

'Busy?' he murmured. 'I suppose the Café takes a lot of time, and then there's that business about your friend. But of course that's over now, isn't it? You must be relieved they've arrested the man. A load off your mind, I'd say?'

'Oh, but we never thought it was the serial killer.' We were near the roundabout now: 'I turn off here,' I said.

He had stopped. He stood looking at me, slightly vacant, as if his thoughts were elsewhere. Then he pulled himself together, grasped my hand in his moist one and said: 'Please go and see her – you will, won't you?'

'Of course I will.' I smiled and extricated myself. And,

as I walked away from him into the hinterland of the housing estate, I thought – why not make time? Miranda was my friend, after all. There was no law which said I had to treat all my friends badly: betray Myra, however fleetingly, ignore Miranda in a crisis.

But how on earth had the Zoo woman, Shelley, managed to get bitten? It sounded weird. There'd never been an accident like that before that I could remember – and you may bet your life that I would not have missed anything in the papers about an accident involving snakes at the Zoo.

I found Anna alone in her office, as before. I sat down on the purple settee.

'William will be here soon. Though I wondered if you'd still be interested. They've arrested a man, haven't they?'

I hesitated. I didn't really want to go into it all yet again: 'I don't believe he was killed by that man. Anyway, they're still questioning the guy.'

'William said Cairo bullied your friend. Thought he was a bit of a wimp as well.'

'Thought Francis was a wimp? Maybe he didn't know him very well,' I said coldly.

She looked at me. 'You can do something useful while you're waiting. Address these envelopes.'

I almost refused, but in the end did as I was told. I didn't mind helping with her mail-out, I just wished she was more tactful.

'Anyone at home?' A male voice boomed from the entrance hall. Tenison-Joliet appeared in the doorway. He gave me a haven't-I-seen-you-somewhere-before look.

'A very good day to you, Anna.' He sat down without waiting for an invitation.

'What can I do for you, Barnaby?'

'Are we going to turn this town around, or are we going to turn this town around! Need your advice. I've been thinking about Marshtown, and I've got a plan. Suppose I run it up the flagpole and see if you salute.'

'Sure, let's hear it.'

'What about this? A Marshtown festival. Summer in the City. Bands, music, a parade – water splash in the canal basin – ' He spoke with manic enthusiasm. Anywhere less suited to a festival was hard to imagine, but it is the destiny of the Tenison-Joliets and Annas of this world to turn water to wine, to roll boulders up mountains, and his energy was such that even I began to be convinced.

Even MM Designs was graciously to be allowed to contribute: 'I have a meeting scheduled with Dean, he's been extremely helpful.'

'Justine knows them quite well.'

'Oh really?' He gazed at me. He had a craggy face, handsome in a way, but the beard and moustache made his red lips look foolishly small and petulant. 'Somewhat pulchritudinously challenged, our Dean, poor chap.' He laughed at his own joke – if that was what it was meant to be.

Anna frowned. 'He can't help his looks.'

'Of course not, of course not.' His laughter boomed forth.

'I'm more his wife's friend,' I said.

'Ah, the beautiful Miranda, the ice queen.'

He managed to turn the words into a sly innuendo, and at once I felt protective towards Miranda. How would he know? I raised my eyebrows slightly to show what I thought of him, but from his smile I guessed that was the reaction he'd hoped for. He wanted to offend – one of those men of God who are compelled to demonstrate they're not afraid of sex, and can be as vulgar as the next person. It was all part of a man-of-the-people act, in touch with the chaps, y'know. He probably had a girlie calendar in his office.

But no, that wouldn't quite do. It wasn't consistent with Sean, with what Anna had said.

Anyway, he was just revolting. I wished he'd go away, but this he showed no sign of doing. He continued to boom on about the festival until Anna managed to stop him by promising to call a meeting to discuss it. I thought I might as well ask him about Mary Mahoney.

He looked surprised. 'Mary?'

'I'm researching the work of a doctor who treated her once – some years ago,' I explained.

'Ah! I can guess what's coming. The great Aaron Cairo. Is that it? I'd heard his methods are making a comeback. A real crusader in his day. Mind you, poor Mary's no advertisement. Doesn't seem to have done her much good.'

Anna said: 'She's OK when she comes in here.'

'We make sure she has her jab.'

'Yes,' said Anna. 'In fact, you can tell, can't you. I mean, she's dressed OK and her hair's cut nicely, but there's still something – that greasy complexion . . . I don't know what it is, the side of her face twitches.'

'She is a very damaged person, Anna,' said Tenison-Joliet, 'and I have a feeling that Cairo or someone up there just churned her up more. Personally I don't believe in taking a tin opener to people, particularly when they're psychotic.'

This didn't sound right to me. 'I thought psychoanalysts didn't try to cure schizophrenics,' I objected. 'I thought they only worked with patients who were more or less in touch with reality.'

'You're too young to remember, my dear,' said Tenison-Joliet, 'but in the sixties there was a group who called themselves radical psychiatrists. For them, the Marys of this world were saner than the rest of us, because they'd understood the true madness of our society. Schizophrenia was a healthy reaction to a sick civilisation. I'm not sure how far Cairo was influenced by that sort of thinking, of course. Poor show in my view making political guinea pigs out of God's sick children. But then from where I stand the good Sigmund Freud's ideas come pretty close to being the work of the devil.'

He was still smiling, but I knew he actually meant it, and, like any feeble agnostic – too much of a wimp even to call myself an atheist – I retreated into embarrassed silence, as if talk of the devil were nothing more than a naff social error, when in fact it was a full-scale ideological assault, a terroristic device, an instrument of oppression. Then I recalled that he was persecuting Myra.

'Do you believe that everyone who disagrees with you is influenced by Satan?' I enquired in a neutral tone of voice.

He stared at me, but, perhaps fortunately, decided he wouldn't be drawn. Instead he rose to his feet and left us to our own devices.

After he'd gone, Anna said: 'Why did I say I'd call his bloody meeting? Can't stand the man.'

'I suppose he actually believes that, as founder of the psychoanalytic movement, Sigmund Freud is roasting in hell at this moment.'

Anna laughed. 'I'm glad you didn't get into an argument with him, that's just the reaction he wants.'

'Sigmund Freud in hell' – I was warming to the theme. 'You could make a wonderful play about that. What would hell be for Freud? Interminable analysis? He'd have to attempt to cure the most evil men in history. Hitler on the couch. The infantile neuroses of Genghis Khan . . .'

'It's only us in the West who think Genghis Khan was a monster.'

'Hi!' A tall, gangling man stood in the doorway. He must have been forty at least, but he was one of those who carry on looking boyish right into old age. Like Francis.

'I saw the born-again bishop in the distance, pompous idiot.'

'He was here. You just missed him.'

'Thank God for that.'

Anna went into the kitchen to make sandwiches. William sat next to me on the purple sofa.

'Anna said you wanted some information about Four Lawns or something, said I might be able to help?'

'I'm probably wasting your time.'

'Depends what you want to know. No problem, anyway.' I liked his smile.

'Anna said you were there when Aaron Cairo was alive. Also a friend of mine, Francis Vaughan.'

'That's right. Anna put me in the picture.'

'Francis had been revising some work of Cairo's, preparing it for a conference, and I know he was worried about some of what he turned up. He became convinced that Cairo hadn't committed suicide, and that something rather strange had been going on at Four Lawns around that time. I – my friend Myra and I – just wondered if you remembered anything that seemed odd. Particularly anything about the patients Cairo was seeing at the time.'

'The main thing I remember was all the fuss about Beverly Smith. She was drowned in the lake – suicide. I'd only recently arrived at the hospital, I was supposed to be Aaron's social worker. It didn't work. We didn't get on. He was very controlling, he wanted to do everything, social worker didn't get a look in. I did family background interviews on new cases, but most of his work was on his research cases, and no one else was allowed near them. He created a mystique about them. Very much part of the way he set himself up as the man on the white charger, coming to rescue the patients from the horror of drugs and electric shocks.'

'So what was the fuss about her death?'

'Well – no mental hospital likes to have a suicide, although inevitably they occur from time to time. It was the circumstances, the way things were hushed up. That was what really finished it for me with Aaron. I had to break the news. Wasn't allowed near them when it was a question of his so-called confrontation therapy, but when it came to telling them we'd let her get drowned, I was the one who did the dirty work. Well – you might argue that was part of my job, depends how you define it, but the really gross bit was I was supposed to lie to them. The official story was the patient had been on her own. But that wasn't true. Her sister was with her when it happened – half sister.'

'Her sister? That didn't come out at the inquest. I've just been reading a report.'

William looked surprised, but didn't ask where: 'An odd family, the Smiths. He'd had some sort of white-collar job – got made redundant, became long-term unemployed. They were sort of sliding down into the underclass. Still had their own house – wasn't very nice, shabby. Mrs Smith basically gave up, let things go. She was his second wife. He was quite an intelligent man, but . . . dour. She was a slob. There was a son and daughter by his first marriage, and then Beverly.

'You see this half-sister had left home, she had cut herself off completely. They hadn't seen or heard from her for – I can't remember how long. Two years, something like that. The brother was around, he was always in trouble. Part of Aaron's confrontation therapy was to involve the whole family. Naturally this half-sister wasn't there. Only then – no one knew how – the girl somehow got to hear that Beverly was in hospital. She came up to see Aaron. Not with the rest of the family, naturally. And after he'd talked to her, Aaron gave strict orders that her parents weren't to know she'd been. He said it was important for Beverly, she needed her sister's support, and the sister would only visit on the understanding her parents didn't get to hear.

'So it was very awkward – well, worse than that – that the sister was actually with Beverly when she drowned. Cairo freaked. No one was to know. Not the police, not the inquest, no one. And Derek Leadbetter supported him. I was amazed. I thought it was illegal, I didn't think there was a choice. The story was the sister would have been endangered, there were hints of abuse. But it was very, very weird. And quite risky. And it made Cairo more unpopular than ever.'

'Unpopular! I thought he was the great hero. That's what Francis thought.'

'Yes, well – Aaron had his supporters. At one time he'd been very popular with patients and their families, but he had so few by that time. And you see towards the end the hospital became very divided. The battle for the top post – the Freudians had it in for Derek. They mounted quite a campaign against him. Not in the hospital itself, but outside – with Aaron as the Trojan horse, the enemy within the gates. It seemed like an attack on the hospital to many of the staff, so most of the nurses supported Derek. Felt the whole thing was unfair.'

The unanswerable question remained: 'So why did Leadbetter support Cairo over the suicide affair?'

William shrugged and made a face: 'They still hated each other, I can tell you that. Derek was determined to get Aaron out, get rid of him. From his point of view Cairo's own suicide was a lucky break.'

Ah – so we were back to the rivalry scenario. Neither that nor the Beverly Smith story was what I'd come to hear. I tried to get back to what seemed like the main point.

'You see, the rumour we heard was that Dr Leadbetter was up to something that wasn't quite . . . above board.'

'Oh, the drugs research, is that what you mean? I was only a humble social worker. We were rather separate from the rest of the hospital culture. It was the nurses and patients who circulated all the gossip. But everyone knew about the drugs research. Some of the staff were all for it. There are loads of psychiatrists, come to that, who are really waiting for "the cure", you know, like it was going to be penicillin all over again. The Freudians have more sense than that at least. They know life bloody gets you in the end. They know there's no cure for unhappiness.'

'But several patients died, didn't they?'

'Yeah, actually. And Aaron backed Leadbetter over that. Yes, when I think about it, I suppose the whole thing was some sort of quid pro quo. I suppose Derek had to give Aaron his full support during the Smith case, because Four Lawns' reputation was at stake. The father tried to kick up a stink about it to begin with, sue the hospital for negligence, blamed Cairo. Derek talked to Mr Smith – managed to persuade him to back down. Aaron must have been grateful for that.'

That had a kind of plausibility – only the timing was wrong: 'That would only work,' I said, 'if Cairo had needed support earlier on. Because the Beverly Smith suicide wasn't long before he died.'

William shot me a keen look. 'You say Francis thought it was murder. But I wondered at the time if that wasn't why Aaron topped himself, quite honestly – couldn't live with what he'd done, whatever that was, exactly. You see, it's hard to explain. I didn't like what Derek was doing – what I thought he was doing. He took unjustified risks with patients' lives, he danced to the drugs companies' tune, he benefited materially, I'm pretty sure there was a kick-back. Of course, he saw to it that the hospital benefited too, but then he got more kudos for that as well. It was unethical even if it wasn't illegal. But at the same time he did believe that he would find a cure, or at least a better treatment. Whereas Aaron absolutely didn't believe, he thought it was terrible, and yet he supported Derek at the end of the day. I always thought Francis should have made more fuss. He didn't like what was going on.'

'Did you? Make a fuss?'

'I tried. But a doctor would have had more clout.'

From politeness I sat there for a while, ate the sandwiches Anna had made, drank the horrible coffee, we talked about Roxburgh's Celtic Front, about the economic situation, about the renaissance of the local football team. I got away as soon as I decently could. I almost ran up the road and into the MM factory forecourt, hoped Dean wouldn't spot me again, unlocked the Lagonda, climbed into the safety of the driving seat and drove away.

So Leadbetter hated Aaron Cairo's guts. They'd covered up for each other. Cairo had to go. He conveniently died. But there was absolutely no proof of anything, we still had nothing but a web of supposition. I had to see Myra now, had to talk it through. But . . . I slowed down. Perhaps I ought to visit Miranda first. I didn't want to, but it seemed mean not to if her friend was ill and she was upset. I reached the roundabout, drove round it twice, unable to make up my mind, and finally came off it in the direction of the Mars house.

I walked up the path, careful to look where I stepped in

case of snakes, and rang the bell. Nothing happened. No one came to the door. I peered in at the window. There was no one there that I could see. I rang again, and after waiting for a little while I went away, secretly relieved, but puzzled too. Then I understood. Of course: Shelley must be in hospital, and Miranda would be at her bedside.

As I reached the Lagonda again I caught sight of a man and a woman walking through the churchyard. It was difficult to see, for they were some way off and half hidden beyond the trees, but I thought the woman was Miranda. Something about the man was vaguely familiar as well. I waved and called, but my voice did not carry that far, and anyway the two of them turned aside and were lost to view. I ran towards the alleyway with its iron posts, hurried through to the graveyard, but there was no one to be seen. I called her name – no response. Only some sweet wrappings drifted along the flagstones. I must have been wrong.

Myra was waiting for me back at the Café. She looked sombre and grim: 'Can you get away for a bit? I need to talk to you. Not here.'

Oh God. She knew. Marky must have told her. 'Well it's a bit difficult, you can see how busy we are and Chloe isn't in today.'

'Let's go somewhere we won't be disturbed.'

'Home?'

Myra shook her head. 'Somewhere no one knows we'd be there. What about Vic's place? It's only down the road.'

Oh God. She did know. She definitely did. She'd decided not to play it cool. She was going to make a scene.

'She might not be there,' I said pathetically.

'I thought you said she works at home all day.'

'Well, but – '

'If she's not there we can always go down on the beach.'

So we drove along the front to Vic's squat. Myra's grim silence somehow stopped me from telling her about William. I was certain we were in for some terrible row.

Vic's immense front door was ajar. I pushed it open and called Vic's name.

'It's great to see you – where've you been?' Her eyes were a little wary. 'Don't touch me, I'm covered in dust.'

I crumpled into the only comfortable chair. Myra went on standing up.

'Justine and I have to talk.'

'Don't mind me. I'll get back to my installation.' She made a face behind Myra's back. I pretended I hadn't seen it.

'It isn't private,' I said. 'Myra just wanted somewhere no one would find us.'

But Vic carried on with her work at the back of the huge double room, making rather a lot of noise with a hammer and a sheet of metal.

Myra said: 'Have you got the photos?'

I nearly fainted with relief. So that was all it was: 'I'm so terribly sorry, but I lost the ticket.'

'You lost it? When? How could you have lost it?'

'I asked Vic to fetch them. I had a phone call to make, so I told her to take the ticket out of my bag. Then, when she didn't come back, I thought I could retrieve the prints anyway, if I give the guy my name, but they weren't there. Vic *had* collected them already. At least, that's what I thought. I came back here to get them.' But I thought I'd better not go into too much detail over this part of the story. 'But she hadn't got them, after all.'

Vic's hammer blows had ceased and she was listening again. 'What have you lost? Why don't we look now?'

'No – it's not here – someone collected them. Don't you remember – I asked you if it was you.'

Myra frowned: 'But I don't understand. I gave you the ticket in the Café.'

'Yes, and I put it in my bag, only then Vic couldn't find it.'

'Who was at the Café?'

'Oh God – the usual people, you know – the *Daily Post* lot ... that woman from the film collective, Elsa ... loads of people I don't really know. It was very crowded because there'd been some sort of performance art thing at the swimming complex – '

'And you left your bag lying around? Yes, of course you did. You always do.'

Gennady had often told me to leave it in the office, but I never did. I needed to have it with me, like a security blanket.

'So someone took it,' she said.

'Well, I'm not sure, I could have dropped it, I suppose.' But I knew how unlikely that was. 'I've just seen Anna's social work friend, I've got lots to tell you,' I said.

She wasn't listening properly. 'I wanted to tell you I got a death threat, too.'

'Too?'

'Don't you remember, Justine – Rosemary Jones got a threatening phone call. Well, I've had one now.'

'Christ. What are we going to do?'

'I don't know.' She stood there, lost in thought.

'Don't you want to hear what Anna's friend had to say?'

'Oh yes – yes, of course.'

She didn't appear to be listening when I started, but when I'd finished, she sighed, and stretched and said: 'Ah. So that's it. At last – I'm beginning to understand. It was all in his notebooks after all.'

'What do you mean? What shall we do?' I stood up.

'I'm going back to the apartment. There's something I have to check. I don't know why I didn't see it before . . . Look, I'll see you in the Café in an hour or two. Wait for me there. And be careful.'

Twenty-three

I was at the Café all day, but Myra didn't return. I rang her apartment and got the machine.

The evening paper was delivered, and Gennady came over with the news. I remember thinking how his head was polished like ivory: no more two-day stubble, he must have shaved it just before coming in. I was seated at my table – alone, luckily.

'Darling – ' He sat down beside me. 'Don't be upset – is maybe not such bad news,' and he showed me the headline. JAIL RIOTS. BENTHAM ABLAZE.

'Oh my *God*.' I raced down the report, but there was no mention of any names. There'd been a mass breakout, an organised event, someone had turned off the electricity to the perimeter fence, arms must have been smuggled in, screws had been taken hostage, part of the prison was on fire.

'They say is organised by Celtic whozzaname. Look.' Gennady turned to an inside page, where there was a feature on Roxburgh. I had to tell you now, right away, someone's talking about it anyway, for sure, sooner or later, didn't want it to come as a shock then.'

'Oh Gennady, I'm touched.'

'You want to go home?'

'No, no. I'll be OK.'

'Or Vic? You want I call Vic?'

'*No*. Better to carry on. No point worrying – nothing I can do.'

He left me the paper and I read it properly. The breakout had taken place in the early hours of the morning, missing even the last editions of the daily papers. If Lennox had got out at 6 a.m. he could have reached the city by now . . . But of course, he wouldn't come back to the city. That was the last thing he'd do. He might not even have got away, although if Roxburgh had organised it, and Lennox had been involved, which I was pretty sure he had, the chances were he was either free, or captured, wounded, even possibly dead.

There was absolutely nothing I could do. I knocked back several cocktails, touched up my lipstick, and joined a group of women journalists I knew.

Then I noticed Gennady's underworld comrade Ivan propping up the bar. He was looking at me. I sauntered over to where he stood: 'Still after my Gaggia machine?'

He turned. His lazy smile was all flirtation but his eyes said something different. To my surprise he took my hand in both of his and lifted it to his lips. As he did so I felt a square of folded card pressed into my palm.

'Sooner have your Lagonda. Unique, one would know it's you anywhere. You're not exactly anonymous.'

'I don't aim to be.'

'No? Sometimes it's better . . . at night. Don't want some bastard following you. If you've been drinking too – much better take a taxi – '

He glanced away, looking for Gennady, saw him, gave his jaunty salute and was gone. I held the paper carefully in my palm and took my time getting out to the kitchen, pausing to speak to Chloe on the way.

The new cook clashed her pans amid clouds of steam and seemed to be in a state of agitation. I wondered if we could trust her, if from now on we'd have to try to vet everyone. She had her back to me. I unfolded the card and looked at it in bewilderment. It was a small oblong, the size and shape of a personal card or one of those cards that cab services push through the letterbox. On it was printed: ARE YOU

SAVED? BE *BORN AGAIN* IN THE LORD, followed by the address of Tenison-Joliet's mission.

I was on the wrong track for a while, jumped to the conclusion I was to go to Marshtown, but then I noticed that '*Born again*' had been underlined in biro. I returned to the main room of the Café, saw Chloe flashing between the tables with her tray shoulder high and waited for her to return to the bar.

'Call me a taxi will you? In your name? Tell it to wait by the swimming pool. I have to go out for a while. And ... I didn't bring a coat and it's cold. If I could just borrow yours – '

She looked at me. 'Don't be away too long, Boss. We're busy tonight.'

'I won't be.'

When I'd enveloped myself in her long, hooded raincoat, two sizes too big for me, and wrapped her soft white stole round my neck, I left by the back door, which led from the kitchen to an alleyway. The alleyway ran in one direction down to the jetty, in the other up towards my apartment block and the swimming pool beyond the car-park. I came out into the open, looking all round me as I wove between the ranks of cars, until I reached the steps leading to the separate swimming pool entrance.

A cab idled by the steps. I gave the driver Chloe's name and my destination, and lost myself in the padded interior.

He took me along the front, turned inland through Belgrano Square and dropped me outside the Galleria. There I paid him off and slipped into the crowds that seethed along the bright thoroughfare. It was only ten o'clock. I crossed the main street, climbed the steps up on to the raised pavement, walked along past shops still open, and restaurants from which came a subdued roaring sound – a hundred people talking – hurried along, looking back over my shoulder every little while, seeing no one visibly following me, dodging forward and sometimes tripping over Chloe's coat, until I came to the endless flights of shallow stairs that led to the cliff. I soon left the noise behind, and the further up I went the quieter it grew. By the time I reached the little square I was on my own. That was much worse than being in a crowd. I looked all around me, listened for alien footsteps. It was so silent up here. But there was no slinking through the shadows now, anyone who saw me would see where I was going, so I walked smartly into the open square towards Born Again Books, my own footsteps sounding clearly in the silence.

I peered through the window, staring at the unfamiliar woman, swathed in a white scarf, my own reflection but so alien, and I wondered who she was and what she was going to do. I went and stood in the doorway. No one came. I tried the doorhandle. The door was unlocked.

The bell no longer jangled. I closed the door softly behind me, and walked forward in the dusk. I was only a little afraid. Because the place was familiar that somehow made it OK. At the back of the shop was a kitchen and the stairs to the upper floors. I called his name softly and started to climb upwards. On the first-floor landing, a door was ajar. I pushed it open. The slim figure stood by the mantelpiece on which a candle, stuck in a bottle, was burning. Next to it lay a handgun. He must have heard me, for he turned.

'Oh Christ! Who are you!'

It wasn't Lennox. Yet the man with the sneering smile was familiar. He wore a lounge suit over an open-necked shirt. In the light of the candle his face looked unhealthy, or perhaps it was just the shadows. He had brown hair which fell over his forehead, and there was nothing special about his looks, yet there was something I couldn't define about his face that made me want to look at it. Perhaps it was his eyes. He came up to me, but didn't touch me, just stood close and looked down at me. I could smell his beery breath. But he wasn't drunk. He smiled.

'Didn't expect to see me, did you?'

'Who are you?' I stared at him, hypnotised. I'd heard the voice before as well.

He said: 'He's asleep. I'll get him.' He took the gun. 'Just wait here.' He left the room and I heard him run up the stairs to the top floor. I waited. This must have been Otto's bedroom. Some of the furniture remained: a narrow bed, a small, cheap office desk, a chair. Footsteps overhead were followed by a murmur of voices. Someone dropped something. There were footsteps on the stairs.

Lennox stood in the doorway. He didn't say anything. They both moved towards me. I stepped back involuntarily. I was frightened again.

'Listen,' said Lennox. 'I need some brass. Not a lot. Just to tide me over. If you get it to Charley here, he'll bring it to me.'

'Why the go-between?'

'It's safer – he's OK. He's not on the run. He's paroled. They'll be watching you.'

On the run. It sounded so bleak, so hopeless. 'But if they know you knew him inside, won't they be watching him as well?'

'Shouldn't think so, they can't watch everyone. Listen, this is how you'll do it.'

I listened. It wasn't difficult, wouldn't even take me long. They wouldn't see us together. When he had finished explaining, he turned to his mate.

'Look, clear off now, will you? I want to be alone with her.'

I went for my early morning swim. Nothing else was as usual, but no one at the pool would be surprised to see me. I launched myself through the gently rocking dark blue water, and even today my thoughts floated away as I ploughed up and down.

I'd withdrawn the money from a wall dispenser. Now I just had to hope the drop would work.

At the pool, the lockers occupied a space between the men's and the women's changing rooms. It was an awkward arrangement. You had to stagger out holding all your belongings, wander round on the slippery floor, find a locker and put your stuff in it. At one time you'd also had to find the attendant, who'd lock it for you, but recently that had changed and now you simply locked it yourself and pinned the key to your costume.

We'd agreed a simple change to the procedure. When I left I was to lock the money in my locker and leave the key hanging on a row of pegs at the rear of the locker area. Charley was to arrive just after I left, so the risk of it going wrong was minimised. He'd promised us it was a system he'd used several times. No problem. If I was worried, I was to contact him at Otto's. He'd still be there.

All I had to do was watch the time. It wasn't even a lot of money, a mere 3,000 ECUs.

I floated through the cool, soothing water. Lennox was crazy to have come back to the city. Even with my help he'd find it difficult to get away. And I wanted him away – I wished he'd gone straight off with Roxburgh, I wished he hadn't come back. I wished he hadn't looked at me. I wished he hadn't put his arms round me. I wished he hadn't talked the way he'd never talked before. And I wished it wasn't true what they say, that you step and do not step into the same river.

And then – well I wished I'd never met Charley. You'll love it when I tell you who he is. I could hear Lennox now, could see his smile when he said it.

'But why didn't you tell me before?'

'I didn't know – I only knew about the gun.'

Twenty-four

I unlocked my front door, dropped my swim bag and walked into the living room. Myra was there. She was looking out on to the roof terrace.

'Where the fuck have you been?' she said. 'You look exhausted.'

'Busy.'

'Me too. Want to hear about it?' She walked around the room. I could tell she was excited.

'I've got things to tell you too.'

'Listen: Leadbetter. It didn't make sense for him to have murdered Cairo. It wasn't as if Cairo knew anything about him and his drug trials that a lot of other people didn't know as well. It made no difference to Leadbetter if Cairo was dead. Nor to Lord Cairo. They were both in the clear because Aaron wasn't going to blow the whistle on anything. And you were absolutely right – the job business just wasn't plausible as a motive.

'But why wasn't Cairo going to do anything about it? And why did Leadbetter cover up for him over the death of Beverly Smith? On the contrary, both of them made sure everything was smoothed over, no really awkward questions got asked. As if the sister had to be protected, as well as the hospital.

'So what about the patients? Mary Mahoney and the twins could be more or less ruled out. The sixth patient was dead, Beverly Smith, so we – like Francis – ruled her out too. And we never really considered the other two. Because Francis didn't seem to have thought it could be them.

'You visited Françoise Lange with Francis, and afterwards he said it had solved it for him – talked about Ward F and all that. As though he hadn't known about the drug trials at the time. Maybe he didn't. He seemed to think it had something to do with all that, anyway. And because he thought that I suppose we did too. That was what the notebook Leadbetter pinched was about: Cairo kept those notes when he was trying to do something about the experiments with drugs. But then he dropped the whole thing.

'I reread all the notes, and I began to see it differently. And when you came back with the story about Beverly Smith and her sister, it all began to make sense. It was clear from Cairo's notes that Beverly and her sister had never got on. That was supposed to be part of Beverly's problem. The older sister – or rather half-sister – hated Beverly, had always been jealous. But then Cairo's notes changed. He reinterpreted it all. Now it was Beverly who was jealous of her sister. Everything was twisted round into its opposite. It was as if Cairo was seeing a different person – the sister was beautiful, saintly, long-suffering, her stepmother neglected her, Beverly even tried to harm her – and so on. And yet if you look at the original details of the case, it wasn't really like that.

'And then what about Rosemary Jones? There was her story of the other woman. But when we see her husband, he says *she* was the other woman herself. In that case, why the photographs, why did he follow Cairo?

'Then I remembered the pyramid spread: the two women. And it dawned on me. Suppose there were two women, not one. Rosemary Jones *was* his mistress – her husband would hardly have lied about that – but then why was she so bitter, so angry? *Because she'd been supplanted.* Perhaps Cairo's relationship with her had largely been to fulfil a basic sexual need. Only then he met another woman and fell romantically in love with her: Beverly's sister.'

'It's plausible,' I said, 'but it's pure supposition.' I thought about it, and suddenly it seemed to me as though that could explain a baffling aspect of the Rosemary Jones story: her claims to have been so fond of Monica Cairo. It could be, I thought, that once Cairo had been unfaithful to them both, she'd managed to forge a sense of common injury, so that patient and nurse had become fellow sisters betrayed instead of rivals. That, however, was supposition too.

'And what about the photos?' continued Myra. 'How did you lose the ticket? It could have just dropped out of your bag, but that isn't very likely. You always zip it up, don't you, and then it also has a flap that closes over with a stud. You thought Vic had taken the ticket and collected the photos, but she hadn't. So someone else had to have known it was there, and been able to get it out of your bag. So who was there when you talked to Vic about collecting the photos? That's what really gave it away.

'There was also the money. Where did it all go? Did all of it really go in blackmail pay-outs to Rosemary Jones? I rang Ruth Gardiner, and got the name of the Cairos' stock-broker from her. Gave him the story that the Cairo family had hired me. Didn't go down too well, and he only told me what I'm sure he told them years ago: that Cairo had sold up an awful lot of stocks and shares, a large sum of money was transferred to his bank account. Cash.

'Well, then I had a better idea. The house. I went round the local estate agents to see who'd sold the house, to see if anyone remembered – that lovely eighteenth-century vicarage, bang in the middle of Marshtown. Even now there isn't much interest in property out there, and there certainly wasn't eight or nine years ago. Anna told me there was just this one agent, Sparrow, who'd been around a long time, and was more or less solely responsible for what gentrification there'd been. So I paid him a visit.

'Well – he did remember. Cairo came to look at the house. It was pretty run down, but he liked it. Then he came back with a girl. She seemed to love the place too. Cairo made an offer. Cash sale – went through like a dream. Sparrow remembered it well, it was during the recession. And it was an unusual sale, it was all to be in her name.

Later, Sparrow noticed it was being done up. One day he was looking at another house in the street, and he saw them drive up, park, get out of the car. And he told me he'd realised at once that it wasn't the same man. This man was younger, but, said Sparrow, "he was no oil painting".

'I knew I'd get nothing from the Mars accountants – even if I could find out the name of the firm. I did a company search instead. When the company was set up, that was all in her name too. You'd have thought her backers' names would have been there too, but it was only her.

'I got back to the Café quite late yesterday evening. Chloe said you'd buggered off somewhere in a hurry. I waited around. I was worried – thought it might be something to do with them. But then Dean came in. Said he had to talk to us. You know what he's like, all smarmy. But last night he was really strange. Came up on to the balcony – I felt quite . . . ugh! Miranda's ill, he told me. Said she was upset because that friend of hers has died, the snake woman. In the end he said it hadn't happened at the Zoo at all. It was up at the house. She got bitten by the snake she gave Miranda. It was her fault, he said, because she couldn't have extracted the fangs properly. He went away in the end. But of course he'll be back.'

The little square was as quiet and dusty as usual. Born Again Books was still unlocked.

We stood by the stairs and called. Silence.

'He must have gone,' I whispered.

'Of course he's gone.'

'I don't mean Lennox.'

We started up the stairs. On the landing the doors were closed. Myra casually opened the one at the back and peered round it. Then she pushed open the door of the front room.

Charley Smith hadn't gone. He was lying on the bed, but he wasn't asleep.

I had once seen a dead body, but never anything like this. There was even blood on the walls. The room smelt like a butcher's shop. He'd been shot again and again, in the neck, in the chest, in the stomach. The pulp that was his body I couldn't look at, yet even more gruesome was the still intact face, like a mask slipped sideways.

Myra backed away. 'Let's get out of here.'

'They'll think Lennox did it.'

'Why did he stay? They were crazy to come here in the first place.'

We'd left the Lagonda in the Galleria car park – the second time I'd been there that day. We sat in it. I couldn't get the sight of all that blood – and the look on Charley Smith's face – out of my mind.

'Lennox said the scene was that Charley was trying to blackmail Miranda,' I said. 'But still – he was her brother. Christ.'

'I don't think she actually did it – any of it. I think Dean does it for her. All part of his devotion to her.'

'Do you call that devotion, or is it just ultimate control?'

'Why the hell didn't Lennox tell you the whole story earlier?'

'All he knew in prison was that Charley got the gun. Charley never said a word about his sister when he was inside, kept it to himself. Didn't want other cons knowing about it, I guess, it was his insurance policy for a rainy day. But yesterday, when Lennox was out, Charley did tell him. He'd always kept track of Miranda, knew she was a big success. After his release he read an item in some paper about the Lost Time Café connection, it may even have been in the reports when Francis died. Did you know I actually saw him, hanging around outside the Café one day? I had no idea who he was then, of course. And another time I think I saw them together, near the house.'

'What are we going to do about Dean?'

'Go to the police and hope for the best, I suppose.'

We went on sitting in the Lagonda. I switched on the radio to hear the news. Some of the escaped prisoners had been recaptured.

'What was Lennox going to do?'

'Going up north to join Roxburgh. I hired a car for him this morning. Used Occam's licence. And I paid cash. We'd arranged I'd leave it here, in this car park, with the keys in the glove thingy. Bit of a risk someone would notice it was unlocked, but – anyway, it's not here now.'

'That was stupid, Justine – to use Occam's licence. They'll trace it to you.'

'I'll cross that bridge when I come to it.'

We went on sitting there. At length Myra said: 'About the snake. Could she have got hold of another one?'

'How? How could she? And she liked the Zoo woman, Sandy, whatever her name was. Shelley.'

'It was a genuine accident, I suppose.'

'Shelley took out its fangs – but perhaps that didn't satisfy Miranda, she wanted a *real* snake, you know.'

'But how would she have got hold of one?'

I thought of Miranda walking up the path with the box she'd held so carefully, and not letting me go in with her that day.

A storm was brewing. The sky was darker than the sea, darker than the tower blocks, the gulls were nowhere to be seen, they were crouched in the cliffs, waiting for the rain to come down.

The faded curtain still drooped across the gritty window of the shop in the little street. We pushed open the door. There was a second door, to the left. Myra pushed it open and I followed her in. A bell clanged in the back somewhere. We stood in the centre of a small room, lined from floor to ceiling with glass tanks. In every tank a coiled reptile – a room lined with snakes. Some flickered a tongue at us; some glared with those leaden beads. One was huge: it had papery white scales and red eyes. Snakes at every turn, they came at me from every part of the room, it was worse, far worse than the reptile house, this room was so small, so claustrophobic, I was going to scream, or faint, or die.

Twenty-five

The Lagonda swooped down the slope and into the car park beneath our block of flats. Our footsteps and the slam of the car doors echoed around the cavernous concrete. Petrol stained the concrete floor and its smell tainted the air.

As we rounded the corner to the lift, Dean uncoiled himself from the pillar against which he'd been leaning.

'Get back in the car,' he said. He was as obsequious as ever. Like always, you never knew quite what he meant. It was always like he ought to be scary, but wasn't.

I even laughed: 'What's the matter? Don't be ridiculous.'

'I've got Charley's gun.'

He had. We walked back to the Lagonda.

He sat in the back. 'Drive along the front – towards the old pier.'

'We need to talk, Dean,' said Myra in a calming tone of voice.

He just laughed. 'Yes, yes indeed.'

As we reached the front, the rains came down. He told me to park in one of the narrow side streets that backed steeply up from the sea. Rain drummed on the roof and swirled down the windscreen, but it wasn't until I tried to leave the car that I felt the full force of the gale. He had got out first, and I knew he had the gun.

The downpour flattened me against the side of the vehicle while the water poured down as if I were standing under a shower. The whole world seemed to have turned to water.

There was no space between the shafts of rain which sluiced over me, relentlessly hosing me down. I staggered against the car, managed to wrench open the door, which hurled backwards, nearly torn off its hinges. He didn't try to stop me. I was already soaked, and as soon as I unfurled the umbrella I'd grabbed from the back, the wind seized and whipped it inside out, jerked it from my hand and spiralled it into the air, whirling away like a gigantic raven gone out of control.

He laughed again. 'Never mind. You won't be needing it.' He was staggering himself as he nudged us towards the sea.

I tottered down the slippery pavement, groping against the wall and at Myra for support and shivering as the wind roared through the narrow wind tunnel of a street. When we reached the front the gale took full possession of us. I still gripped the wall at the corner, but the howling monster came at me, prising me away in an attempt to hurl me across the road and towards the railings, beyond which the sea boiled and churned, rearing and roaring this way and that in a turmoil of brown and yellow hills, a rubble of solid matter bearing no relationship to the calm grey water I knew. It leapt and crashed up over the railings on to the paving stones, and spat pebbles while the wind whirled the shingle up so that the sky rained stones. A deckchair was lifted aloft and sailed through the air. Canvas ripped away from the booths; doors were torn off and clattered along the road.

I was hardly conscious of Dean and Myra now. We were wrenched apart, pulled and flung different ways, no energy for anything except to keep upright.

Why didn't he shoot us right away? He'd been prised loose from the wall and was reeling across the road. In my terror I staggered to and fro and almost made a run for it. But he was still there on our heels, he still had the gun.

I edged along towards the pier, clinging to the walls of the buildings while the gale tried to claw me away. The awning of the Ocean View Hotel groaned and the gale bellowed underneath it, filling it like a bursting bladder. The front stretched ahead of me, filled with water, the sky bruised purple. The stucco buildings glared in eerie whiteness, thunder rolled boulders across the sky.

The three of us were alone. No other human beings were mad enough to be out in this. This was a post-human world. I pushed forward, leaning away from the force of the wind, and with almost a sense of exhilaration, nothing left to lose, felt my shirt and my silk trousers stuck as tightly to my body as a second skin.

I was keeping my head down but I knew he was still behind us, driving us forward towards the old pier. The battering of the gale and the sea and the rain drowned all other sounds and when I looked back his figure, drenched like me, enveloped in a grey garment, struggling silently forward in slow motion, was like a figure in a dream.

The disused pier gleamed through the torrents of rain. The gale had already torn away some of the rusty metal on the broken roof.

Every step was a battle with the gale. Even gripping the railings, it was a struggle to propel myself along without becoming airborne. Now the pier was only a few yards away.

He forced us through the shelter of the pier entrance and out on to the pier itself. It stretched towards the sea, with its broken kiosks, and rusting railings. It swayed where it jutted over the water, and I could hear the rusting piles creaking in protest at the battering they were getting from the churning lumps of sea.

I stood there, terrified. I dared not go out further and there was nothing to hold on to.

'Dean!' shouted Myra above the noise. 'Listen. You must listen.' She staggered and almost fell, gripped hold of me.

For a moment he paused. Then he lurched forward himself, pushed by the wind. It almost lifted him up, flapping the skirts of his greatcoat. He stumbled, reached for the pier railing. He seemed to wave his arm. No, he was taking aim. I shrank back. Whichever it was, in letting go of the railing he had loosed himself to the wind, and in a moment it had lifted him and was shaking him like a rat. His coat ballooned up, he staggered, grabbed for the rails. He grappled with them for a moment. Then with a rending sound they collapsed outwards. I heard his scream as he disappeared after them.

'Quick – back!' yelled Myra, grabbing at me. We both fell and now I was crawling away towards the safety of the entrance and the road, an eternity beyond.

The gale created deafness. Nothing could be heard but itself. When the groaning pier cracked as the rusting beams broke like sticks, that was part of the sound of the storm.

The pier was moving. The whole structure shifted, collapsing downwards, caving in almost as if it were melting. A rift widened between the boards and with a gathering of sound louder than thunder and than the sea itself the structure slipped in slow motion into the sea. It took only a few minutes, and now I was staring out at just a few yards of duckboard and the tip of a wrought-iron pavilion surfacing above the ploughed-up water.

The gale was as strong as ever. As I veered away from the flying pebbles and across the road I saw Myra struggling towards me, it seemed, her head bent against the elements. I screamed her name. When she got close I saw her face was streaked with blood.

It felt better to be holding someone's arm. We walked along, bent by the wind as if we'd aged fifty years. We reached the Ocean View Hotel. I dragged her up the steps.

The manageress stared at us like we were drowned cats. When I looked down, there was actually a puddle – well, more like a lake – on the carpet where we were standing. Myra gave a plausible version of what had happened. They called emergency. We decided to stay in the hotel until the storm was over.

It was only after we'd ordered room service that we began to talk. I curled up on a sofa by the window and watched the storm. Tonight there were no lights glittering through the rain, their reflections smeared on the tarry road surface. There was no TV either, and the ephebe who wheeled in the room service trolly told us pylons were down and most of the city had no electricity. The Ocean View had its own generator of course.

I tried to put a call through to the Café, but had no luck.

'How did your face get cut?' I asked Myra.

She looked surprised. 'I don't know – from the shingle whirling about? Or perhaps it was when I tripped over and fell – but never mind about that.'

'Why did Dean go out on the pier? He did intend to kill us, didn't he?'

'I guess so.' Myra dabbed her face gingerly. 'He'd shot Charley. And yet . . . there was always that element of farce about him. Clumsy, awkward, a botched job, even his own death.'

'It wasn't a botched job what he did to Charley.'

'Charley must have got in touch with them. When they met, Charley must have told him about Lennox.'

'So Dean knew we knew.'

Later I lay in the dark, alone in the biggest bed in the world. The wind had died down. I listened to the sirens that wailed in the distance: the sound zigzagged mournfully up and down the stormlocked city. I liked the sound of the sirens. It was like the city outside was old Manhattan, and in my dreams Miranda was there, a blonde in a black and white movie, with death in her eyes and a gun in her hand, brought low but not defeated by the men she'd betrayed.

In the morning they sent us a paper with our breakfast. The city had woken to trees and cables blown down. There'd been fifteen deaths and many roads were blocked by fallen trees. Office workers were told to stay at home. Schools were closed, hospitals on emergency alert. The pier had collapsed. The body of a man had been fished from the sea.

'What are you thinking about?'

'I'm thinking about Miranda,' I said.

Twenty-six

       I got across the city, despite the chaos, by avoiding the expressways and taking a back route through side streets. I rang Miranda's doorbell.

Nothing happened. I waited. Surely she was there. I put my hand up to ring the bell a second time when suddenly the door opened as if my movement had caused it to do so.

Miranda stared at me. Her hair was uncombed and seemed paler than usual, her face rather redder. For one fleeting moment I saw her brother, as she stared out at me, with a suspicious, unfocused look.

She said nothing, but swung the door wide. The room had always looked half finished, but now I could see a film of dust on the floor. Newspapers were lying about unfolded in messy piles. There was used crockery on the dining table. Cushions on sofas were creased and dented with the impression of whoever had last sat there.

'So you heard. Let's have a drink. Now where did I put the whisky?' She stood stock still and looked vacantly round, paused, seeming to forget what it was she was looking for.

I didn't drink whisky and certainly not at this time of day, but it seemed beside the point to say so. I watched her uneasily as she walked slowly, too deliberately, towards the back of the room. She grasped the bottle from where it stood on the table, and gripped the table's edge for a moment.

'I'm sorry the place is in such a mess, darling.'

'Miranda – '

'So you heard. That was quick. I only just heard myself

. . . Yesterday, I think it was yesterday.' She didn't wait for my response, but wandered away to the back of the house. I heard a crash. After about five minutes she came back with two tumblers. She poured whisky into them, then brought them into the front part of the room, where she placed them on the floor. She flung herself down on the sofa. Her robe fell open and she pulled at it vaguely without bothering to cover herself up.

'What did you say, darling?'

'Is there any way I can help?'

'No. No, I don't think you can, really. I mean, what could you do, it's too late, isn't it?'

I leant against the wall. I watched her. I was on my guard. I was not going to sit down.

She swung her legs to the floor and stared up at me, suddenly hostile. 'Why have you come here?' she cried.

I said nothing, because I didn't know. To confront her seemed pointless now. Why had I even thought of it?

She seemed to forget about her question. 'It wasn't my fault, you know. It was a horrible accident. I tried to tell her about the snake, she laughed, she didn't believe me.'

My mind wasn't working too well. I couldn't think why she was talking about the snake, but, reminded of it, I looked cautiously round the room.

'Why did she have to die, Justine? It isn't fair. It isn't *fair* just when everything was going so well.'

I didn't know why I'd come. I certainly hadn't come to break the news about Dean, but it looked as if I would have to. I'd foolishly assumed he would already have been identified, that she'd already have heard. I hugged myself nervously. The nails of my right hand dug into my left arm.

'Miranda,' I said. I swallowed. 'I've got some bad news. It's Dean. There's been an accident.'

'Dean was always bad news. I hate him. Did you know that? You must have. Don't tell me you didn't know. It's a physical thing. He crawled all over my life . . . The funny thing is, I'm frightened now. I never used to be frightened of him, but now I am. I think he knew about the snake. I think he egged Shelley on, pretended I was just joking.'

She took a sip of whisky – a very small sip, very ladylike: 'Stupid, I wasn't frightened before.' She paused. When she spoke again it was as if she were starting from the beginning again. 'I can't stand Dean. And I'm frightened of him, you know. Did you know that? You can't even begin to realise how frightened I am of Dean. Have you any idea, the remotest idea what he's like? The longer we're together the more frightening he is. I thought I'd get used to him.' She shook her head slowly, and smiled. 'Never. I got the snake for him, really. Only he was too clever.'

'But he adored you, he was devoted to you.'

She laughed. 'It's awful to be worshipped. You never had that experience? No. I don't suppose you have. Certainly not with that pretty boy of yours.'

'But surely Dean really did love you, Miranda, it wasn't one of those sick obsessions . . . surely?'

'He's jealous. Even of you – of Shelley – all my women friends.' Her eyes opened wide in innocent amazement. 'I mean – what's the problem? I said to him: aren't I supposed to have *friends*, darling?'

'Oh come on, Miranda! You know the score. Why bother to deny it? Nobody cares. Everyone's doing it. Why, it's actually *fashionable*, for Christ's sake.'

I had such mixed feelings about that. Who wouldn't rather be an outlaw?

'What is – what d'you mean?'

'Dykes. Lesbians. You know.'

She flung herself back against the cushions, glared at me. 'Oh you're all the same. You're obsessed. I am *not* a lesbian.'

I thought I would sit down after all. Might make her feel more relaxed. So I sat on a dining chair that was set against the wall.

'It's all been so hard for you, then,' I said in a soothing voice.

'Hard?' She swallowed some more whisky. It was unnerving to see her losing control. How tightly reined in she'd always been. That must always have been a big effort: perpetual vigilance. Now the hard edges were going soft, her body going slack, the contours of her face collapsing. I couldn't even hear the razor in her voice any more.

'They're all the same, you know. Men – they're all the fucking same – adore you, *adore you*, don't give me that. Dean adores me all right, he adored me so much he said he'd deal with Aaron. I thought, when he'd done whatever he was going to do, I'd be through with him as well. I didn't need him, I had Aaron's money, didn't I.'

I risked a question. 'Why didn't you just leave Aaron?'

She laughed. 'Don't worry, that was the idea. But after his bloody wife died he got big ideas. Marriage, children, the lot. He threatened to take back the money. I was afraid of losing all that. It was partly my own fault, I suppose. I acted all innocent, said I couldn't *possibly* do it with him till we were married. What a joke.'

She stood up suddenly. I only just managed not to leap up myself, in fright. But I stayed put, leant back against the wall and gripped the seat of the chair, my heart thumping so loud I was surprised she didn't hear it. She walked about the room and then sat down again.

'To be quite honest,' and now her voice was getting quite blurred, 'I could never understand what Aaron saw in me. I really couldn't. But I suppose I was someone to look after, all the children he'd never had. His little girl. He called me his angel. Only he didn't really want an angel. Still, I never did do it with him, you know, never. *Not once.*' She laughed. 'Can you believe that? What a fool he was.

'Charley told me Bev was in hospital, said Aaron wanted to see everyone in the family. Said Bev was the way she was because of the family. Charley said I should go. I was afraid they'd ask questions, find out about Bev and us at home. But Charley said it'd look worse not to go. They might even try and trace me. Go, he said, and tell them they musn't say a word, make out like you were abused or something.'

She was more or less talking to herself, and drinking as though she were drinking alone. Which she was. I was afraid to say anything, as if by drawing attention to myself I'd bring her back to the present, but I was equally afraid to say nothing, afraid that if she forgot about me for too long, my presence would come as a shock, she might do something weird when she came down to earth and remembered she had an audience.

'What were you afraid they'd find out?' I asked.

Her eyes slewed round. 'Oh . . . *you* know, I'd made her do these mad things, get her into trouble, it was all for a laugh really, she was dumb to start with, completely random actually, but I suppose you could say we frightened her out of her brains.' She started to laugh. 'If you could have seen her at times!' She put her hand to her face, she was convulsed, laughing till she cried. 'There was one time we almost persuaded her to throw herself off a balcony, I'll never forget the look on her face. Do you have brothers and sisters, darling? You don't, do you, so you wouldn't understand. And you never lived in a stinking little house with cardboard walls, so you couldn't possibly imagine what it's like to be banged up with people you loathe. I always knew I was different. Charley was OK, we both had brains, came from our mother. But my stepmother, grief, and my sister, God, was she stupid. I think stupid people should be strangled at birth.'

She was laughing again; she was beginning to go round in circles.

'So Aaron helped you to get away.'

'Aaron.' She raised her glass. 'Here's to Aaron. He was a pushover. He loved being a benefactor. I could see I'd had an effect. So I went up there again. Looked good. Looked like I cared about my sister. I don't suppose she liked it much, but then she was the mad one, wasn't she . . . and finally one day I managed to engineer it, he gave me a lift home. D'you think I'd ever been in a car like that before? Once bitten, forever smitten, that was me. Not with him, needless to say. Actually, it was hard work. It wasn't easy. He had scruples. Riddled with them . . .

'She'd be sitting there, zonked out. "She's cutting herself again," the nurse would say. "Perhaps you can talk to her, make her see sense." So I'd talk to her. "Dad's going to kill you," I'd say, I'd tell her anything so she'd go and cut herself up again, try to kill herself, so I could go on going up to the hospital and see Aaron. I'd tell them I was worried, that I needed to talk to the doctor. They'd say he was too busy, or he wasn't there, but I made them give him the message, and after a few weeks I found out he had these clinics in the centre of the city. That made it easier – no more trek out to the bin. I used to have to hitch rides, a man nearly raped me once.'

I believed her. Her glass was empty. She looked around for the bottle.

'Why am I telling you all this? You must be bored out of your skull, darling. And you're not *drinking*.' And suddenly, unnervingly, she was back in familiar Miranda mode: sharp, brittle, glossy, apparently not drunk at all.

'I am.' I raised my glass. 'Go on,' I said. 'Please go on. It's fascinating.' Then I thought: oh God, what a stupid, insensitive thing to say.

She looked at me, and her eyes started to swivel again. 'Fascinating . . . *fascinating* . . . it's not fas-cin-a-ting, not fas-cin-a-ting at all. It's deadly. What I had to do – what I had to go through to get where I am, what I had to put up with. Aaron was so boring, so boring you can't believe. I had to listen to all his trials and tribulations about his bloody wife: it was all in secret, we had to be careful, he never took me anywhere nice, I was almost a prisoner in the poky little flat he bought me, miles away from anywhere. But it was near his outpatient clinic, off the China Road, so he was pleased.

'Charley was the only one who knew. First I thought I'd die, I was so lonely. Then I had this idea. I told Aaron

I wanted to go to art school. It was brilliant, he could pay for my education.

'He knew it was lonely for me. He didn't like it, but in the end he agreed, found out about all the courses, and there I was. It was like going to heaven. I was going to be a dress designer. It was great.

'And then I met Dean. I think I met Dean the day I was born. "You and I – we're made for each other," he said. And we were! The way – handcuffs are made for criminals, darling. The way the noose is made for the neck. Torturer and victim.

'He was the year above me. I had the talent. And he soon found out I had the money too. He had the business brain. It was the perfect set-up. As soon as I'd finished my training, Aaron started me off. Financed the whole thing. Put in all the capital. Things could not have been better. Dean was always so smart. He said to make sure the flat was in my name, and to get as much as I could out of Aaron, get it while it lasted. "You never know what'll happen," he said.

'It wasn't that difficult, you know. Aaron was worried about his own health as well as hers. He bought shares in my name. Even there he was careful, never missed a trick. Didn't use the family stockbrokers, oh no. Did it through a different firm. Gave me a whole lot of diamonds, too. Bought me some paintings. He wanted to be sure I'd be OK if anything happened to him. Which of course it did.' She started to laugh again. 'Poor old Aaron – if only he'd known.

'So I had Aaron for the money, and Dean for the business, and I had my own little flat as well.

'If only Aaron's bloody wife hadn't died. That took us all by surprise. She could have gone on for years. By which time Aaron himself might have died. But she died. And the shit hit the fan. That stupid black bitch started to make trouble. And there was Aaron saying if I didn't marry him he was going to stop the money. But he never guessed about Beverly. He was so stupid. They were all so stupid, really. All except Dean. He knew. You gave her a little push, didn't you, he said, but I suppose it was just in fun. Just tell them you can't swim, it'll be OK.'

I saw her ploughing through the blue water of the pool.

'Aaron was going crazy, his wife only dead two months and he was saying we had to get married properly, I had to meet his family, we had to have children, I couldn't believe it. And then I thought of Dean. I knew he'd do anything for me, but I never thought he'd *dare* to . . . the thought of going to bed with him, it simply never crossed my mind, it would have just been too disgusting – far worse than Aaron. But I never thought of that.'

She put her face in her hands, and I saw she was crying, tears oozing down her cheeks. She looked in my direction, a pleading, bewildered expression. 'I mean, what would you have done? What was I supposed to do? I'd have died if I'd had to marry Aaron – but I never dreamt Dean was going to . . . he just said to get him to meet me. Not in the flat. He said to say I was going to a concert in the Botanical Gardens, and I'd meet him afterwards.

'I didn't actually go to the concert. I just walked round to the exit nearest the concert, waited for him by the gate. I guessed he'd be early, he was always the gentleman, never kept me waiting, and so I was earlier still. I was there when he drove up, said I'd got sick of it. I got in, and said I wanted to drive around. I said I wanted to talk. I acted like I was upset. Well I was. I . . . I didn't know what was going to happen, but I was frightened, I felt uneasy. I got him to drive me to the place Dean and I had agreed – there's a side road, it's very quiet at night. I asked him to stop the car, I said I wanted to walk around. There was a moon, I acted like I was feeling all romantic. It was a warm night. I'd made sure the windows were open. And then Dean stepped out of the bushes and – oh God, it was awful, I was afraid he'd hit me too. There was blood all over my dress, my lovely white dress . . . Dean gave me his jacket, we ran off through the bushes. We didn't even remember to wipe off all my finger-prints, there must have been some. But you see that didn't matter, because they had no way of connecting him to me. Everything had been done in my name. The only thing I had to be frightened about was whether he'd told his family, his lawyer, if he'd set the wheels in motion – but he hadn't. It was all hunky dory, everything was fine.'

'How did Dean get hold of a gun?' I asked, although of course I already knew.

She looked at me as if I were stupid. 'Charley, of course. He was only sixteen, but he knew all about getting a gun. There were pubs off China Road, he said, the drugs and guns scenes, easy as falling off a log.

'Afterwards I said, I don't know how to thank you, Dean. I don't know why you've done this for me, I don't know what to say. But of course we'll go shares in the business. You deserve nothing less, I said.

'I thought I was being really generous, I wasn't even sure I really meant it. He didn't say anything, there was this funny silence, so I turned to look at him, and he had this – expression on his face, I can't describe it, and he said, "I think I deserve rather more, Mrs Mars."

'I didn't take it in – Mrs Mars. It must have shown on my face, for he got angry-looking as he looked at me, and after a while he put his fat hand on my neck, and laughed in a bitter, horrible way. You really thought you had a choice, did you? I thought you were smarter than that, he said, why d'you think I went through all this? Why did you think I did this for you? Did you think I did it for fun? Or for money?

'I looked at him. I just could not believe it. He came close to me and put his arms round me and held me tight. I'd never let him touch me before. But now if he hadn't been holding me, I think I'd have fallen to the ground. We'll get married, he said. I didn't like his smell: too much aftershave.

'I tried to talk to Charley, but he was no help. He couldn't see the problem. We paid Charley off. We all agreed it was better not to meet for a while, none of us wanted the gun traced back to him. It seemed better not to stay in touch. Mu-uch better not to keep in touch. Charley understood.

And Dean and I got married. Dad didn't know his second name. Didn't know he existed. They couldn't trace me, they didn't connect me with Miranda Mars, I was always Mandy to them. Miranda fucking Mars. What a laugh. They probably read about me in the papers when I did Saffron's · wedding dress. It was in all the tabloids.

'I never wanted him. It was just so unfair that there always had to be Dean. Dean – Dean – Dean. Whichever way I turned, he was always there, blocking out the future, hiding the view . . .'

She stood up suddenly and started to walk around. She paced up and down, circling towards the back of the room and then back towards me.

I felt no different from how I'd always felt: a certain affection, a certain fascination, but also that sense of distance, we'd always been very *public* friends. Brittle in the end. It was as if her antics and affectations still simply amused me. I felt myself smiling in that same indulgent way.

'Why are you smiling like that? You think this is all so-oo funny, don't you – you always were so patronising, you always thought I was a vulgar little bitch.'

'Hey, come on, what's the matter? That's not true. I was only smiling because you – ' You're like a child, I'd been going to say. Just taking what she wants like any toddler. Ramming out a sticky fist and making a grab. And screaming with rage and frustration when she doesn't get it.

'Miranda,' I said boldly – I wasn't afraid of her at all – 'What happened to Francis?'

'Dean had to deal with him too,' she muttered, 'he was getting too close. We got nervous. It was my idea to make it look like the serial killer. That was a really good idea. Brilliant. Dean didn't want to do it, he said Francis hadn't a clue, but I made him. He was a pain about it all. And then we didn't know quite what to do when you and Myra started poking around. It was hilarious – you told me what you were doing, you told me everything.' She laughed and laughed. 'Oh dear, it was so funny really, you simply told me everything you were doing . . . oh dear, I can't stop laughing.'

'Miranda, you're upset. You can't go on like this. You've got to sit down and decide what to do.'

'You think you know so much. You think you know so fucking much. You don't know anything. D'you know what it's like to be brought up like me, with Dad and that half-wit slob of a stepmother? What d'you know about anything?'

She came and stood over me and now, too late, I felt fear. 'I hoped you'd come here. You haven't seen him, have you? My pet, I mean. Dean said he'd get you here, he promised me . . . You've seen Dean, haven't you? He'll be back soon, you know.'

She moved off again, whirled around. 'It's really your fault Shelley got hurt. I thought she'd pull through. You took me that day. To the snake shop. I never wanted Shelley to pull the fangs. I wanted a real one. So I got rid of the one she gave me and now I have Goebbels. You want to see Goebbels, don't you? I don't know quite what to do with him now, he's been so naughty, he bit Shelley, you know, that naughty boy, but it wasn't his fault, he didn't mean to.'

And there it was: the cardboard box. She was picking it up. How could I not have noticed it until now? The long, cardboard boot box papered with grey marbled paper – for of course I'd seen it before. I remembered it lying on the seat of the Lagonda. I remembered her carrying it into the house. She held it out and took a step towards me. I slid sideways up off the chair and put it between her and me as I backed towards the door. She was still lurching towards me but she stumbled and tripped and that gave me time to pull open the door and bang it behind me as the box went hurtling to the floor.

Twenty-seven

I rammed the Lagonda through the narrow side streets, only just missing parked cars, shot out into the seedy back end of the twentieth century which was the main road, and veered wildly on to the roundabout. But however fast I drove I couldn't escape the thought of the snake, which writhed across my field of vision, rippled along the floor of the car and twined round the wheel. I'd heard of how snakes in Australia would somehow manage to slither up into cars, in Southern Carolina they'd drop out of trees and through the open sun roof, in Africa a whole packed busload of passengers jammed together in terror while a green mamba slithered from head to head.

There might have been more than one. How was I to know? I felt snakes all around me. I was surrounded by snakes. I looked down at the floor and almost rammed the car in front. I slammed the brakes on and the car behind almost rammed into me. I could see the driver in the rear mirror: a black guy, hooting, putting his finger to his head and then flinging his hands in the air to express his view of my driving.

I drove on, more slowly. The snakes were receding. I no longer felt them crawling through my clothes, over my foot, along my shoulders. I had no idea where I was going, but I supposed it was in the general direction of the Café. Myra wouldn't be there, though; in spite of the hurricane she'd told me she had to go to the Channel Nine Studio.

I drove slower and slower. I'd run away. I'd panicked.

Unnecessarily. Miranda would never have tried to kill me. As I drifted along the highway past the grey, boarded-up factory buildings and the broken-down houses I tried to remember what had actually happened. She'd shown me the box. She'd taken off the lid. She'd taken a step or two in my direction, but she hadn't threatened me in so many words.

'You think you know so much.' I'd heard a threat where possibly none had been spoken.

She was mad. That didn't mean she'd had me in mind for her next victim. She'd let me run away. She hadn't tried to stop me. What had happened wasn't even that clear in my head.

Finally I took a left and stopped in a gloomy side road. I leaned forward, my arms and forehead resting on the steering wheel. I knew now I'd done the wrong thing, I'd taken the coward's way out: the sign of a true coward – to take flight at an imaginary danger, a danger that was not even real.

I sat there wondering whether I'd have been braver if she'd threatened me with a gun or had held a knife in her hand. It would have been different then. That would have been an unmistakable threat, but when she'd taken a step towards me she could have simply wanted to show me her secret, her treasure. She was that mad. I just didn't know.

'You want to see my silent friend.'

I wondered what she was doing now. Packing up. Going away. No – just sitting there too drunk to do anything. She didn't even realise Dean was dead, but one thing I did know: without Dean she'd never be able to carry on. It had been Dean that held her together, kept her going.

Now that I knew all about her, or more at least than I'd ever known before, I felt only her pathos – although pathos may seem a strange word to use about a woman who'd had three men murdered and filched a fortune into the bargain, driven her sister mad, and then drowned her.

Pathos: in her greed, in the way her plump hands had seized every sweet in the shop window for fear of missing it all; in her pleading look when she'd explained. 'I was only eighteen years old.' Pathos had even reached the blind blue of her eyes as they opened wide at the memories: if you'd known what it was like – to be a child in that house – and her heart-rending look of bewilderment and pain when she thought of Shelley dead.

Suppose I told the police what Miranda had told me. All it amounted to was a dangerous snake on the loose, and all the police would want to know was whether Miranda had a licence to keep it.

Officially there was nothing more to solve. Dean Mars's death by drowning had been an accident. Francis had been the 'gay slayer's' last but one victim. Aaron Cairo had died years ago. No one had found Charley's body yet, so far as I knew, but no doubt that would be put down to some drug feud.

Something was worrying me. I sat there thinking and thinking. Something to do with the house. Something to do with Miranda. Something to do with Dean.

When I finally remembered I set off to look for a phone booth. I spoke to Gennady, and then I drove back the way I'd come.

I parked the other side of the church. I walked through the churchyard, past the mossy gravestones. Must have been Charley I'd seen her with there that day. It was quiet, still, deserted. The solitude of the place was peaceful and yet this place was always a little creepy. I walked on, past the old iron posts and along the alleyway, and turned into the enclave of old houses. I rounded the corner and came to Miranda's street. How quiet it was. Someone in one of the houses began to play the piano. They played well. A torrent of notes poured into the empty air. The music rippled with life, tumbling over and over.

I walked into the garden, up to the front door. I stepped carefully so that my footsteps should make no noise and to make sure I didn't tread on a snake. I put my hand to the bell, but took it away again. I listened. Silence. I crept round the side of the house. A twig cracked where I stepped on it. I stopped. Nothing happened. I moved on, trying to avoid dead leaves, gliding over the dry grass as though I were a ghost myself. Or a snake.

I rounded the corner. The french windows at the back were open. I edged slowly forward until I could just about look into the room.

From where I stood I could see Miranda's legs sticking out from the sofa. They seemed to be at a slightly awkward angle, and they didn't move at all. I waited. Nothing happened.

I stepped over the sill, making no noise. It was horrible. I hoped she'd move, and hoped even more that she wouldn't. I was too afraid to go forward, yet a ghastly curiosity drew me, a slow horror as I stepped on the polished boards. The boards were relatively safe: you'd see the snake a mile off.

I glided forward until I could almost see her face. I saw then that the box – *the* box – was open, empty, on the floor. For I don't know how long I stayed still, petrified – literally, I mean: turned to stone.

I shook off the paralysis, let my feet sound on the boards. I called her name.

Then I shrieked, for suddenly her arm slumped sideways, sticking out in the air.

She was dead. Her face was greyish and there was foam on her lips. I couldn't see the snake, but I knew it must be somewhere on the sofa, in the room, or ... anywhere, it could be anywhere.

I stared at her. I couldn't see where she'd been bitten. It must have happened just after I'd left, or she might still have been alive. It might even not have been too late to save her.

I don't know how long I stood there before I heard a noise at the top of the stairs. I almost thought it must be the ghost of Dean as I whirled round.

'I want my daddy!' The child peeped down from the top of the stairs, clutching her blanket. Her hair was messed; she must have just woken up. She began to sob, staring at me with those big round brown eyes like drops of black coffee. Her sobs were like hiccups.

'Isobel.' I held out my arms. She didn't move. I started slowly up the stairs myself, still with open arms. She put one leg down on to the next step. 'Isobel.'

She shrank away against the stairs and shook her head very sadly. 'I want my daddy. Nanny gone away.'

But when I picked her up, she didn't struggle and I was able to press her face into my shoulder, so that she didn't see her mother as I hurried from the room.

I walked out into the garden again, looking carefully where I trod. I carried her round to the front of the house. Just as we reached the gate I heard a car vroom to a halt. Its door slammed.

The three of them stood there: Gennady, Vic and Myra. When Myra saw us she stopped in her tracks. She said: 'Oh *shit!*' and began to laugh. But then she saw that I was crying, and she came up and put her arms round us both.

Twenty-eight

Myra said: 'It was there all the time in the cards, you know.' She was fanning out her pack, face up.

'This was the first spread,' she said, when she had picked out ten cards and arranged them in the Celtic Cross. 'You remember it ended with treachery and betrayal.' She pointed to the Knave, stealing away with the swords from the tents against the yellow morning sky.

Gennady wasn't so interested in the cards. 'But how you found out?' he said, 'I don't understand.'

Chloe brought another tray of drinks and snacks up to the balcony. We'd been drinking steadily for some time. Isobel was asleep on the sofa. Vic had her arm round me.

'Well, you remember when Miranda came on the scene,' said Myra.

'Yes. Why did she come looking for us?' I asked.

'I guess she was worried,' said Myra. 'Do you remember at the Aaron Cairo concert how she was waving and smiling and then she suddenly disappeared?'

'Yes.' I could picture it still, that sudden change of expression, the abrupt turning away. 'I thought she was with someone,' I said. 'Some man seemed to come up beside her.'

'No. It was because *Francis* reappeared beside us at that moment. She recognised him, and she was afraid he'd recognise her. He'd been away in Boston at the time of Aaron's death, but that was only a three-month visit. She must have seen him, met him, even, at the hospital. Aaron had been treating Beverly for several years.

'But once she'd seen Francis with us she was in a dilemma. It was a reason for steering clear of us, but it was also a reason for getting to know us. Because we knew him and because he was promoting all the new interest in Cairo's work, she'd hear about anything awkward that might come to light. If she hung around with us, that is. It was still on her mind, wasn't it? Why was she at the concert at all? That proves it was still important to her, that she never stopped worrying about it, never once.

'Of course I thought nothing of it at the time, but she always came to the Café on women's night, the one night she could be sure that Francis wouldn't be there.'

'So she was never interested in us, never liked us at all,' I said. 'I suppose the Bohemian Collection was just a smoke-screen, an excuse.'

'No, no, she was intrigued as well, she wanted to get to know you anyway. She really liked you, Justine, you know she did, and I'm sure she was shrewd enough to see how brilliant the fashion angle would be.

'She had an extra bit of luck, because Rusty tagged along and – ' But Myra stopped suddenly, because Gennady was staring hard at her, daring her to give the game away in front of Chloe. 'Well,' she continued, recovering, 'Rusty heard all the gossip when Francis was around, and I expect she passed it on – quite innocently.'

'You know when I began to know something was wrong,' I said, 'it was when I told her about Rosemary Jones. Miranda knew she was black – but I hadn't told her. So she must have known her before. I didn't realise at the time – only much later.'

I thought how I'd laughed at the serial killer's landlord for not realising what his lodger was. It didn't seem so funny now that it turned out we'd been just as blind.

'Miranda's brother Charley met up with Lennox in prison and got interested. Maybe he noticed Lennox had visits from a posh-looking woman friend, got talking to Lennox, found out all about it. You probably told Lennox, didn't you, Justine, that you'd met Miranda on the train?'

'Wrote to him about her, actually.'

'Men like Charley Smith are such opportunists. No doubt he kept tabs on his sister, knew how well she was doing, touched her for money from time to time. He found out from Lennox that Miranda had got to know you. Later he heard that you were worried about Francis, that Francis was rooting around in Cairo's past.'

'But Lennox never talked about things like that,' I objected. 'I did tell him those things, but I'm not sure he was listening, I don't suppose he remembered, and he certainly wouldn't have passed it on – too busy being wowed by Roxburgh. He just wasn't interested in things like that, you know, gossip, personalities.'

'Yes, but Charley was, he could have wheedled it out of him.'

Gennady said: 'They are banged up together? This is very big coincidence.'

'Not really – Bentham is the prison they send those sort of offenders to: small-time politicos like Lennox, and medium-time drug dealers and armed robbers like Charley Smith. And they're always moving prisoners around. I believe the idea is to stop too much fraternisation, but on the other hand it means that prisoners get to know an awful lot of other prisoners, even if not so well.'

'Lennox isn't that small time,' I said.

Myra shot me a pitying look. 'Anyway, Charley got to hear about Francis. Then his release date came up and he was out. Maybe he approached Miranda and got a dusty answer. Maybe not. But he certainly got in touch with Francis. He could prove to Francis that Cairo *was* indeed murdered, and no doubt he felt confident of getting something in return. Money, to be precise. Whether Francis would have been willing to pay him is another story, of course. More likely he'd have wanted him to testify.

'We don't know if he and Francis ever met, but in any case by this time Miranda and Dean must have been getting really nervous about Francis. They decided he had to go.

Dean must just have followed him one evening – remember, Francis didn't drive – and ambushed him somehow.

'So Francis was out of the way. But the problem hadn't gone away. *We* were still there. What were they going to do about us? As if that weren't bad enough, everything was beginning to unravel between the two of them. Miranda had finally had enough of Dean. But how could she get rid of him? I suppose Shelley – unintentionally of course – gave her the idea of the snake.'

'Miranda was a snake,' said Gennady. Chloe was sitting close to him. She looked white and shocked.

'No,' said Myra, 'Miranda wasn't a snake.'

She gathered the cards together, shuffled them, started to lay them out again, a pyramid this time.

'This was the second spread. I'm doing it from memory, but I think it's more or less right.

'There were so many cards reversed, and then the cards of fertility and creativity.' Myra pointed to them: the two images of women glowing yellow and white.

'This spread was all about Miranda,' she said. 'It wasn't about Aaron Cairo or Francis at all. It's Miranda always carrying the heavy burden from the past, pretending nothing happened, dissociating herself from it all, in total denial – yet the denial never worked. And she was a creative person, but at such a cost . . .'

For a long time she stared in silence at the bright cards, then swept them into a heap once more, tidied them into an orderly pack, and put them away.

'Why was she so obsessed with snakes?' I wondered.

'She could never be like a snake, she was the opposite of a snake,' said Myra.

'Haven't you ever read about the Indian serpent rituals of New Mexico? The Indians considered man an inferior being, not swift like the antelope or strong like the bear. Unlike human beings, the animals, they thought, do wholly what they have to do. A snake, too, is always true to its own nature. Miranda never was true to hers.'

'Wasn't she?' How could Myra be so sure?

'Yet the question remains,' said Myra, 'what is the true nature of the snake? To human beings it has always seemed the most symbolic of all creatures. But what does it symbolise? Is it death, on account of its poison? Is it healing, because of its legendary wisdom? Is it immortality, because it sheds its skin and is reborn?'

Poor Miranda. What had she wanted? What had her true nature been? For her, the snake had meant death and she had brought death to so many others – to Aaron, to Francis, to Charley, to Shelley, to Dean. Yet she'd wanted life, had wanted to live. I thought of her radiant beauty. I thought of Aaron Cairo, the healer who wasn't a saint after all. And then I thought of Francis who had died looking for the truth about his hero.

I stood up, looked out from the balcony at the scene below. The Café was in full swing. The jazz pianist was playing, there were voices, there was laughter, there was life. The show went on.